DEAD BY DESIGN

A DETECTIVE DEANS MYSTERY

JAMES D MORTAIN

MANVERS PUBLISHING

Get one of my eBooks for FREE!

Join my exclusive *Crime Scene Team* and cop a bargain!

Find details at the back of this book.

DEAD BY DESIGN

A DETECTIVE DEANS MYSTERY

by

JAMES D MORTAIN

Cover design by Jessica Bell
Editing by Debz Hobbs-Wyatt

ISBN: 978-0-9935687-3-2

Manvers Publishing
Bideford
Devon
EX39 3QH

For my wife Rachael, without whom, dreams would mean nothing and sacrifice would have no purpose.

PROLOGUE

BATH 1975

George Fenwick leaned back against the cushions of his new cane Peacock armchair and admired the stonework of his freshly crazy-paved patio area.

His daughter, Samantha, had made fun of him ever since he purchased the wicker furniture, saying it looked more like a royal throne. Now that the final concrete slab was laid and set, he could finally take his place upon his 'throne' and enjoy the delights of his lush and verdant garden.

He smiled to himself and returned a lit pine match to the tip of his imported Montecristo cigar and sucked his cheeks until the leaves glowed orange once again. He inhaled a lungful of the sweet tasting Cuban smoke and watched Sammy playing on her bespoke oak swing at the far end of the garden, under the shade of the majestic weeping willows.

Her mother died three years before. It was sudden and shocking, and as a six-year-old at the time, it knocked the stuffing out of the poor little girl, but now, she was able to have fun again. When the time was right, he would too.

George tapped his shoe on the thick paving slab beneath his chair and a smile curled upwards from the corner of his mouth. Life was good, life was great and now, things would only get better.

Sammy came running over to him. 'Daddy, can I have a bottle of cola, please?'

George smiled, 'Of course you can, Sammy. Why not bring one back for Daddy, there's a good girl.'

Samantha skipped off towards the house, leaving George to his thoughts. He was making significant improvements to the home, Sammy was doing well at school and tomorrow, George was taking the new E-Type Jaguar Coupe for a test-drive. It had long been a desire of his to have a flash set of wheels to drive along Pulteney Street and impress the neighbours even further, and now that he was able to, nothing was going to stop him.

He scratched beneath his ear. *Where is Sammy?* He looked back towards the house, but there was no sign of her. He leaned his head against the high fan of the tall wicker chair and closed his eyes.

A fly buzzing around his face caused more than a degree of annoyance. He swatted the air, took a satisfying deep breath and listened to the birds chirping happily in the nearby trees.

Samantha returned soon after. 'Daddy we haven't got any Coke.'

'We do, Sammy. Look closer.'

'But Daddy, there isn't—'

'Sammy,' George said glaring at her. 'Look in the pantry, you will see a crate on the floor, I know it's there, I only bought it yesterday.'

'But I did look there—'

'Look harder,' George said. 'I'm hot and I want a drink. You really do not want me to have to get up out of this seat…?'

Sammy stood in front of him. Her arms rigid by her side. Her eyes wide and unblinking.

George suddenly sprang up from the seat and grabbed Sammy by the shoulders. 'Come on, Samantha, step out of my sunshine and get me that ruddy drink.'

Samantha let out a squeal, turned quickly away, and her long tousled hair slapped her in the face.

Standing two paces away from him, she huffed loudly and stomped back towards the house.

George sank back into his chair, shaking his head and mumbling something beneath his breath about a 'lazy, ungrateful brat', he returned his cigar to his lips and puffed with more vigour, creating a blur of smoke around his head.

This was turning into a very pleasant day, if only he had that drink!

The flies continued to bug him, buzzing close to his face. He puffed more smoke and blew it in the general direction from where they appeared to be coming – which unusually was beneath his seat. Several insects were getting through the shield of smoke and pitching around his neckline. It was a warm July day, and he was perspiring. He could feel the dampness of his skin around his collar and continued to waft his free hand around his head as he did his best to relax, leaning back in his luxurious new armchair, eyes closed and face turned towards the sun.

'Daddy, I can't get in the pantry, the door is locked,' Sammy shouted running back towards him.

'Jesus Christ!' George spluttered and sprang up from the comfort of the seat. 'I said to you, that if I had to move…'

Sammy stopped dead in her tracks and covered her face with her hands. She looked at him and let out a shrill scream.

'What the hell is wrong now?' George said making his way with a heavy foot towards her.

Sammy cowered away and screamed again.

'The pantry is not locked. You were in it five minutes ago! For Christ's sake!' he shouted. His teeth were bared and his shoulders were tight.

'Daddy what have you done?' Sammy mouthed, breathlessly, taking two steps backwards.

'What the hell are you talking about?' George seethed as he stomped beyond her towards the concrete steps leading up to the back door.

'Daddy you're bleeding—'

'I am most certainly not bleeding.'

Samantha screamed again and George turned angrily.

'Daddy, your shirt has turned red.'

George looked down and frowned as he shook his head, his shirt was fine.

'Right,' he snapped. 'I've no idea what has gotten into you, but you are no longer having a Coke. I'm not going to tolerate any more of your nonsense.'

George climbed the steps and looked back towards his daughter. She was standing ten feet into the garden and she was still clutching her mouth.

He grumbled and walked into the kitchen and made direct for the pantry. He opened the door and there on the floor was the unopened crate of cola that he had picked up the day before.

How the hell could she miss that? He sighed deeply and removed one of the bottles, yanked off the cap with a nearby bottle opener and made his way back towards the door.

'I bloody meant it,' he mumbled to himself. 'She's not having one. All this fantasising—'

George suddenly stopped. His eyes were wide and gaping. He took several backwards steps the way he had just come, turned about, and looked at his reflection in the window.

Mouth ajar, he leaned in closer. His shirt was crimson red; in fact, it was seeping with blood. He cautiously looked back down at himself and he shook his head. His shirt was still pale blue. There was nothing on it. He quickly looked back into the reflection of the window and the bottle of pop dropped from his hand and splashed in an arc of exploding bubbles.

He leaned in again and looked at his throat. Small wells of blood were oozing from under the surface. He reached for his neck and rubbed beneath his ear as another small balloon of red gloop burst from his skin.

Frantically he rubbed the area, but the more he did so, the more the blood leached out.

'Daddy, Daddy, are you okay?' Samantha's voice came from outside the door.

George quickly turned. 'Stay there, Sammy. Don't come in.'

'But Daddy—'

'I mean it, Sammy. Stay the hell outside...' George turned back to his reflection and saw a perfect line from ear to ear of weeping blood under his jawline. He gripped his neck with both hands and tried to stem the flow of blood, but the more he tried, the quicker it flowed.

'Daddy!' Samantha screamed. She was in the kitchen.

George faced her with horror in his eyes. He cried out 'Don't see me' and waved her away with a completely blood-dripping hand. He turned back to the window and his heart stopped.

Written on the glass in his blood, were the words:

IT BELONGS TO ME.

'Peter?' George breathed.

He turned and ran to the top of the steps. He looked over to his chair on the patio – the entire area was now infested with flies and the sound of buzzing filled the air. He noticed Sammy two steps below him, pointing up at him, her other hand across her mouth.

George followed the direction of her finger, it was pointing at his chest. He looked down – his shirt was pale blue once again. He rubbed his neck – there was nothing. He looked back towards the chair – the flies had gone. He settled on Sammy. She was now crying and laughing at the same time. George held out his arms and Sammy came running into his secure grasp.

George looked around him in slow motion – to the patio – over his shoulder at the doorway to the kitchen and finally back down at his hands. He rested his chin on the top of Sammy's head and directed his eyes once again on the patio area.

'He's back...' George whispered. 'Oh God... Peter... Peter.'

CHAPTER ONE

Detective Andrew Deans backed wearily onto the narrow patch of concrete at the front of his semi-detached house. He was fortunate: parking spaces, let alone driveways, came at a premium in Bath – but that was one reason why they had chosen to live on the outskirts.

The engine stayed running. Deans stared ahead, eyes swollen and heavy. He blinked once, long and slow, and uncurled his fingers from the leather steering wheel that he had gripped so tightly for the last three hours – like peeling chipolatas from flypaper. He killed the engine and dragged his heels to the front door.

The hallway was dark, cold and silent. He dropped his bag beside the telephone table, threw his keys on top and went straight through to the kitchen without turning on any lights. He ran water through the pipes for thirty seconds, filled the kettle and opened the wall cabinet. Instead of taking a mug, he reached for a heavy glass tumbler and searched for the bottle.

He moved through to the living room, lit only from a beam of streetlight sneaking in through a gap in the drapes, and he was already into his second glass of Jameson's before the water had boiled. He slumped onto the sofa, kicked off his shoes without unlacing them, and rested the nape of his neck against the cool brown leather. Maria filled his head. Delightful, ditsy, fragile Maria. He took another swig without lifting his head, the hard-hitting spirit splintering the back of his throat. He sucked a shallow breath from the solemn air and closed his eyes. If only he had listened to her; he would not have gone to Devon, would not have become so catastrophically immersed in the Amy Poole murder, would not have flirted with fantasy evidence, and would still be sitting beside her.

A heavy noise above his head snatched his breath away. He gawked at the ceiling, as if he had the superhuman ability to see through plasterboard, his jaw wide and slack.

There it was again.

He slammed the glass onto the coffee table, whisky splashing onto the back of his hand, and he raced for the stairs, taking them two at a time.

Their bedroom door was closed but was framed with light seeping from inside the room. Deans burst in, his anticipation beyond ecstasy.

'Maria,' Deans whimpered.

His wife faced him, kneeling tall on top of the bed sheets.

'Do it,' an urgent voice sounded from somewhere behind him.

Deans shot around, his arms held before him ready to embrace Maria, but they dropped like concrete blocks when he saw Ash Babbage emerging from the shadows of the back wall.

'Do it, now.' Ferocity spewed from Babbage's lips.

Deans spun back facing Maria; her face was wild and desperate. It was only then that he registered the arm across her forehead.

'Maria,' he shrieked, lunging forwards but falling short. Then he saw it: the glint of steel chasing the clenched fist beneath her chin followed by the sickening nick and popping sound of sliced muscle and sinew.

'Maria! No!' he screamed, clawing the fringe of the duvet but making no ground.

The corners of her mouth lifted for a millisecond, and her hands gently cradled the mound of her stomach.

And then he awoke… and she was gone.

CHAPTER TWO

Sweat drenched Deans' clothes. He swung his legs around off the sofa and hugged his knees. The clock on the DVD player showed 05:33. Two hours to go until his first day back on duty.

He had received visits from colleagues – most of them genuine – but he still seethed at having to justify his final forty-eight hours, before *that* day.

Getting ready did not come naturally. There was nothing ordinary about this day. And at just gone seven a.m., he locked the house and made his way to the office.

For once, his skipper, Detective Sergeant Savage was at his desk before Deans had arrived.

'Hello, Deano. You okay, buddy?' Savage asked.

'Shit the bed, Mick?' Deans replied, diverting the question.

'Thought you might appreciate a little company… before the others arrive. I knew you'd be in early.'

'Yeah, well.' Deans wheeled his seat out from under his desk and sat down.

Savage stood up and patted Deans on the shoulder. 'Brew?'

Deans nodded and Savage left the room.

It had only been a short break, but Deans felt like the new boy all over again. He peered around the room, his pulse spluttering and his heart banging through his rib cage. His eyes settled on the case files stacked on the corner of his desk, untouched for three weeks, and he heaved a despondent sigh.

Savage returned shortly after, a mug in each hand. 'I am going to be honest, Deano. Bloody good to have you back.'

'Thanks,' Deans said taking one of the coffees.

'It's been busy,' Savage continued. 'The guys have been snowed under with jobs.'

Deans inclined his head and closed his eyes.

'Not saying that you have to do any more than you are willing to,' Savage quickly qualified.

'I'm ready, Mick,' Deans said softly.

'I'm sorry, Deano. I didn't mean it to sound... the others are managing just fine. You can take it easy... until you're ready – properly ready.'

'I don't want preferential treatment. I'd rather be busy than...' Deans stopped speaking and turned away.

'There's a job, Deano,' Savage said hesitantly. 'Came in early this morning.' His face tightened. 'Don't feel obliged. It's not going to be nice.'

'Tell me what it is,' Deans said.

Savage narrowed his gaze and paused a beat. 'Suicide pact.' He did not elaborate until Deans looked at him again. 'Young couple. Found this morning,' Savage said.

Deans bunched his eyes. *Why did the first job have to involve death?*

'That's fine,' he said quietly.

'I can give it to Mitch,' Savage responded. 'He could use a decent job for his end-of-year performance review.'

'It's fine,' Deans repeated. 'I'll take it.'

Savage bobbed his head. 'Thanks, Deano. I know the others will be pleased you're back.'

Yep, Deans thought and drank his coffee.

Detective Constable Daisy Harper and DC Damien Mitchell came in just after eight. Deans couldn't tell who was more awkward, him or them. Everyone dealt with these situations differently; Daisy simply threw her arms around Deans' neck, gave him a kiss on the cheek and welcomed him back with kind words. Mitchell greeted him as if Deans had not been away.

'Alright, guys,' Savage said, flopping a wad of papers onto the desk in front of him. 'I'm delighted to announce that Deano is back with us, but we've got a fresh job, a suicide pact.'

Harper and Mitchell groaned, but before they could grumble, Savage stepped in to save their embarrassment. 'Deano has already offered to take the job.'

'No, that's okay,' Harper said at once correcting her apathy, 'I can juggle my workload. Give it to me.'

'Dais,' Deans said. 'It's okay. I want to take it.'

She cast him a *bless you* look from across the desk.

'I'm going to head out to the scene with Deano,' Savage continued, scooping up the papers, 'but you guys have to pick up anything else that comes in today, alright?'

The others agreed willingly.

'The duty inspector is waiting for us at the scene. Deano, are you good to go?' Savage asked.

Deans accepted, and a short while later they were in transit.

Deans drove. Savage had an ardent dislike for taking the wheel, especially in poor weather, and this was a dank and miserable early December morning, but Deans was finally glad to be out of the house.

'So?' Savage eventually said. 'Have the quacks got you on anything?'

'A-ha,' Deans uttered.

'Occy-Health?' Savage asked.

Deans nodded.

'Any more… news?' Savage probed hesitantly.

Deans shook his head, kept his eyes on the vehicle thirty feet in front of them.

Savage was still for a moment. 'I know I have said it before, but I'm truly sorry, Deano.'

Deans' eyes flicked to his wedding band and his fingers tightened on the steering wheel.

'You need a beer any time, I'm your man,' Savage continued.

Deans nodded again. He knew Savage meant it.

Half a minute slipped by until Deans spoke. 'Tell me more about this job,' he said.

'Right, yeah. It's a couple in their late thirties. Called in by one of the neighbours earlier this morning. Both snuffed it in bed.'

Deans blinked rapidly but did not take his eyes from the road ahead.

'There's a child,' Savage continued, 'with one of the night shift officers.' He huffed. 'We are still waiting on Social Services to make some kind of bloody decision. I'm told CSI are already on scene.' He turned to Deans. 'We just need to check it out, Deano. Make sure that nothing has been missed and get the hell out of there. We'll be back in the office by eleven.'

'Sounds odd,' Deans said.

'Yeah, they don't happen very often.'

'Why leave a child?' Deans questioned.

'Why take your own life, Deano? Or that of your missus—' Savage stopped abruptly, cleared his throat and looked out through the passenger window.

They barely spoke again for the rest of the journey.

Deans parked behind a CSI van. Forensic officers, Bradley and

Parsons, were waiting to meet them. A veritable double-act – not so much Crockett and Tubbs; more Laurel and Hardy.

'Hi fellas,' Parsons said in his usual jaunty fashion and extended Deans a special nod and wink.

'What's the state of play?' Savage asked.

'Ready for you guys to dive-in. Bodies are still *in-situ*,' Parsons replied.

'Anything, Nate?' Deans asked Parsons.

'Nothing obvious, but wait until you see their faces – like something from a horror movie,' Parsons grinned.

'Can you guys slide these on, please?' Bradley said, holding out packaged forensic paper suits. 'Probably not required, but you never know.'

As they traipsed towards the front of the house, Deans' shoulders tightened and he stopped ten paces short of the door.

'Come on, Deano,' Savage encouraged, 'before it pisses down with rain.'

Deans looked up at the brooding sky, then at the three-storey Georgian terraced house, and at each of the ten front-facing windows. He shivered inside and continued walking.

They gave their names to the officer on point duty and entered the sizeable dust-sheet-clad hallway, like a set from an eighties music video – minus the big hair. The house was clearly in the early stages of a major renovation. The room was cool and the smell of damp masonry clung to the air.

Bradley walked at the head of the white-paper-hooded train as they clunked their way up the wooden stairway in respectful silence, Deans at the rear.

On reaching the second floor, Bradley stood outside of one of the many dark wooden doorways, and just as downstairs, dust-sheets covered the floor like fondant.

Bradley pushed the door inwards and stepped aside as the room opened before them.

Savage entered first. Deans stopped one step beyond the threshold.

The room was bright – unlike anything Deans had seen in the property up to now – and a whiff of recently applied paint filled his nostrils.

Deans centred his gaze on the bed before him, sheets pulled back, and two naked corpses lying entangled in the centre of the mattress, and then he noticed the open windows.

'I take it we've discounted carbon monoxide,' he whispered in Savage's ear.

'If it was carbon monoxide, we'd be fucked already,' Savage said casually.

'It's a house under renovation, it has to be a possibility.'

'Perhaps we should get one of the canaries downstairs to sniff the boiler,' Savage said, squeezing Deans' shoulder gently.

'She's quite fit considering,' Parsons commented.

'What? Considering she's dead, you sick fucker,' Savage barked.

'No – considering her little'n is still a baby. She obviously kept herself trim. That's all I'm saying,' Parsons said.

'What are you like?' Bradley sniggered. 'I'm surprised you haven't asked her out yet. At least this one can't run away.'

Amidst the banter, Deans was taking in the room. The Moses basket inches from the edge of the bed. The bedside cabinets with a thick novel on her side – bookmark hanging out like a tongue and a car magazine on his side, pages open wide. He focussed on the puckered bed covers at the foot of the mattress and the graphic faces of both deceased persons, their bodies tightly entwined. Deans looked along the wall behind him and saw a tall a chest of drawers with nothing more than a baby monitor sitting on the top.

'Has anyone had a good look around the place?' Deans asked the duty inspector, who had just joined them in the room.

'My guys did a cursory search. Nothing stands out,' the inspector replied.

'Deano and I will mooch around and we'll tie up again downstairs,' Savage said.

The others agreed and moved away, leaving Deans and Savage staring in silence at the naked bodies lying before them.

'Are you up for this, Deano?' Savage asked, eventually.

Deans thought for a moment and then concurred.

'I can easily give the case to Mitch. You can have a backseat role?'

'It's time I was back on the horse, Mick.' Deans had not taken his eyes away from the female. She was of similar age to Maria and had the same raven-black hair.

'Major Crime won't touch this, unless we suspect murder,' Savage said. 'It could be yours for a while.'

Deans turned and faced Savage. 'We'd better crack on then.'

CHAPTER THREE

Three hours later, and the bodies had been removed to the mortuary. Deans was now alone inside the house. He had toured the property several times. It was a cavernous old place, and in dire need of updating. The victims were named Mike and Helen Rose. They had only been living there for three months. It appeared that they were renovating the home one room at a time, beginning with the bedroom they shared with the baby. The kitchen was clearly a work in progress, but it had one of those large American-style fridge freezers – the kind you could practically walk inside. It looked new and was stocked full of fresh food, milk and several bottles of white wine. Deans had spoken to the neighbour who had alerted the police after what she described as hearing screams while she was outside in the street with her recycling bin at five a.m. She thought they were having a domestic ding-dong so called the police. She confirmed that she did not really know much about them – said they seemed a normal, young couple with an eight-month-old daughter, named Molly. Both worked. He had a high-powered job in Bristol. She was in advertising. The Roses had certainly embarked on a challenging renovation, which made their deaths even more puzzling to Deans.

A loud *clunk* from upstairs grabbed Deans' attention. He moved silently to the base of the stairs and looked up to the first level. The hairs on his arms lifted in the cool still air.

'Mick, is that you?' he called out.

There was another *bump* – sounding as if it had come from the second floor.

Deans frowned. He knew he was alone; Mick had left ages ago with the CSI Chuckle Brothers and said he would return once he had sorted out a few issues back at the station. Mick was not exactly svelte-like and Deans was certain he had not missed his return. Deans' chest pounded through his shirt.

'Mick?' he called out again, but not at full volume. He listened intently for a reply, but heard silence.

He began up the steps and felt his pulse quickening.

Thud.

Deans stopped dead in his tracks and held his breath.

He waited ten, maybe fifteen seconds, and then crept forward.

He moved beyond the first level of rooms, his eyes looking as far ahead as the winding stairs would allow and he made his way to the source of the noise; the couple's bedroom. He hesitated with his hand on the door handle and felt something unusual, something he had experienced only recently.

He became aware of his juddering breath but felt a strong desire to look inside the room. He took a deep gulp of air, pushed down on the handle and shoved the door inwards.

He saw it at once; something obviously different from before: a large, golden picture frame now lying face down on the floor, on Mike's side of the bed.

Deans turned to the window. It was still open and the mesh veils were billowing inside the room. Death was still in his nostrils, but he gently lowered the sash window and tightened the latch.

He looked over toward the bed and could still make out their body impressions in the mattress. He moved back over to the fallen frame, keeping half an eye on the dented white bed linen. He pulled a deep morbid breath from the air and in one swift movement, heaved the frame up from the floor and stared at it for a while.

It was an oil portrait of the family. Mum and Dad were cradling the little one. Deans ran his thumb carefully along the intricately designed edge of the frame. It was a grand and expensive looking portrayal of pride and love. An abstract departure from the Pompeii-esque remains he had earlier seen.

He looked at the wall and frowned. There was no hook.

He heard the *thump, thump, thump* of slow and deliberate footsteps coming up the stairs. A chill dropped through his spine like a boulder of ice tossed into a deep well.

He waited, still holding the picture out in front of him and counted – three, four, five more heavy steps. They were getting louder and slowing.

Deans threw the picture onto the bed and hurriedly closed the angle of the opened door, leaving just enough space to peek through. His breathing was shallow and the hairs were standing up on his ice-cold arms. He patted his pockets; he had nothing with which to defend himself. Each step was now growing louder and practically upon him.

The front door slammed shut.

'Deano,' he heard being shouted from downstairs.

It was Savage.

Deans did not respond. His eyes were trained on the space between himself and the top of the stairs.

'Deano, you here, mate?' Savage bellowed.

Deans' skin prickled with adrenalin. The sound of footsteps had stopped the moment Savage had entered the house.

'I'll… I'll be right down,' Deans shouted from behind the door.

He heard the heavy plod and panting of Savage stomping up the second flight of stairs.

Deans stepped back away from the door and breathed.

'Where are you?' Savage called out.

'In here,' Deans said, lifting the picture from the bed and gently leaning it, portrait side to the wall.

'Ah,' Savage puffed. 'I was calling you.' He wiped a hand across his brow.

Deans stared at him.

'I need you to trace the previous owners,' Savage said getting his breath back. 'We've spoken to Helen's mother.' He shook his head and smiled between gasps of air. 'She reckons all manner of things have been going on in this house.'

'What things?' Deans asked without hesitating.

Savage gave Deans a quizzical look. 'Odd things,' he said.

'Like what?' Deans asked.

Savage cast him a dismissive look from beneath his clammy brow. 'The kind of things a woman who has just lost a daughter would say. This house was advertised through Fox's Estates. I need you to chase up the agent and find the details of the sellers. Pay them a visit and try to establish a recent history.'

'Of what?' Deans asked.

'Of the house,' Savage smiled wryly. 'Of the house.'

CHAPTER FOUR

Fox Country Estates was located in a prime position for the obscenely wealthy, just metres from the Royal Crescent in Bath. Deans liked this part of town. It was uncluttered, peaceful, historic, and romantic. He entered the shop and was immediately greeted by a well-groomed agent.

'Good afternoon, sir,' the agent said. 'Just browsing, or might I offer assistance with something in particular?'

Deans sniffed in a lungful of leather-soaked air. He loved that aroma. It was comforting and warm.

'I'm looking to speak with the manager, if possible,' Deans replied, noticing the two luxurious brown hide sofas.

'Of course,' the agent replied. 'I will check to see if Miss Small is available. May I ask if this concerns a sale or purchase, sir?'

Deans looked around the room. They were alone. 'Police enquiry,' he said.

'Oh!' the agent said. 'Certainly, sir. Can I offer you a drink while you wait?' He stretched a hand out in the direction of a fancy-looking coffee maker.

Wait? Deans questioned silently in his mind. *How long does it take to grab the manager?* He smiled at the agent. 'Lovely,' he said.

Deans did not hesitate and the moment the agent had stepped out of the room he was into the coffee and a comfortable lounge on one of the sofas.

He scanned the advertised properties as he sipped from his steaming cup. One-point-five million, one-eight – these were high-end properties, even for Bath.

'Hello again, sir,' the agent said awkwardly approaching Deans. 'Miranda will be with you very shortly.'

The agent backed away with a low bow.

Deans smiled. They obviously did not get many visits from the cops.

Not long after, a woman walked into the room from the rear part of the building.

'Hello,' she said. Her voice was flat, like Deans was inter-rupting her from important business. 'My name is Miranda Small. I am the manager.'

Deans placed his designer cup and saucer onto the small glass table, stood from the comfort of the sofa and shook her hand.

'Would you care to come with me, please?' she said and walked back the way she had come.

'How can I help?' she asked, leading Deans up a narrow flight of winding stairs to a pristinely tidy first floor office.

Even though the window was open, Deans could smell the remnants of a recently smoked cigarette.

'I'm interested in one of your properties from a recent sale,' Deans said, following her pointed arm to a chair opposite her desk, which he took with a smile and a nod.

She shook her head and placed both hands flat onto the desk. 'I'm sorry, why should the police be interested in that?'

'I'm merely following a line of enquiry,' Deans said. 'Please be assured there is nothing you or the company need be concerned with.'

Her mouth twitched and nearly broke into a smile... nearly. It

was obvious she was hoping for more information. She wasn't
going to get it.

'Well… alright,' she said eventually, taking her own seat.
'Where exactly are we talking?'

'The Willows, Bathwick,' Deans said and noticed her eyes
flicker and narrow a little at the corners.

Ms Small leaned back in her seat.

'You know the house?' Deans asked. He already had that
answer loud and clear.

The manager looked away and shuffled her bottom in the
chair. 'Yes…' she said moving her hands behind the desk and into
her lap. 'I know The Willows.'

'What can you tell me?' Deans asked.

She twitched and blinked rapidly. 'It was a straightforward
sale,' she replied down to her desk. 'No hiccups and certainly no
issues that we were made aware of by any party involved in the
transaction.'

Deans smiled and waited a beat before speaking. 'I'm interested in the sale: who the vendors were, where they are now, and
how I can get hold of them?'

'Um, I'm not sure I can—'

'No one is in trouble,' Deans interrupted. 'But I must trace
them and this appears to be the only way.'

The manager frowned. 'Well, have you not considered asking
the new occupiers?'

Deans matched her concerned features. 'I would have,' he
said, 'had they still been alive.' He gave her an uncompromising
stare.

After a few seconds she stood up from the chair. 'I'll find the
portfolio,' she said and left the room.

'Okay, how can I help?' she asked returning only seconds later.
She was clutching a beige folio file pressed tightly into her body.

'Firstly, when did the exchange take place?' Deans said, his
day-book open and his pen at the ready.

The manager got herself comfortable in her chair and opened the cover. She cleared her throat as she turned the pages.

'September the fifteenth. Friday,' she said peering at Deans over the top of the folder.

'Sold by?' Deans asked.

'The executor was Samantha Fenwick,' the manager replied with a flat tone and without looking at the information contained within the folder.

Deans squinted. 'Executor... she didn't live there?'

'Actually, I believe she did,' the manager said. She was acting on behalf of her father, who as I understand now lives in a care home.'

Deans looked down at his day-book. He had picked up on a tinge of attitude in the manager's tone.

'Can you let me have the contact details of the vendor, please?' he asked.

'Yes,' she replied.

'Thanks,' Deans said looking at her directly in the eye. Something though, was clearly amiss. 'Anything else about the sale – how much did it go for?'

The manager shifted uncomfortably in her seat and looked away.

Here we go. He lowered his pen and smiled.

He watched her fiddle with the pages of the folder. He could tell she was not reading any of the content.

'Well... this property was unusual for us to take.' She looked up at Deans.

He signalled for her to continue.

'Not the bricks and mortar,' she said. 'In fact to have a complete house of this kind, in its original form and in that locality is our specialty.' She brushed invisible lint from her jacket lapel, straightened herself in the seat and wiped the front of her jacket again. 'But not at that price.'

'Go on,' Deans prompted.

She turned away briefly and then looked back. 'We put the property on for four hundred and ninety-five thousand pounds.'

'And what did it fetch?' Deans asked.

'Four hundred and ninety-five thousand pounds.'

Her neck stiffened, and she looked along her nose at Deans. 'On the first day.'

Deans shrugged. 'And?'

The manager drew a controlled breath. 'That was a nine hundred and fifty thousand pound property.'

Deans nodded. 'I guessed it was pricey from my visit there. Why so cheap?' he asked.

'The vendor... the vendor was adamant in her mind that the property should sell with immediacy. I must say, against our best attempts to dissuade her,' the manager said.

'Why do you suppose that was?' Deans asked quietly, leaning in closer to the desk. A little body language technique – they were now sharing a secret.

The manager's eyes were free from explanation. 'I really don't know,' she said.

'How did the buyer pay?' Deans asked.

'Cash – outright,' the manager said without looking at the file.

'Lucky them,' Deans jibed. 'How much mortgage did the vendor owe?'

The manager shook her head. 'Um—'

'I'm not recording this information anywhere,' Deans said. 'Just for my benefit it would be useful to know?'

The manager covered her mouth with her long slender fingers. 'None, to the best of my knowledge.'

Deans sucked in through his teeth. Now, he had two dead bodies, an expensive house sold for half the market value and an increasingly unsettled feeling about the investigation.

Was he ready for this?

CHAPTER FIVE

'Hello.' The phone was answered in a dozy and slurred response.

'Good evening,' Deans said. 'Is this Samantha Fenwick?'

'Um… yeah.'

'My name is Andy Deans. I'm a detective with Falcon Road Criminal Investigation Department. I'm sorry to trouble you, there is nothing to worry about. I just need to ask you a few questions about your time at The Willows in Bathwick, if I may?'

A faint groan filled the earpiece, followed by a short pause.

'Why, what's this about?' she mumbled.

'I'd rather see you in person,' Deans said.

'See me?' She sounded confused.

'Yes. Are you free for me to come by this evening?' Deans asked.

'Not really.'

'This is important, Mrs Fenwick.'

'Well, you tell me what it's about and I will see if I am available.' Her words were barely coherent.

Deans slapped his pen onto his day-book. 'Look, I need to speak with you regarding your time at The Willows, that's all.'

There was no reply.

'Hello,' Deans said impatiently.

'Well, how long will it take?'

'I can't say, Mrs Fenwick, but probably only a few minutes.'

'Miss.'

'Sorry?'

'You keep calling me Mrs. I'm a Miss. Miss Fenwick.'

'My apologies, Miss Fenwick. So, can I say I will see you this evening?'

'I suppose so. Are you coming to me?'

'Yes, that would be no problem at all. Where do you live?'

'Travis Street flats.'

Deans recoiled. 'Okay,' he said. 'And the number?'

'Thirty-seven,' she replied – though it sounded more like *thirzeven*.

'Shall we say at six p.m. tonight, then?'

Deans waited eagerly for her reply.

'Okay,' she finally said.

Deans ended the call and, confused, stared at her address in his day-book.

All the local cops knew Travis Street Flats. Some spent more time there than in their own homes. For a time in the early nineties, it had been a no go zone, especially if you were solo crewed. Two police cars and four officers was a minimum: two officers to deal with whatever was happening, and the other unit to prevent the unoccupied police car from being trashed. These days the council housed the *unfortunates* within its walls – the smack and piss-heads and incumbent bone-idle. It was certainly not the address of someone that up until recently had resided in the relative opulence of The Willows. Such a change in circumstances seemed inconceivable.

Deans interrogated the police intelligence systems. It was clear as he read the data that Miss Fenwick was one of the few Travis residents that had not received a visit from the police in recent times – a remarkable achievement in itself. Maybe that accounted for her reluctance to see him; her head was buried so deep in the sand, the crazy world she co-inhabited simply span around her arse.

But a big question stuck in Deans' mind: what happened to the four hundred and ninety-five grand?

Deans arrived ten minutes early.

From the outside, the flats appeared relatively modern, faced in the familiar, buttery Bath sandstone. The building sprawled over three storeys, with a maze of stairwells, a number of different entrances and no clear order to the room numbering.

Deans went to the recognised 'main entrance', buzzed 37 on the wall-mounted intercom, and waited with an ear tuned to the small perforated stainless steel box.

'Alright, officer?' a voice came from behind him.

Deans turned to see a young man with the generic appearance of one of the residents, sporting a smart-arsed grin on his face as if he had just exposed a secret agent in the midst of a clandestine operation.

Deans wasn't wearing a uniform, but cops stood out in a place like this.

'Alright, mate,' Deans replied, as the youth scuttled off, digging a hand into the pocket of his grubby light-grey tracksuit bottoms – held up around his upper thighs by a magic force of nature.

No doubts, this shit-bag was the drumbeater; *the filth are about.*

'Hello?' a weary voice sounded through the intercom speaker.

'Miss Fenwick, it's Andy Deans from the CID. We spoke earlier.'

He heard a buzz and a click and tugged at the door to let him inside the building.

If the flats looked tidy from the outside, they looked a dreadful mess from within its walls. The floors were scuffed and dirty. The walls were peeling beneath the mosaic of colourful stains. The general odour was the same as any other doss-house, or public toilet frequented by the ne'er-do-wells of society – a subtle blend of months' old body sweat, cannabis, urine, vomit, alcohol and excrement. If Dior bottled it, *Wretch* or *Heave* would make a suitable branding.

Deans made his way up to the next level, carefully avoiding any wet patches on the floor.

He went along two false corridors before finally coming to number thirty-seven. At least this one still had an intact number on the door.

He knocked loudly on the door and waited.

After thirty more seconds, he tapped again, and this time lifted the letterbox and called out. 'Miss Fenwick, it's Andy Deans.'

He waited some more and then heard the sound of a key being turned, followed by another, and then a sliding bolt.

The door started to open inward, but then stopped abruptly to the twang of a security chain at full tension.

A pair of sluggish eyes appeared in the opening and looked out, but not directly at him.

Deans held his warrant badge in front of his chin and angled himself to be within her line of sight.

'Hello, Miss Fenwick. I am Andy Deans. Can I come in, please?'

She blinked with painful slowness, and after a tortuous ten seconds raised her brows in recognition of who he was.

The door closed. The security chain rattled, and the door opened to its fullest extent.

'May I come in?' Deans asked after a moment, hovering at the threshold to the door.

Miss Fenwick laboured a wave, inviting Deans inside, and replaced each security measure in an excruciating and uncoordinated display of why not to touch heroin.

She slouched through the narrow hallway without a spoken

word and moved into an area that could just about be described as a living room.

Deans followed silently behind her.

The windows were blacked out with thick drapes and two small table lamps dimly lit the room with rouge coloured shading.

Miss Fenwick placed herself down in an armchair in front of a battered pine coffee table, upon which, numerous bottles of cheap cider, Rizla papers, cigarette tabs and general crap was randomly spread.

The room was a disaster zone, but Deans had seen worse. One bonus though: at least she did not appear to have pets. Less poo for him to step in.

This is going to be hard work.

'Miss Fenwick,' he said. 'Thank you for seeing me.'

She did not react.

'The reason I have asked to see you, is to chat to you about your time living at The Willows.'

She turned lethargically towards him and squinted through watery, black eyes. Her wiry, grey hair took on a witch-like rose hue from the lamp light behind her.

'The Willows,' she gargled, and her face attempted a smile.

'How long did you live there?' Deans asked. He had not bothered to open his day-book, and his pen was still deep inside his suit jacket pocket.

'All my life,' she said eventually.

'Do you mind if I ask your age?'

'Fifty-one.'

Fuck me, another good reason not to use heroin. She did not look a day over seventy.

'And how long have you lived here?' Deans asked looking around the room.

She raised a clawed hand towards her forehead and held it there for a moment.

'Since we sold The Willows,' she slurred.

30

'We?' Deans repeated. 'You just said, "We sold". Who did you live there with?'

'Dad,' her throat crackled.

'And is he still around, may I ask?'

She did not answer.

Deans noticed her head gradually drooping as if she was falling asleep.

'Miss Fenwick. Is your father still alive?'

'Um...Yeah,' she mumbled down to her chest.

'Where does he live now?' Deans asked. He could see her lids becoming heavy. He checked his watch. 'Miss Fenwick, where is he now?'

'Care home,' she garbled.

'Care home? How long has he been living in a care home?'

One of her dirty talons scratched the corner of her forehead.

'Two...' she slurred.

'Two what... months?'

She started to cackle and her head dropped back as if it was only prevented from rolling off her shoulders by the connecting skin between her chest and her ears.

'Who looks after the proceeds from the estate?' Deans asked loudly. His lips were tightening.

She rocked her head back and forth and momentum brought it upright again. Her beady eyes sought out a cider bottle on the table and she dragged it towards her. 'I do,' she said.

Christ!

He watched her struggle with the ballast in the bottom of the plastic bottle, as it got closer to her lips.

'Is your mother still around?' he asked.

'Dead,' she replied quickly.

'Brothers, sisters?'

She waited until she finished her mouthful of cider before answering.

'Nope.'

Deans rubbed his face. 'Your mother – was she buried, cremated?'

Miss Fenwick groaned and chuckled quietly. 'Buried,' she eventually replied.

'Where is she buried?' Deans asked.

Miss Fenwick forced her head up to peer at Deans. 'It's not Mum,' she spluttered.

Deans shook his head. 'What's not Mum?'

'The reason you are here.' Miss Fenwick kept staring at Deans. 'It's not Mum,' she repeated.

'Why am I here?' Deans asked, narrowing his gaze.

She leaned forward with a groan and directed more cider towards her lips.

'Charlie,' she said between gulps.

'Charlie,' Deans mirrored.

'Char-lie,' she repeated as if Deans had not understood her the first time.

Deans scrunched up his face. 'I'm sorry,' he said, 'I don't know what you're talking about?'

Miss Fenwick hugged the bottle of cider to her bosom and formed a self-satisfied half-smile.

'The ghost,' she said after a few more seconds.

Deans felt his scalp creep. He did not move. Did not speak, and he realised he was holding his breath.

'What ghost?'

'Char-lie,' she repeated.

Yeah, I get that, you skanky old crow.

'Who is Charlie? And please, don't say "the ghost".'

'He won't like you being there,' she said, partaking in more alcohol.

'Who, your dad?'

Miss Fenwick spluttered and chuckled with barely the energy to force air beyond her lips.

Deans huffed and checked his watch again.

'What am I doing here?' he mumbled beneath his breath and peered at the pathetic individual sharing his air.

'I will have to speak with your dad,' he said.

She shrugged, or at least that was how the small movement in her shoulder appeared to Deans.

'Which care home did you say he was in?' Deans asked.

'Lansdown Grange,' she replied, placing the cider bottle onto the edge of the table while attempting to conceal a crumpled fold of silver foil that Deans had clocked the moment he entered the room.

Deans knew of the Grange – one of Bath's original Georgian masterpieces, occupying a lofty position over the city. But the location wasn't what it was famed for – it was the price tag.

'Do you pay for your dad's stay?' Deans asked.

She shook her head.

Deans frowned.

'What happened to the money from the sale of The Willows?' *Apart from what you have pissed up a wall and jabbed into your veins.*

Miss Fenwick mumbled incoherently and stretched forwards.

Deans made it easy for her. 'Is the money in a bank?' he asked.

She slowly acknowledged him, her eyes rolling into the back of her head.

Deans pursed his lips and shook his head. *The best part of five hundred grand in the hands of this bloody imbecile.*

'I'll let myself out,' he said. *It'll be quicker*

.

CHAPTER SIX

It had been three weeks since Deans last spoke to Denise Moon.

Throughout the Amy Poole investigation, Denise had been his one true ally and trusted friend.

Amy Poole was the murder victim of his last job. A job that drew him away from home and from his wife, Maria. A job that had changed every conceivable belief and understanding of the world as he knew it. A job that had ruined the person he used to be and created the person he had become.

Denise Moon's insight into the paranormal world of the after-life had confused him and yet, her final words to him still lingered.

He was alone in one of the empty offices that had dominated the nick since austerity measures dictated the futures of many of his colleagues. He was sitting on top of a desk with his feet planted on a chair in front of him. The room was dark, other than stray street light from the council car park adjacent to the station. Nobody walking by the office would see him, and he hoped the closed door would shield his words.

He dropped his head. Did he have the courage to speak to Denise... and was he ready for the answer?

He looked at his phone quivering in his hand. He steeled himself and allowed the call to ring beyond the three times of his earlier attempt.

Denise answered with the familiar, satin warmth of her voice.

'Hello, Denise,' Deans said.

There was a pause before she spoke. 'Andy! How are you?'

'Fine,' he said gulping. 'I'm fine, thanks.'

There was an instance of silence.

'Andy, I'm terribly sorry about your wife.'

Deans did not answer.

'How have you been keeping?'

'You know.'

'I was unsure whether to bother you,' she said.

'It's fine,' he said. 'Look, I need some advice.'

'Yes, of course.'

Deans hesitated, looking towards the door. 'Do ghosts really exist?' he asked after a beat.

'Ghosts? Well, yes,' she answered. 'You know they do... why? What's happened?'

'I'm dealing with a job—'

'You're at work?'

'I had to,' he groaned, and rubbed the large *pasty-ridge* formed scar behind his left ear.

'No you didn't. You should be looking after yourself—'

'I am,' he cut in. 'This way I'm not...' He stopped himself finishing the sentence.

'I'm sorry, Andy. You must do whatever is right for you. Tell me about this...job.' Deans walked to the door and looked through the glass into the darkened hallway.

'I understand I have experienced... *stuff* before,' he mumbled, 'but can a ghost make noises – like day-to-day noises; walking, moving objects, that sort of thing?'

'Yes, they can,' she replied without hesitation.

Bugger.

'Have you encountered another spirit?' Denise asked.

'I think so.'

'Andy, you need to take care. You are in a particularly vulnerable state now. Not all spirits are like Amy.'

Deans did not answer.

'Where is the investigation?' Denise asked after a silence.

'Bath – a double... *suicide.*'

'Something has happened for you to ask that question,' she said.

Deans walked to the window and stared out into the night sky with hollow eyes.

'Do you want me to visit and see you? It might do you good just to chat about—'

'Would you?'

'Yes, of course. I can probably rearrange my appointments—'

'I'd like you to come up,' he said.

'I might sort something over the next day or two. How does that sound?'

'I'll almost certainly be at work, but I can meet you at the train station,' he said.

'Okay.'

Deans stared out at nothing in particular and his eyes glazed over.

'Andy?' Denise said. 'Are you still there?'

'Did you know?' Deans asked and waited.

He heard a heavy breath in the earpiece.

'"Don't give up, whatever happens," that's what you said to me when I saw you last in North Devon. You had been crying—'

'No,' she said softly. 'No, I didn't know about Maria.'

Deans fell silent.

The line was quiet for many more seconds until Denise filled the void. 'I realised *something* wasn't right, but I could never have predicted—'

'How?' Deans asked speaking over her. 'How could you realise?'

'The guardians,' Denise replied. 'The guardians watch over us all – watch over you – remember?'

Warmth radiated from deep inside his chest and spread throughout his torso. He looked down and touched his shirt.

'Do I have other... *abilities*?' he asked.

'You have unparalleled abilities, Andy. I have never come across anyone with your potential.'

'Would that include visionary foresight?'

'Quite possibly.'

His body sagged and he bunched his eyes.

'Andy?'

'I...' he hesitated, struggling to find the words he wanted to say. 'I keep having...dreams,' he said.

'What sort of dreams?' Deans sucked air deep inside his chest and held it for a moment.

'Am I seeing the past...or the future?' he asked hesitantly.

Denise did not answer straight away.

'What kind of dreams, Andy?'

He took the phone away from his ear and lowered it down by his side. He drifted off and looking out through the window, watched a young couple in the car park below. The woman walked around the front of the car and joined the man. They embraced for a long moment. They were in love – Deans could tell. The ache in his heart intensified.

'Andy?' he heard Denise asking. 'What kind of dreams?'

He tore his eyes away from the couple and raised the phone back to his lips.

'Horrific.'

'Maria?' Denise asked.

Deans stared at the floor. 'I wake before...'

'Your safety net,' Denise said.

Deans nodded. 'I guess so.'

'Do you want to talk about it?'

Deans shrugged and looked through the window again. The couple had moved on. His breath fogged the glass and he studied it for a moment.

'I walk in on her execution,' he said and closed his eyes. 'I can do nothing about it.'

'Do you see who is responsible?' Denise asked.

'Ash Babbage… and someone else.'

Denise did not speak.

'Why do I keep having the same dream?' he asked. He listened and waited for Denise to answer.

Her breathing became louder.

'You feel guilty for not being there for her when she was taken; that's you walking in onto something bad and you are not in control. You need to regain that feeling through the dream. Create anything to give you back that power. Own the dream; change the reality.'

Deans shook his head. 'I realise now that I am in a dream, but I'm completely helpless—'

'As you are in real life,' Denise cut in. 'Own the dream. Change your reality…'

Own the dream. He never wanted to experience the dream again, let alone dictate to it.

CHAPTER SEVEN

Deans had slept reasonably well and for the first time in days he had not had *that dream*. Denise told him over the phone that she would treat him remotely – whatever that might mean. Maybe she had done something to help. He certainly felt more energised.

He placed the whisky bottle back into the kitchen cupboard, walked to the bathroom, and swilled his mouth with Listerine. He stared at the face looking back at him in the mirror – he barely recognised himself.

The landline began to ring in the bedroom. Deans bolted from the bathroom and picked up. 'Hello, Maria?' he answered quickly.

'Good morning,' came the breezy reply. 'Is this Mr Deans?'

'Who's calling?' Deans asked.

'Is this Mr Andrew Deans?' the voice replied.

'Yes, yes, I'm Mr bloody Andrew Deans. Who is this?'

'Can I take your month of birth to verify who you are please?'

'I know who I am. Who are you?' Deans barked.

'Your month of birth please, sir?'

'February. It's February... the 12th if you really must know. Who is this?'

'Thank you, Mr Deans. This is the fertility clinic. I'm sure you understand the reason for our confidentiality checks.'

'Oh, yes... sorry. Sorry, I'm having a bit of a rough time at the moment.'

'That's okay, I understand,' the still breezy voice said. 'We are just checking that everything is okay?'

'Why wouldn't it be?'

'You and your wife missed an appointment with us on Tuesday and we were just making sure you were still happy to continue with the treatment? Or, perhaps if you would like to speak with your consultant about anything?'

Deans didn't speak. He lowered the phone from his ear and peered over at Maria's side of the bed – her favourite teddy – 'Bob' sitting expectantly on her pillow awaiting her return. A tickle of chilled air crawled up the back of his spine. He rubbed the nape of his neck with his free hand.

'Mr Deans?' the voice said after a few delayed seconds.

'Yes,' Deans said returning the receiver to speak. 'I'm sorry for the missed appointment,' he said in a blank voice. 'Maria... Maria isn't here at the moment. Can we call you back to make another appointment, please?'

'I can make one for you now if you would prefer?'

'No. No. Thanks, but... I need... I need to speak to my wife before I make any decisions.'

'Well okay, that's absolutely fine. Just to make you aware though, that your consultant is having an extended holiday this Christmas and has advised us that you shouldn't leave the next appointment any longer than two more weeks from now. Is that okay?'

'Yeah... I understand. Um, I'll talk to Maria when I see her next.'

'Okay, that's wonderful. Take care and pass on our best wishes to your wife.'

Deans looked at *Bob* again. 'Yeah,' he said. 'Thanks.'

He sloped across to the wardrobe, dug out the least crinkled work shirt and slowly dressed in a subdued daze. He stopped buttoning his shirt and waited.

He held his breath and listened carefully. Scanning the room, he walked slowly over to the window and peered outside through a gap in the slats. His eyes narrowed as he searched the area in front of his property. He pulled his fingers away and the metallic blinds sprang back into position.

Deans walked to the hallway and stopped. He sniffed the air, held it deep within his lungs and closed his eyes. *It's not her*, he thought and returned to the bedroom. He peered at *Bob*. 'See you later tonight, mate,' he said and closed the door.

The office was in the centre of Bath, a short, or long thirty minute walk, depending on how it was viewed.

The moment he arrived Deans saw Savage coming out from the DI's office. He was frowning and came straight over to Deans.

'I've just been speaking with DI Thornton on the phone,' Savage said. 'He wants you to contact him this morning. He said it was urgent.'

Deans checked his phone. 'He hasn't tried to contact me. What does he want?'

Savage bobbed his shoulders and spoke in covert tones. 'Just give him a call. Use the boss's office; he's not in there at the moment.'

Deans' eyes burned wide, and he headed straight for the small office at the back of the room, slamming the door behind him.

He fumbled for the number stored on his phone and waited impatiently for DI Thornton to answer his call.

'Thornton,' the response eventually came.

Deans was so anxious to speak, he forgot to say who he was. 'My skipper said you needed to speak to me. Is there news?' he spluttered.

'I'm sorry,' the DI said. 'Is this Andrew?'

'Yeah, yeah. Do you have news?'

'Thanks for getting back to me so soon, Andrew,' Thornton said. He sounded business-like. 'Any chance you could pop over this morning?'

Pop over? Deans rubbed his face vigorously. 'Is there news?' he asked again.

'Let's talk when you come over,' Thornton replied.

There's news.

'I'll come over right away,' he said, his heart leaping through his chest.

'Good,' Thornton replied. 'Shall we say, around ten o'clock?'

'I'm on my way now.' Deans ended the call and rushed back out into the office.

Savage was standing, waiting for him.

'Deano?' he asked.

'I've gotta go,' Deans said scooping up the contents of his day-bag and grabbing a set of car keys from the rack. 'He's got news.'

'Are you alright?' Savage asked, but Deans was already jogging out of the door.

Deans arrived at the Major Crime Investigation Team (MCIT) offices in central Bristol, and hurried his way through the security doors, running up to the second floor, to where the incident room was located. Even though he was a detective of the same police constabulary, he was not granted automatic access in to this particular department.

He peered through a clear panel of the door and rapped on the glass with his knuckles.

Three detectives sitting at their desks a matter of feet away did a spectacular job of ignoring him.

Bollocks to it.

Deans booted the base of the door with the toe-end of his shoe.

A female officer looked up from her computer screen and glared at him.

Get off your arse now. He beckoned her across to him with a wave.

She rose reluctantly from her chair and came to the door. 'Yes,' she said obtusely.

'I'm Andy Deans.'

She gazed at the ID badge hanging on a lanyard from his neck and shrugged in a disinterested fashion.

Deans' face tightened. 'Andy Deans,' he repeated. 'Maria Deans' husband.'

'Oh!' the officer said, looking over her shoulder towards the other two detectives at the table. 'I'm sorry,' she said. 'Please, come in.' She stood aside and held the door wide open.

'DI Thornton phoned me,' Deans said. 'He wanted to see me.'

The officer's skin was now a crimson glow. 'Um… can you just wait here?' she said. 'I'll go and see if he's ready.'

Ready? He instinctively checked his phone. No messages.

'Would you like a drink?' the detective asked coming back into the room. 'He's going to be a few more minutes.'

Deans shook his head.

He shifted uneasily on his feet and looked around the room. He had previously worked in this very same office when detectives had been seconded from outer districts to aid the MCIT during a spree of gang murders in Bristol. His eyes settled on the white-board in the corner of the room. **'OPERATION ENGAGE'** was penned in bold black letters. He repeated the words in his head and prayed they were; engaged.

The female detective broke Deans' trance. 'You…' she said hesitating, 'you work at Falcon Road nick, don't you?'

Deans silently confirmed.

'I love Bath, I do. I come down every year with my boyfriend for the Christmas market. He's meeting me this weekend and we're going over.'

Deans' brow furrowed. *Come down?*

'Andrew!'

The recognisable Bristolian tones of DI Thornton came from the other end of the room.

Deans dipped his head to the female detective and walked over, shaking Thornton's hand.

'Come on through, Andrew. Thanks for trekking over to see us.' He held Deans' stare for a significant moment. 'Come in to my office,' he said.

The DI led the way through another open plan office with enough seating for at least thirty officers, and stood aside his glass-walled fishbowl office in the corner of the room.

'Take a seat,' he said, nudging the door closed with his bottom, yet remained standing himself.

Deans complied and stared wide-eyed at Thornton.

The DI hovered for a measured moment and then sat next to him.

Deans' knee bobbed uncontrollably. He looked the DI square in the face. 'You have news,' he said.

The DI's lips constricted, he shook his head and lifted a twitching a finger above his head.

Two suits Deans did not recognise entered the room and stood in front of him.

'Andrew, these detectives want to ask you some questions,' the DI said rising to his feet and standing closer towards the door.

Deans looked at the two officers and then raked a glance at Thornton who returned an apologetic smile.

'You are fucking kidding me,' Deans said, stiffening his arms and shoulders.

'Just follow the chaps please, Andrew,' Thornton said. 'Let's not make this any more difficult than it already is.'

Deans stood slowly from his seat. His body buzzed with adrenalin as it prepared to fight. He looked back into the main office as a group of heads ducked down behind their computer screens like a mob of meerkats seeking shelter.

The DI was already outside his office directing the officers with an outstretched arm. 'This way please, lads.'

As Deans neared the DI, he stopped and faced him, toe-to-toe.

'Come on,' the DI whispered. 'Please.'

'Come on, bud,' one of the others officers said to Deans.

Deans curled his lip and followed them through the foyer into a small room with a table and three chairs. He looked above the door. There was a small camera.

The first detective did not speak but gestured with his hand for Deans to sit in the chair facing the camera, and the two detectives took their seats opposite him.

Deans hovered for a moment and considered his situation, before himself taking the 'hot' seat.

Deans glared at the mute detectives and jabbed a hand towards the camera knowing that Thornton was watching.

'What the fuck is this?' he seethed. 'Are you arresting me?'

The second detective spoke over Deans' angry rant.

'I am Detective Richardson. This is Detective Davies. We just have a few questions of you.'

'Am I under caution?' Deans asked.

'Did you hear us caution you?' Davies said sarcastically.

Deans glowered at Davies who had his day-book out on the desk and his pen at the ready.

He was one of those cops you could instantly tell spent far too much time in the gym, looking at himself in the mirror. He was wearing a short-sleeved shirt, exposing a thick black tribal tattoo on his sizeable bicep.

Deans gazed up at the camera. His jaw locked tight.

'Describe your relationship with Denise Moon?' Richardson asked.

Deans lowered his focus onto Richardson, pouted his bottom lip and shook his head.

Richardson half-smiled. 'This is low-key stuff, Detective Deans—'

'Cut the shite,' Deans said. 'I'm really not in the mood.'

'Suffer with moods do we?' Davies asked smugly.

Deans glared at him again.

Davies lowered his pen onto his day-book and wrapped the palm of one hand around a clenched fist.

'Your wife has been missing for coming on a month now, Detective,' Davies said.

'Nineteen days,' Deans retorted immediately.

'Nineteen days, that's right,' Davies beamed with a two-hundred-quid cosmetic smile. 'And *we* are trying to make sure she's not missing for twenty, thirty, or sixty days,' he sneered.

You condescending bastard.

'Where are you both from?' Deans asked. 'I must have missed that part when you introduced yourselves.'

Davies flicked a sideways glance.

'Dyfed Powys Police,' Richardson answered.

Dyfed Powys fucking police, Deans repeated in his head. He looked up at the camera. Cops never investigate officers of their own force – not for the serious stuff, anyway.

He folded his arms and leaned back against the chair.

'I want someone with me before I answer any other questions,' he said.

'Andrew…' Richardson said. 'Come on. We all want the same thing.'

Deans slammed both hands onto the table with a loud whack. 'Do we? Do *we* want the same things?'

He made a point of looking at their fingers.

'Neither of you are married,' he said. 'Or if you are, you're trying to hide it. You don't know what I'm thinking. You don't know the pain—'

'Well, how about you start by telling us then,' Davies said, all matter of fact and Hollywood smile.

'Just for the record,' Deans said, jabbing a pointed finger towards Davies. 'I've met a few wankers in this job over the years, but I reckon you're right up there with the best of them.'

'Andrew,' Richardson said, patting down the flames. 'Come on, please. We are not against you.'

Deans glared at Richardson. 'Get that twat out of here,' he said nodding towards Davies. 'And get me Thornton.'

Richardson huffed and ran fingers through his beard. He looked over at Davies and gestured for him to leave the room.

Davies stood up with a challenging snarl and stare.

Deans did not speak until he saw Thornton at the door. 'What the fuck is this?' Deans shouted before Thornton had the chance to come inside the room.

'Andrew, you know procedure. Come on. Cooperate for all our sakes,' Thornton said.

'Did Mick Savage know this was going to happen?' Deans raged.

Thornton shook his head.

Deans clamped his jaw. Being belligerent was not going to help Maria, and while they were seeing who could piss the highest up the urinal wall, presumably, nothing was being done to find his wife.

He scowled at Thornton. 'Just ask me what you need to know and then get back out there and find my wife.'

Thornton was poker-faced.

Richardson spoke, 'Maria left you before she went missing.'

'Questions, not statements,' Deans barked. 'That's getting us nowhere.'

Richardson smiled. 'Okay. Were you having an affair?'

'No,' Deans said quickly. 'Next question?'

'Why would Maria leave the stability of her home having just found out she was pregnant?' Richardson asked.

Deans stared forcefully at his interrogator and shook his head.

'Describe what you thought about the pregnancy,' Richardson asked calmly.

Deans looked away and blinked for the first time in minutes. He pictured Maria.

'I was delighted,' he uttered. 'Meant the world to us.' He snarled at Richardson. 'Means *everything* to me.'

Richardson jogged his head and took notes in his day-book.

'If it meant so much,' he said down to his page, 'why were you away from home so often?'

Deans snorted a false snicker.

'Where are you now, Richardson? You're not at home. You're not even on your own patch. Who's to say your partner isn't banging the next door neighbour, fucking your inspector, or sobbing into a pillow because you're not there?'

Deans screwed up his face.

'We, none of us, know the impact the job has on our other halves, because the job is everything. The job is *The Job*. Has to be... regardless of the outcome to our personal lives.'

Thornton stood up and pointed at Richardson. 'That's enough, now. I've heard enough.' He held out a hand to Deans. 'Come on, Andy.'

CHAPTER EIGHT

Neither of them spoke until they reached the DI's fish bowl office.

'There is something you need to see,' Thornton said softly.

Deans stopped in the doorway.

'Please,' Thornton said. 'Come in. Close the door.'

Deans looked over his shoulder. It was just the two of them –
and the gang of meerkats, now shielded behind their screens.

Thornton's features softened, but his brow twitched. 'This
investigation has escalated, Andy.' He sniffed loudly. 'We believe
we have… evidence.'

Deans stiffened. 'Evidence of what?'

Thornton cleared his throat. 'I'm afraid…' he said hesitating.
'…I'm afraid we are now treating Maria's disappearance as
murder.'

Blood plummeted into Deans' feet and he wobbled.

Thornton moved towards his desk and spoke as he walked.
'I'm afraid I must ask you to sign a declaration that will allow officers to look into your bank and internet activity.'

Deans could not speak. Could not move.

Thornton lifted a sheet from his desk and held it outstretched
in front of Deans. It was a Data Protection Authority – the kind

Deans used on a regular basis to satisfy the legal loopholes when looking into specific areas of a person's life – such as bank transfers.

'It'll make life easier, Andy,' Thornton said. 'For you. For everyone.' He waved the form so that it made a rippling noise in front of Dean's face. Thornton stepped closer. 'Please?'

He placed the document in Deans' hand and handed him his Parker pen.

'For what it might be worth to you, Andy. This is a hell of a thing and I know you have nothing to worry about.'

Deans looked at him, his eyes heavy and moist. He stepped over to the desk and gave his signature.

'There's something else,' Thornton said quietly. 'I want you to view something.'

A bead of wetness dropped down Deans' cheek.

'Shall we go to the video suite?' Thornton asked moving for the door.

Video suite?

Deans acquiesced and followed in Thornton's footsteps, head bowed.

The DI led Deans into the tech part of the building and entered another secure area. A male officer was sitting alone before a mosaic of screens in the darkened room.

'Gav, this is Andy Deans,' the DI announced.

Gav stood up and shook Deans by the hand. 'I'm sorry about your missus, mate,' Gav said and sat back down in his chair.

'Gav, the starting point, please?' the DI said and turned to Deans. 'We were able to trace Maria from her last bank transaction.'

Deans nodded and wiped his nose along the back of his hand.

'Are you okay, Andy?' Thornton asked, handing Deans a wad of paper tissues.

Deans grunted.

A large monitor on the wall brought light to their faces and showed a still image of a woman walking into a building from the outside.

Deans instinctively stepped toward the screen and his stomach tightened.

'Play it forward,' Thornton said softly.

The frame rolled forward. The woman was closing her umbrella in the doorway while struggling to keep hold of a department store shopping bag. She walked forwards and out of shot.

'Is that Maria?' Thornton asked.

'Yes,' Deans said breathlessly. With all his will, he wanted to leap into the screen and wrap her in his arms.

'That is the Natwest Bank on Milsom Street,' Thornton said.

Deans noticed that Thornton was watching him, rather than the footage on the screen.

The camera angle changed and was now looking into the bank from above the door. Maria was third in line at the counter.

'How much did Maria withdraw?' Deans whispered.

'She didn't,' Thornton said. 'She made a balance enquiry.'

Deans blinked.

'She has online banking, right?' Thornton asked after a short pause.

Deans nodded, not taking his eyes away from Maria.

'If she'd been shopping, she would have been checking her account balance – suggesting to me she was looking to buy something else,' Deans said.

'Me too,' Thornton said. 'But sadly we don't have any other transactions.'

Deans turned to Thornton. 'Then this is the start of our window.'

Thornton held out a hand.

'We've got more,' he said and motioned to the techie.

The image on the screen changed.

Deans was now looking at an area he knew well – the Southgate shopping development – only a few minutes' walk from the nick.

'Watch top left,' Thornton said.

Deans trained his eyes that way. He saw the streaming Christmas decorations, shop window displays and bright festive lights.

'It's quick,' Thornton said.

Deans immediately noticed Maria's yellow and black floral birdcage umbrella amongst a throng of people.

He ducked and bobbed his head as she moved away from the camera, but he was unable to make her out clearly in the crowd. She was walking in the direction of the train station. Suddenly her umbrella dropped to the ground.

'Where is she?' Deans asked, frantically combing the screen.

He turned to the techie, 'Play that back bit-by-bit.'

Thornton consented, and the screen flickered with accelerated movement.

Deans' eyes burned on each still frame that slowly clicked by and he settled on the final image of Maria's umbrella now lying upturned on the floor.

'Is that it?' Deans barked.

'That's all we have at this time,' Thornton said.

'Who was behind Maria?' Deans asked, his voice booming in the silent room.

'We don't know,' Thornton said folding his arms.

'But you will? You've got more footage to review – right?' Deans barked.

Thornton shook his head. 'We were hoping for more.'

'What about those people?' Deans was almost shouting now.

'We are doing our best, Andrew.'

Deans glared at Thornton. 'There are over sixty police controlled cameras in Bath city centre, not to mention the hundreds of privately operated ones, and you're trying to tell me those people appeared from nowhere and vanished into thin air?'

'It's a start,' Thornton said.

'A fucking start?'

Deans' teeth were bared. He pointed angrily at the screen. 'That's my wife.'

The DI stood firm.

'My wife,' Deans repeated stepping closer to the screen, jabbing the glass with his fingertip and causing puddles to appear on the LCD screen.

The techie was about to complain about Deans' finger, but then must have thought better of it and closed his mouth again.

'And that looks to me like the moment my wife has been nabbed—'

'We don't know that, Andrew,' Thornton interrupted and stepped into Deans' personal space.

'Then you tell me what that was,' Deans snapped loudly.

Thornton held Deans' stare and he looked Deans up and down.

'Don't worry. I'm going to find out.'

CHAPTER NINE

Deans stormed up the two flights of stairs and beckoned Savage to follow him into one of the disused offices. 'Maria has been kidnapped,' Deans said.

'What?' Savage's voice raised several octaves.

'Right here,' Deans said stabbing a finger towards the window. 'Under our bloody noses. I watched it for myself on CCTV.'

Savage frowned and shook his head. 'What?' he said again.

'They think I had something to do with it. I've just been grilled by two Taffy officers.' Deans glared at Savage. 'Did you know about this?' he snarled.

'No. Absolutely not,' Savage pleaded. 'Deano, that's ridiculous—'

'Tell me about it,' Deans said. 'I still can't believe it.'

Savage walked over to the door and locked it from the inside. 'Were you formally arrested?' he asked.

'No,' Deans said. 'They weren't that professional… bastards.'

'What about Thornton?' Savage asked. 'He never said a thing to me.'

'It's been upped to a murder enquiry.' Deans looked away.

'Shit!' Savage spat. 'I am sorry, Deano.'

'It was a trap,' Deans said. 'Seems I was the only one who didn't have a clue what was happening.'

Savage shook his head. 'Not the case from this end. We've been kept well out of the loop from the sound of things. What is all this about CCTV?'

'I'm going out there now,' Deans said. 'Southgate. She was taken at the entrance to the covered section.'

'I think you need to lay off, Deano. You were told from the outset not to get involved by DI Thornton.'

'How can I not get involved when the team entrusted with finding my wife are pissing up the wrong tree and wasting valuable time?'

'Deano, you don't need this crap. Let it be somebody else's problem.'

Deans glared at Savage. 'This *is* my problem – twenty-four-seven. Not thirty-seven contracted hours per week. There is no escape for me, no cosy nights in with the missus, and I will do whatever it takes to find my wife.'

Savage groaned. 'In that case,' he said pulling on his raincoat, 'I'm coming with you. I need to make sure you don't drop in the shit.'

They grabbed their go-bags and walked the short distance to the shopping centre. Deans headed directly for the spot where he saw Maria's umbrella on the floor from the CCTV footage. The Christmas shoppers were out in force, making it difficult not to be swept along in their tide. Deans planted himself in their path and was bumped and barged in the process. He looked back towards the CCTV camera and scanned the walls nearest to him. There were no cameras obviously closer.

'Was it here?' Savage asked.

Deans nodded and carried on looking around him.

'How could she go from this place?' Savage asked. 'People would have been everywhere.'

'They were. Come on,' Deans said and walked with a purpose towards the outlet store opposite them.

Savage followed and Deans went up to the counter and flashed his warrant card from his wallet.

'Hi,' he said to the young man serving. 'Manager, please.'

The lad looked at Deans' badge and pressed a button causing a bell to sound on the wall behind his head.

A flustered woman came to the desk, all huffy and puffy.

'What is it now,' she said to the lad. 'I told you already that I am trying to cash-up.'

The lad signalled over at Deans and Savage, and Deans showed the woman his badge.

'Again?' she said. 'Can't keep you lot away.'

Deans scowled and looked at Savage.

'Do you have a moment, please?' Deans asked. 'I appreciate you are busy and this will not take long.'

'Come on,' she said with a defeated groan and walked back the way she'd come.

Deans and Savage followed and exchanged the same troubled glance.

She took them into a back office – typical retail set-up – desk, computer, kettle, mugs on a round tin tray, comfortable chair, and general mess and clutter.

'I just need to make sure I'm not duplicating work,' Deans said. 'But what have the police been here for recently?'

'Well, that stolen coat,' the manager said as if Deans should know the ins-and-outs of every shoplifting in town.

'That's not why we are here,' Deans replied.

'Is it the CCTV outside… again?' the woman wheezed.

Savage stepped forwards. 'Again?'

'Who else has asked you for the CCTV?' Deans questioned more directly. 'When – when were you asked?'

'I can't remember... two, maybe three weeks ago,' she shrugged.

Deans scowled and looked at Savage.

'And did you have CCTV to hand over?' Savage asked.

'Well, obviously,' she said sarcastically.

'Can we see it now?' Deans asked looking over to the old-fashioned VHS recording equipment.

'Well, no,' she snapped. 'Not until you lot come back and fix the machine you broke.'

'Has it worked since that time?' Deans asked.

'No it hasn't,' she replied tartly.

'What did the CCTV show?' Deans asked with a determined voice.

The woman looked at him as if he was an idiot and shook her head.

'The lady – the umbrella lady,' she replied curtly. 'The stuff you lot wanted in the first place.'

Deans lunged towards the equipment.

Savage reacted first. 'What are you doing?' he said pulling Deans back.

'Seizing the recorder—'

'Deano, you can't.' Savage held Deans' arm tightly preventing him from grabbing the machine.

Deans grimaced. 'We need that footage.'

'I know, mate,' Savage said trying to calm Deans down. 'Let me chat to Thornton, see what's happening.'

Deans relaxed his arms and spoke to the manager again. 'Do you remember who came to collect the CCTV?'

The manager shrugged. 'How am I supposed to remember everyone that comes in here?'

'Did they leave a card... a contact number?'

She shook her head.

'Suit or uniform?' Deans pressed.

She pulled a face and raised her eyes to the ceiling. 'He was in a suit. Smart-looking. Just like you two.'

Savage suggested that they go to a coffee shop for a chat and a cool down. Deans was in no fit state to return to the office and a caffeine fix was probably a good idea. Savage took the lead and thankfully found them a decent place.

They sat in silence with their drinks. Savage watching Deans continuously.

'I've been thinking,' Savage said eventually.

'Me too,' Deans replied.

'I'd do everything by the book if I were you, Deano. There are obviously things in play that neither of us knows about.'

Deans bowed his head.

Savage slurped his drink and tugged the tip of his ear like it was a piece of rubber.

'What's on your mind?' Deans asked. 'Just come out with it.'

Savage stared down at the table and fiddled with his mug.

'Did I have anything to do with it?' Deans asked. 'Is that what you were thinking?'

Savage looked up and held Deans' eye.

'You know where I was Mick,' Deans said.

'I know where you say you were. But none of us were there with you, Deano.'

Deans lowered his chin and looked at Savage through his brooding lids.

'Come on, Deano. I've got your back—'

'But?'

Savage blinked and peered into his cup.

'But?' Deans repeated more assertively.

'Look, I understand the Amy Poole investigation took a toll on you. Put pressures on you and Maria I could never fully appreciate.' Savage shook his head. 'I didn't know you were trying for kids – having treatment. Christ! Why did you allow yourself to get so involved in Devon?'

Deans lowered his gaze and began twisting his cup in the saucer.

'I'm just saying, Deano. If that was me—'

'But it wasn't,' Deans snapped. 'And you have no comprehension about what has happened to me over the last few weeks.'

Savage scratched the side of his nose and bobbed his head.

'Are you still in touch with that woman?' he asked.

Deans nodded once.

Savage huffed. 'She's the reason your life has become so screwed up, and you don't seem to see that.'

Deans smiled insincerely and gently rocked his head. 'Fine,' he said.

'I'm trying to help,' Savage said. 'Trying to give you warning.'

Deans narrowed his stare and brought his cup to his lips with both hands.

'Are you going to see her again?' Savage asked.

Deans took a considered sip from his coffee and licked the froth from the top of his lip before answering. 'More than likely,' he replied.

'Well then...' Savage planted both hands flat onto the table as if he was about to perform a push-up. 'I think we'd better go and get a proper drink.'

CHAPTER TEN

Savage took Deans to the Bunker – a trendy, subterranean wine bar below the busy pavements of George Street. With a near guarantee of not being surrounded by shit-bags, this was a safe bet for two cops to hang out and have a serious chat. Savage had already called the office, spoken to the late tour skipper, DS Reynolds, and told him not to expect them back, and to inform the rest of the team he would see them in the morning.

Savage was a self-proclaimed wine connoisseur. He probably talked a load of bollocks, but Deans did not know any the better; it was either red or white.

Savage shouted in a thirty quid bottle of Argentinian red and they found an alcove furthest from the music where talking was less of a challenge.

'How's the double-death going?' Savage asked.

Deans sipped from his glass. 'Okay.'

Savage gave him a fleeting glance.

'Come on, Mick,' Deans said. 'What's really on your mind? Don't treat me like a bloody idiot.'

Savage smiled. It was as if just a few sips of the vino had already loosened him up.

'Okay,' he said. 'Cards on the table.'

The dim lighting made it difficult for Deans to read Savage's eyes.

'Human Resources have been in contact with me over the last few days. They are concerned about your... capacity... considering—'

'And what about you, Mick?' Deans interrupted. 'Are you concerned?'

'Deano, you know I'm supportive of you on this. Would I have given you the double-death if I was concerned about your ability?' Savage stopped talking and fiddled with the long slender stem of his glass. 'I have to be seen doing the right thing, that's all.'

'Which is?'

'Your welfare, Deano.'

They locked eyes and Savage turned away and took a couple of quick sips from his glass.

'Have Occupational Health been in contact with you this week?' he asked.

Deans nodded, took a sip. 'I've got an appointment with them on Monday.'

'Good,' Savage said and placed both hands flat on the table.

Deans made a point of noticing the gesture.

'Look, I'm worried about you, Deano. The entire department is worried. It's a hell of a shock—'

'And I'm dealing with it.'

Savage dipped his gaze and shook his head. 'What about Babbage?'

Deans' cheeks flushed and he shifted in his seat. He lifted his wine glass towards his face and created a shield between himself and Savage.

'What do you mean?' he asked and took a drawn out sip.

'Come on, Deano. You must want to wring his neck. It sounded like he practically coughed to Maria's disappearance.'

Deans shrugged. 'What can I do? He's on remand in a Devon prison and their force is investigating him.'

'Deano…' Savage wavered and checked over his shoulder. 'Deano, all that stuff about psychics and ghosts?'

So, that's what this is really about. Deans placed his glass down onto the table and rested his chin on top of his interlocked knuckles.

'It's just…' Savage continued. 'I think you do need to see a proper doctor, or something—'

'Or something?'

'You know?'

'No, Mick. I don't know.' Deans leaned back against the hard wooden rungs of the chair and stared at Savage. 'I trusted you with that information, Mick.'

'Come on, Deano. Really? Do you honestly believe half of that *stuff* happened?'

'I confided in you. I needed someone I could trust. You have no idea what I went through—'

'No, I don't.'

Another weighty silence followed.

'What have you told Human Resources?' Deans asked.

'Nothing, Deano. Not about that. Christ, how would it make me sound?'

Deans could not believe what he was hearing.

Savage sunk the rest of his glass and poured himself another as he spoke.

'Deano, the current climate… well, you're familiar with how it is. I just don't want to lose you because you've made it easy for HR to get rid of you.' He waved a dismissive hand. 'Just saying, Deano. Just saying.'

There it is. I'm on my own.

CHAPTER ELEVEN

Next day Deans went to work with a thick head. He had played along with Savage, extracting any snippets of information that might help him, or he should be wary of, but the more Savage drank the more he wanted to divulge his own domestic strife. At least Deans did not have to rehearse his own real life drama.

His plan for the day was simple: return to The Willows and mooch about for answers. But what he needed most was to be on his own. The Roses' post mortems were fixed for ten-thirty, commencing with Helen Rose. In fairness to Savage, he had insisted Deans should not be involved in the examinations – probably a wise call.

Savage was not around, Mitchell was in Southmead at the post mortem and Harper was away from her desk.

Deans sat in front of his computer screen, shoulders rounded and his back hunched. Even the third coffee of the morning was doing little to help his motivation.

His eyes settled on a Jiffy envelope on the corner of his desk. He put his coffee down and picked up the package. He noticed the STORM LOG reference number for the double-death written on the corner – probably copied from the press release on the force website.

Deans twirled the Royal Mail package in his hands before setting it back down on the desk in front of him.

He took another swig of coffee, hooked a little finger under the flap and peeled it open. He squeezed the edges together and peered into the parcel. There was a CD case.

He frowned, poured it out onto the desk and reached for a pair of forensic gloves. It was always better to be safe than sorry.

The disk was unmarked. He angled it towards the window-light – it did have something recorded onto it.

He grabbed a laptop and put the disk inside. As the machine readied itself, Deans picked up the envelope and studied it again. There was no sign where it had come from, other than a Swindon postmark.

The computer whirred and whined as the disk loaded, and a small thumbnail file appeared in the centre of the screen.

Deans leaned in closer.

His interest piqued, he double clicked the small square and reached for his mug of coffee.

The image expanded and his jaw fell open. He was looking at the Roses' bedroom – with them inside – and they were still alive.

He dropped his mug to the desk and could not take his eyes away from the screen. *Why film yourselves?*

The bedroom was dark, but everything inside could be easily seen from the sage-green sheen of night-vision photography. As he continued to watch, Mr Rose rolled away from his wife. Deans heard the baby murmur from somewhere inside the Moses basket located directly alongside Mrs Rose and Deans quickly increased the volume, and then it began:

Mrs Rose suddenly lashed out with her hands and screamed wildly waking Mr Rose. The pair simultaneously sat upright, their eyes glowing fluorescent green in the night-vision. The baby began to cry. Mr Rose kicked out with a frenzied attempt to move higher up the bed and Mrs Rose covered her face with her hands and dived behind the small of his back. Both were yelling and screaming loudly. A bright flash of light interrupted the recording and the footage vanished for a second or two.

"Argh… Argh… Argh," Mr Rose howled. Mrs Rose whimpered behind the shield of her hands and pressed herself up against the headboard. Mr Rose lunged over his wife completely covering her from view.

Deans could hear her muffled voice crying out for "Molly", and then, just as quickly, she fell silent. No more crying, no more whimpering, no more calling out for her daughter.

Deans was transfixed and could then hear Mr Rose pleading repeatedly, "No. No. No." He pulled Mrs Rose out from beneath him and ran his hands through her hair, exposing her anguished and twisted face to the camera. Suddenly, an orb of white light moved from above Mrs Rose's head towards the cot. Deans leaned in closer to the screen and watched the light hover above the child for a brief moment, and then race back towards the bed. Mr Rose let out one final blood-curdling squeal before he too fell silent and motionless.

Deans blinked moisture back into his eyes and mouthed, *holy shit*. Their body positions were now exactly as he had seen them at the scene.

The baby suddenly chuckled – no mistake. Neither a gargle nor an incoherent infant emission – a giggle – one hundred percent.

Deans gaped at the cot. The baby's hands appeared on the lip of the wicker basket and then its head.

Is that possible? The baby looked directly into the lens of the camera and Deans' heart jumped a beat. The baby appeared to be watching Deans – *watching him.*

Deans shot back in the chair. He did not blink, even though his eyes were burning wide.

The baby made another noise.

Deans shook his head and swiftly stopped the recording.

His finger hovered above the computer mouse. He surely did not just hear what he thought he heard?

He finally blinked the discomfort from his eyes and rewound the footage by twenty seconds. His mouth was ajar and his breathing hurried. He nudged the volume to maximum and hit the play button once again.

There is was. He hadn't misheard it. The baby had spoken – just three words, but enough. Enough to scare the living crap out of Deans.

"I see you."

Mitchell returned to the office within the hour. He bounded over to Deans and slipped a report onto the desk.

'You okay, Deano?' Mitchell asked sitting opposite him.

Deans didn't look up.

'Have you heard something?' Mitchell asked softly. 'You don't look too well.'

Deans shook his head.

'Post Mortem results,' Mitchell said, 'on that report.'

Deans heaved a sigh, but did not answer.

'Cardiac arrest,' Mitchell said, 'both of them.'

Deans nodded.

'Initial toxicology has failed to identify a contributing cause,' Mitchell said. 'The pathologist is considering further examinations.'

'Won't do any good,' Deans said, finally looking up over the top of the laptop.

'Why not?' Mitchell asked.

'Because there aren't any tests to prove what they died from.'

CHAPTER TWELVE

Deans figured the DVD footage was recorded from the baby-cam he had seen in the Roses' bedroom. He had struggled on the internet to find a camera brand that recorded footage, however, did discover several disturbing news articles relating to 'hacked' baby-cams, where external parties had intercepted insecure units for their own criminal vices. He had watched the DVD again – the extinction of life was no easier for the seventh, as it was the first time of viewing. If anything, the more he saw it the more distressed he felt. Perhaps he was not ready for *this*?

He had kept the DI informed about the DVD, but up until now, had not disclosed everything he had seen on it, or believed he had viewed on it.

'Sir,' Deans said tapping quietly on the open door to the DI's office. 'I'd like to send this disk and envelope away for forensics. We need to find who sent it.'

'For the suicide job?' the DI asked, still working on his computer. 'It's nothing that we need to worry about.'

Deans shook his head. 'It's not a suicide, Boss.'

The DI faced Deans and for a moment just stared at him. He pointed to a chair and Deans sat down.

'What's on your mind, Deano?' the DI asked.

'I don't believe they intended to die,' Deans said. 'The DVD suggests…' he paused – it was now all or nothing, '…well it suggests external influences were responsible.'

The DI shook his head and shrugged a shoulder. 'External influences?' he repeated. 'Surely it shows two people reacting to whatever they've digested? Their final, violent bodily responses to an as yet unidentified toxin.'

Deans looked down to his feet. 'I know I've been distracted—'

'Nobody could criticise you for that, Deano. You are having a hellish time.'

Deans looked the DI square in the face. 'Those two people didn't die by design,' he said. 'They were petrified.'

The DI unscrewed the lid on his bottle of sparkling water with a sharp hiss. Deans could hear each slow revolution of the twisting cap and subsequent throaty gulp of liquid. The DI wiped his lips with the back of his hand and secured the bottle once more. He looked at Deans again and smiled.

'They may have been petrified by what was happening to their bodies, Deano,' he said.

'No.'

The DI tilted his head and exposed the palm of his hands.

'Okay then,' he said calmly. 'Tell me what they died from?'

Deans took a deep breath. 'Boss… there is something in that house.'

The DI sat back and swivelled in his chair. He peered at Deans and bounced one foot on the floor. After a short delay, he gestured *go on* with his hand.

'The DVD shows a light source…' Deans stopped himself and shook his head. 'No. It shows an orb of energy hovering over the couple, right at the moment they perish. That same energy is seen to retreat to the end of the bed as the footage stops.'

The DI's features tightened. 'Energy?'

Deans stood up and walked over the DI. 'I felt it when I was at the house. *Something* else is in there, and it killed those two people.'

The DI was unblinking. He drew a slow and silent breath, making his shirt buttons strain as his chest filled. 'Deano, close the door a minute, would you?' Deans did as instructed and returned beside the DI.

'How is it going with Occupational Health?'

Here we go. 'Boss, I'm not losing my mind.'

'I don't believe I asked that.'

Deans huffed. 'It's fine. I'm on sleepers.' He shrugged. 'I'm doing what they tell me, seeing them when I'm supposed to—'

'And no adverse reactions to anything?'

Deans squinted. 'No.'

'How about Thornton – is he keeping you well informed?'

Deans looked away, suddenly felt guilty for taking his mind away from Maria.

'I make sure he keeps me updated.' The DI gave Deans a concerned stare. 'Are you really ready to be back, Deano?'

'Absolutely,' Deans said without hesitating.

The DI cast him a sympathetic smile. He scratched the side of his face and leaned in closer towards Deans.

'What do you propose we do at the house... with this... *energy*?' he asked.

Deans shrugged. 'I dunno.'

'Well then, why is this... *thing* there?'

Deans shrugged again. 'I dunno? But we should find out.'

He noticed the DI clenching and releasing his fist as if giving an invisible stress ball a vigorous workout.

'And how would we do that?' the DI asked.

'I'd like to chat to the old man in the nursing home. See what he knows?' Deans said.

The DI did not respond.

'I need to speak to him,' Deans said, 'and his smack-head daughter.'

The DI reached for his fizzy bottle and took another considered drink.

Deans waited until the bottle was back on the desk.

'And I need to find whoever sent me that DVD,' he said.

The DI raised his brows.

'And I want to bring somebody else into the house – to help me have a proper look around.'

'Miss Moon?' the DI asked.

Deans blinked and turned his head slightly to the door. *Has Mick said something?*

He looked back at the boss and conceded.

The DI tapped the end of his pen against his front teeth, not taking his eyes away from Deans.

'Okay,' he said, eventually. 'It's all yours. Do whatever you need to. Take as long as you need. Work the hours you want, but don't sacrifice yourself... or the reputation of this department.'

CHAPTER THIRTEEN

DC Sarah Gold was at her desk in the Devon Major Crime Investigation Team when Sergeant Jackson burst into the room and demanded that she join him.

DC Gold was still the officer in charge (OIC) of the Amy Poole murder investigation. Denise Moon's associate and apprentice, Ash Babbage, had been remanded to custody following his partial admissions to her murder during interview with Deans, and Gold had been taking control of each element of the investigation since that time; ensuring the strongest case could be built and presented to the Crown Prosecution Service (CPS).

DS Jackson was her skipper and had been overseeing the investigation. She got on fairly well with him and it certainly helped her that he was a lecherous old bastard, and she was attractive. Jackson had insisted from the outset that Gold take the lead investigative role in the case, despite her youthful experience as a detective.

He was waiting in the hallway with his usual skeletal frown and rancid breath.

'Follow me,' he said and took them into an empty room where he slammed the door shut.

'Sarge?' Gold queried.

He looked at her through his beady eyes.

Gold was quite repulsed by him and thought that he looked like a tortoise; with his leathery, taught features.

He pinched his lips together and panted loudly through his nose.

'What have you done?' he asked.

'I don't know,' she said, taking a backward step. 'I haven't done anything… have I?'

'The case is blown now,' Jackson vented.

'Sarge?'

'The CPS had no choice but to disclose to Babbage that the case evidence has been destroyed.'

'What?' Gold spluttered. 'What evidence? What are you talking about?'

'Jesus!' Jackson said behind clenched teeth. 'All the bloody evidence against Babbage that you authorised for destruction. It's gone. It's all bloody well gone.'

Gold covered her mouth with a hand. Tears began to form in the corner of her eyes. She shook her head. 'But… I haven't…'

'I've got the report,' Jackson seethed. 'You authorised destruction last week, and the officers in detained property didn't know any better. It was your responsibility to ensure the safe keeping of those exhibits.'

Gold shook her head, her hand still covering her open mouth. 'I didn't,' she pleaded again.

'And now Babbage has got a shit-hot barrister from London and we have to go before a judge to explain how *we* made such a catastrophic balls up with the evidence.'

Gold could barely move. Could not believe what she was hearing.

Jackson thrust his spiny finger near her face. 'This is down to you. This is your cock-up and you are going to face the music.'

CHAPTER FOURTEEN

Deans felt a pressure lift from his shoulders. The green light was all he needed. He had not been entirely straight with the DI; he did know what was required and how to go about it. And now he was on his way to the nursing home to see the old man, George Fenwick.

He pulled off the main road and followed a long shingle driveway towards the large Georgian manor house that for the last seventeen years had been used as a luxury private nursing home. He had driven past the entrance many times before, but this was his first venture inside the grounds.

Tall evergreen trees sheathed by six-foot-high mesh boots lined both sides of the entrance road every twenty metres or so. The gardens were pristine. Moisture on the baize-flat lawns shimmered like crystals in the wintry morning sunshine.

He parked short of the entrance and looked over at the valley in the distance. He could see Solisbury Hill, just as he could from his kitchen window at home. He sucked in a deep breath and forced himself back into character.

'Hello,' a breezy voice came from the intercom beside the door.

It was positioned such that Deans had to crouch over to speak. Better placed for guests or residents in wheelchairs.

'Good morning,' Deans said. 'My name is DC Deans from Falcon Road CID. I was hoping to talk to the manager if I may, please?'

'Is she expecting you?'

'No. I don't think so.'

'Hold on.' The intercom clicked and fell silent.

Deans used the opportunity to check his phone for messages – there was nothing.

The door opened and a young, uniformed bleached-blonde girl – probably still in her teens, greeted him with a friendly and outgoing smile.

'Can I see some ID, please?' she asked.

'Of course,' Deans said, his warrant card already poised in his hand.

The girl peered at the card, smiled and welcomed Deans inside the doorway.

'Hold on here a moment,' she said. 'I'll fetch the duty supervisor for you.'

Deans looked around. The thin striped red and black carpet was just as he had expected; dark, resilient and spongy under foot. He glanced at the staff identity board and immediately focussed on the three members of staff not wearing light-grey uniforms – *higher up the food chain,* he thought.

He could never imagine himself doing a carer's role, but if he ever made oak tree age, he would happily spend his final days in a place like this… if only he could afford to.

A woman in a smart trouser suit approached.

'Good morning,' she said; her face an unconcealed question mark.

'Good morning,' Deans replied, shaking her hand. 'I'm terribly sorry to trouble you. I'm a detective from Falcon Road CID.' He again flashed his badge but this time the wallet was taken from him and studied in detail.

'Please don't be alarmed,' Deans said, his hand at the ready for the return of his identity card. 'I'm here to ask about one of your residents, if possible, please?'

'Who are you looking for?' the suited woman said, waving away the girl in grey.

'George Fenwick?' Deans said.

The woman's features became more inquisitive and Deans noticed her recoil her head – ever so slightly.

'Yes. George is one of our residents,' she said. 'May I know what this is about specifically?'

'And can I ask your position here, please?' Deans responded.

'Sally Jarvis,' she said nudging her square-rimmed glasses higher up her nose. 'Team Leader.'

'Hi, Sally,' Deans said. 'Could we speak somewhere a little more private, please?'

She frowned. 'Yes, of course. Come this way.'

She led Deans further into the building – to a large office strewn with folders and papers.

'Please close the door – if you wish?' she said taking a seat beneath a large bay window that looked out onto the shingle car park at the front of the building.

Deans followed her outstretched arm to one of the three high-armed chairs in front of the desk. It was like sitting before a head-mistress.

'I'm investigating two unexplained deaths at George Fenwick's previous address,' Deans said.

Sally frowned and shook her head.

'I'd like to chat with George about the house and his time living there,' Deans continued.

'Ha, ha,' Sally laughed dismissively. 'You won't get much out of dear old George. He's got more than a touch of senility, bless him,' she chuckled. 'I'll even bet that he thinks you are Peter.'

Deans smiled politely. 'Who is Peter?'

'None of us know. Not any relative that we've come across. But Peter often comes up in conversation.'

Deans' eyes lengthened. 'George is capable of conversation, then?'

'Well, yes. You'll get something out of him, but it may not be relevant to what you have asked.'

'I understand,' Deans smiled.

'Okay,' Sally said standing up from her chair. 'Let me run it by him first. He doesn't get many visitors,' she said, almost apologising for the fact.

Deans waited until Sally was gone and then walked over to the window.

He could see a large conservatory with elderly residents sitting around the edge near to the windows. He noticed Sally come into view and approach a lone figure sitting in a high backed armchair.

Deans watched their interaction carefully. Sally leaned in, but the old boy did not move. She remained for another thirty seconds before turning away and making her way back out of the conservatory.

Deans returned to his seat and a short time later Sally re-entered the office.

'Well, he's awake at least,' she said.

Deans smiled.

'So, is it okay for me to see Mr Fenwick?' he asked.

'Well, yes. I think I'd better hover though,' she said. 'For your sake – in case he flies off to Planet George.'

Deans held out his hand. 'After you then,' he said.

They walked through the impressive foyer with its triple-width stairway and split landings, through to a smaller, but no less imposing, drawing room with well-stocked book shelves and a number of elderly faces dotted around the outside of the room. Deans dipped his head at those who registered his presence.

They entered the long conservatory and Deans zoomed in on George, twenty feet ahead.

He was sitting an arm's length from the window with a thick travel rug over his knees. The conservatory was baking hot as it was – most pleasant on such a fresh morning.

'This is George,' Sally announced loudly as they reached the chair from behind the frail old gentleman.

George did not move.

'George,' Sally called loudly, deliberately walking in front of him. 'George, you have a visitor.'

Deans followed and stood alongside Sally.

George stirred and slowly faced them, his eyes a bleeding metallic grey.

'Hello, George,' Deans said warmly. 'My name is Andrew Deans.'

'Peter?' the old boy croaked.

Sally turned to Deans and smiled.

'No, George,' Deans said. 'My name is Andrew Deans. I'm a police officer.'

Deans waited for some kind of recognition, but nothing came.

'Have you brought my lunch?' George asked.

'No, George,' Sally said kneeling before him. 'You've just had your breakfast. You'll have to wait a little bit longer for lunch.'

She turned to Deans with a broad grin. 'He has a wonderful appetite,' she said proudly.

'What's your favourite meal, George?' Deans asked, trying to find a way in – but all he got was silence.

Sally then spoke in a normal, less child-like tone. 'This is fairly standard for George; an initial acknowledgement that we are here, and then he drifts off when we don't produce food.'

Deans nodded, still looking at the old fella.

'When did you last see Peter?' Deans asked.

Sally took a half step backwards and stared at Deans.

George looked ahead, slowly clawing at the tartan blanket that covered his knees.

'Is he an old friend – perhaps a relative?'

There was not so much as a flicker from the molten eyes.

'You've got your answer,' Sally said. 'George won't be able to respond to any more of your questions today.'

Deans sucked in silently through his teeth. 'Well, it's been nice to meet you, George.'

He faced Sally who was already holding an outstretched arm back out of the conservatory.

Sally started to walk away ahead of Deans. 'All he thinks about is his stomach,' she said, 'and Peter.'

As Deans took the final two steps away from the conservatory, he glanced over his shoulder and George was looking directly back at him.

'Do you mind if I ask?' Deans said walking back through the foyer. 'But how much does it cost to become a resident at this lovely retreat?'

'I'm sorry, but we don't discuss personal finances with anyone unless the residents allow it,' Sally said.

'I was considering more about myself,' Deans beamed. 'Just wondering how much pension to keep to one side.'

'I don't think you need to worry about that, just yet,' Sally retorted, shaking Deans by the hand.

'Thank you for your time, and for allowing me to see George,' Deans said. 'He's quite the character.'

Sally held the entrance door open for Deans to walk out. 'You're welcome,' she said. 'Nice to meet you.'

CHAPTER FIFTEEN

Samantha Fenwick did not look surprised to see Deans at the door again.

The drapes were still drawn even though it was now a gloriously sunny day outside.

'Tell me everything about Charlie,' Deans said, standing over her as she slouched, barely alert in the armchair.

She smiled and uncapped a bottle of cider with a hiss of escaping gas.

'Two people have died,' Deans said more assertively.

Samantha shrugged and angled the bottle up to her lips.

Deans watched and waited for her to lower the drink.

'I saw… *it*,' he said.

He noticed Samantha blink clarity into her eyes and she swivelled her head to face him. Her eyes held his for a brief moment and then she turned away.

'Then he has chosen you,' she said.

'For what?' Deans asked quickly.

She reached forwards for her bottle and Deans swatted her hand away.

'Chosen for what?' he said more forcefully.

Samantha held her hand out for the booze and refused to look at him.

Deans moved the cider bottle further away from her.

'Give me my bottle and I will tell you,' she said, not relinquishing her attention from the alcohol.

Deans huffed and handed it back.

She hugged it close to her body like a child cherishing a teddy bear.

Deans dragged the table back away and knelt down directly in front of Samantha.

'What has Charlie chosen me for?' he asked calmly.

She shrugged nonchalantly. 'You'll be next.'

'For what?' Deans' voice was now prickly and loud.

The bottle inched into her mouth. 'His fun,' she said with a smile.

Deans cocked his head. 'Who was Charlie?'

Samantha faced away, not for any other purpose other than to avoid the question.

'Who was Charlie?' Deans shouted this time.

Samantha went to drink again, but Deans wrestled the bottle from her hand, spilling alcohol on to the floor.

'Who the fuck was Charlie, Samantha?'

She lowered her head. The split-ends of her matted and greying hair curled up on the heavily stained carpet.

'I'm not going anywhere until you tell me,' Deans insisted.

'This is police brutality,' Samantha snapped.

'Give it a rest,' Deans said. He had heard that so many times it had become a given. People did not want him tapping on their doors, and thanks to sensationalist television and dodgy police series, people thought it was the way to get rid of a cop on their doorstep – wrong!

'Sooner you tell me, sooner I'm out of here,' Deans said rolling his eyes.

Samantha bared her decaying pegs. 'He was dad's business partner. Now, give me back my bottle.'

'Why is he in the house?' Deans asked.

She shrugged and kept her arms outstretched. 'My bottle?'

'No answer, no bottle,' Deans said, hiding it from her view behind his back.

'You lot can't do anything about it, now,' she said with a smirk.

'What business was your dad into?' Deans asked.

'Why are you so interested in my dad?' Samantha asked cautiously.

'Because he's hiding something,' Deans said.

Samantha drew back and her stare became intense.

There we go.

'You don't know nothing,' she spat.

'And that's why I'm asking,' Deans smiled.

'I isn't telling you nothing.' The venom of her voice confirmed to Deans that *something* needed extracting from either her, or her father.

Deans stood up. 'Well, maybe I'll just go and ask your dad then.' He reached out with her bottle and leaned in close to her face. 'I know he isn't as senile as the care home believes. If he's done something...' Deans held onto the bottle as her hand tugged it back towards her, '...well, I don't care how old he is.'

There was a moment of silence.

Deans stepped backwards and noticed Samantha's hands trembling, but did not think that was the result of two minutes without alcohol. She lowered her head and dug her fingernails deep into the nape of her neck.

'There isn't a ghost,' she said down at her lap. 'I was messing with you.' She glanced up at Deans and shoved her dirty gnawed fingers into her mouth.

She lowered her gaze and teased her lips open with the end of the cider bottle.

'I want you to go now,' she said.

· · ·

Deans sat at his desk staring at the blank computer screen. He had not felt the desire to turn it on since returning from seeing Samantha Fenwick. The remainder of the team buzzed around him.

The final shift of a set was always more productive than the others; nobody wanted to leave their jobs half-baked for their return in a few days' time.

Deans checked his phone – 4:50 p.m. No messages.

Thornton and his team would now also be leaving for the day. Another twenty-four-hours with no news. Day 20.

He had arranged to visit Maria's parents at seven; to go over the same old ground, hearing the same what-ifs, appearing to be in more control than they were. But tonight he was planning on letting them down.

CHAPTER SIXTEEN

Three hours later and Deans was in North Devon. The journey had given him a good opportunity to catch up with his thoughts.

He rounded a corner onto the estate and pulled in between two parked cars. The house was thirty metres further along the road.

He turned off the engine and sat transfixed to the front of Babbage's property. He had not considered what he was going to do once he had arrived, but just being there felt like he was doing something... at last.

It was a black night and the stiff wind caused the street lamps to rock like they were waving at him. The dashboard clock glowed 8:45 p.m. He ran his tongue around his dry lips. *God, I need a drink.*

There had been little movement in the half-an-hour he had been there; a couple of dog walkers braving the gusts, a few passing cars, but not much else.

He heaved a despondent breath and punched her number into his phone. Denise Moon answered on the third ring.

'Hi, Denise. It's Andy Deans,' he said.

'Andy! Are you okay?' she asked anxiously.

'I'm in the area and I was wondering if I could—'

'Please, come on over,' she said over the top of him. 'Where are you now?'

Deans felt a smouldering in his chest where his heart should be. His eyes tracked back towards the house.

'Torworthy,' he said.

'It's late – are you staying in Devon tonight?'

'Haven't thought about it.'

'Have you eaten anything?'

'No.'

Denise chuckled. 'Not much has changed has it?'

'Some things have,' he replied with a broken voice.

Denise did not speak straight away and then asked, 'Do you remember how to get here?'

'Yeah.'

'See you shortly then,' she said and the call ended.

Denise welcomed Deans with a hug.

'Coffee?' she asked.

'Can I stay?' he replied.

'Of course.' Her smile was as generous as she was.

'Got anything stronger then?' Deans asked.

She winked. 'Take a seat,' she said and walked over to the kitchen area.

'It's lovely to see you, Andy,' Denise said, half-filling two bulbous glasses with red wine. She joined him at the kitchen table and tilted her drink towards his with a clink of glass.

Denise watched him with a questioning smile.

'What?' Deans asked.

Her mouth twitched upwards at the corners. 'How long have you and Maria been together?'

Deans blinked and gave himself five seconds before answering. 'Eleven years.'

'How did you meet?'

He looked at Denise, tilted his head and lowered his glass. 'It was when I was a PC. I was at a friend's barbeque and Maria was there with her boyfriend at that time.'

Denise dropped Deans a school teacher type glance over the top of her glass.

'No, it wasn't anything like that,' Deans said. 'I actually knew him, loosely speaking. We used to play for the same rugby club, but not in the same team.'

'So what happened?'

'We had a good night, we all got drunk and at some point during the evening Maria gave me her number.'

Denise's brows were practically touching the ceiling. Deans chuckled and took a sip from his wine.

'Was it love at first sight?'

Deans stared into the bottom of his glass and he allowed himself a half-smile. 'I fell in love with her voice at first.'

Denise hinted for Deans to continue.

He rolled his head and sucked air in slowly through his partly-opened mouth. 'Maria's family moved to Bath from Ireland when she was a teenager. She had a voice that was like soft velvet to the ears.'

Denise grinned and Deans realised that he was smiling properly for the first time in weeks. He snorted and looked back down into his glass.

'So you called Maria?' Denise said.

Deans shook his head. 'No. She had a boyfriend. I'm not into that sort of thing.'

'Then how did you two come together?'

Deans looked away coyly and smiled again. 'She wrote me a note and left it at the front office.'

'What did the note say?'

Deans blinked and drifted off.

Another fifteen seconds went by, but Denise did not interrupt.

'The note was simple – straight to the point,' Deans said. He rubbed the side of his face and the smile returned. 'That was something else about Maria, she knew how to be direct.'

'Well, come on, what did it say?'

'Oh… Um… something like; I'm now single. So are you. Let's do something about it.'

'And you did?'

Deans paused and took a gulp of merlot. 'Yep, we did.'

'And you never looked back.'

Deans' eyes narrowed and he scratched the back of his neck. He shook his head.

'And then you were married,' Denise pressed. 'Where did you go on honeymoon?'

'Africa. We did a safari honeymoon. It was incredible.' He made an *hmm* noise in his throat and held a reminiscing smile for a moment.

Denise watched him, didn't interrupt.

'We had a lot of amazing holidays at the beginning,' he continued. 'South East Asia, the Caribbean, Mexico…'

'Then what happened?'

Deans puffed air out from his nostrils and stared into his glass again. He rolled the remaining contents around and around and then gulped it all down.

Denise pushed the opened bottle closer toward him and he picked it up, pouring a large quantity into his glass. He took another glug. 'Then we decided to have children.'

Denise leaned back slowly in the chair. 'How long were you trying?' she asked softly.

He bunched his lips and wiped his mouth with his fingertips. 'Five…' he shrugged, '…maybe six years.'

'Were you given a reason?'

He shook his head and looked away, down at the floor.

'There's no shame,' Denise whispered.

'I'm not ashamed,' he quickly replied. 'I'm just sorry.'

'You mustn't blame yourself—'

He heaved a deep breath and stared at Denise. 'It was me coming home at three a.m. Me pulling eighteen hour shifts. None of that would have helped—'

'But those are the realities of life, Andy. You have an incredibly stressful job. A job that demands so much from you, and Maria.'

Deans nodded. 'Yeah, well – I'm now paying the ultimate price for the bloody job.'

'Be proud of who you are and what you do for so many different people, Andy. You will always be a police officer, it runs through your core, I can tell.'

Deans heaved a despondent breath and took another large mouthful of wine. 'Yeah, maybe.'

They sat silently for a number of minutes and then Deans looked at Denise with a penetrating stare that he held for a long moment.

'Is she dead?' he asked.

The corners of Denise's mouth twitched and she placed her glass quietly onto the table and nudged it away with the tip of a finger.

'I don't know,' she said. Her eyes narrowed slightly and her nostrils flared.

'It's okay,' Deans said. 'Nothing can shock me – not anymore.'

He watched her jaw muscles tighten. She reached for her glass and took a long drink.

'The guardians told me to protect you,' she said.

'From what?'

She looked up from her glass. 'From yourself.'

'Meaning?'

She sipped her wine again and looked at him over the top of the glass. 'You are very special.'

Deans folded his arms.

Denise half-smiled. 'Being a detective makes your gift exceptional.' She broke eye contact and purposefully leaned in toward him. 'And a personal loss in your life is going to take your ability to unfathomable levels.'

'I don't want the gift,' Deans said in a dull, monotone voice. 'I want my life back – my wife – my unborn child.'

'Of course,' Denise answered awkwardly. She blinked in quick-fire succession and fiddled with the slender stem of her glass.

Deans did not move. He watched her uncertainty with interest.

'I've lost them – haven't I?' he said.

Denise wiped her lips with the back of a finger drawn slowly across her mouth. 'Nothing is certain,' she said.

'Was it Babbage?' Deans asked.

She stiffened. 'The guardians will guide me how best to protect you,' she said.

Deans squinted. 'Why me – I don't understand?' Denise took another long and deliberate drink from her glass before answering.

'It's meant to be.'

CHAPTER SEVENTEEN

Deans had awoken by five-thirty. He had slept well, or at least, he had endured no night terrors. Denise had given him liquid mouth drops, said they would realign his energies and said he was going to need them for the *conflict* ahead. He had agreed to take them on one basis: that Denise return with him to Bath.

He had left Denise at the house. She said she had a full client list at the clinic, but in any event, Deans had plans of his own.

He was in luck; Detective Ranford from Torworthy CID was on duty and came into the foyer within moments of learning Deans was there. That was just as well; a feral young woman with pungent body odour had taken a shine to Deans. The room was only so big, and so far, she had followed him around two laps of the public reception area.

Detective Ranford had been Deans' partner on the Operation Bejewel Action Team when they were investigating Amy Poole's murder. He was Deans' go to man for local knowledge and help.

'Andy,' Ranford said, giving Deans a man-hug. 'What are you doing down here, mate?' Ranford appeared slightly skittish but happy to see Deans.

'Just visiting,' Deans said.

Ranford squeezed Deans a little tighter. 'It's great to see you.' He patted Deans on the back and took a step away, looking Deans in the eye. 'I heard about your wife.' His face dropped. 'I'm so sorry. Sergeant Jackson told everyone.' He tilted an inquisitive look. 'Any progress?'

Deans lowered his head and replied softly, 'No news, I'm afraid.'

'I'm sorry,' Ranford said again. 'Just popping in to say hello?'

'No. I was hoping we could chat?'

'Of course,' Ranford replied.

'Unless you have other stuff—'

Ranford wafted the suggestion back. 'Not at all, Andy. Not at all.' He shrugged. 'I'm on my own today – been a nightmare. Double-hander in the bin, but I'm on top of it. It will probably do me some good to step away for ten minutes. Fancy a coffee?'

'Too bloody right,' Deans replied. 'I won't keep you long, I promise.'

Ranford waved his hand again. 'Honestly, Andy. It is no problem. It's great to see you.'

They left the foyer and walked up the stairs to the CID office.

Deans peered at the duo of desks. The office was back to how it looked before the murder squad moved into town. Ranford's partner, Detective Mansfield, was absent from his desk, as ever.

'Where is Op Bejewel being run from now?' Deans asked, still marvelling at Mansfield's clean and tidy work surface.

'Exeter HQ,' Ranford said. 'After Babbage was remanded they all upped and left as quickly as they had come. Only Sergeant Jackson pops in from time-to-time.' Ranford shrugged and pushed the corners of his files together, as if he was levelling a pack of cards. 'Don't know why? He never seems to do that much.'

Deans stroked the contour of his jaw. 'You guys didn't get caught up with the investigation any further?'

'Nah!' Ranford said. 'Manny and I were told we couldn't be released from district duties.'

Ranford scratched the side of his nose. 'I would have liked to have seen it out, to be honest. All that work…'

'Where is Manny today?' Deans asked looking again at Mansfield's desk.

Ranford bobbed a shoulder. 'He was here this morning – been investigating a series of robberies these past few days. Loads of enquiries, tons of stress…' He flashed his eyelids and smiled.

Deans understood and smiled back.

'So,' Ranford said. 'How can I help?'

Deans shuffled his feet and paused a moment before answering. 'What happened with Babbage after Jackson released me from the investigation?'

Ranford frowned. 'Let me just grab those drinks.' He touched Deans' arm and left the room.

Deans heaved a sigh and looked around the narrow two-desk office. His eyes set on a Post-It label; one of many, stuck on the edges of Mansfield's computer screen. There was a handwritten telephone number; one that he immediately recognised.

Ranford came back into the room and handed Deans his coffee.

'Yeah, anyway… so after you left Sarah Gold interviewed Babbage again with Sergeant Jackson…' Ranford hesitated and took a sip of coffee. 'Well, Babbage went mute. Wouldn't answer a single bloody question.' Ranford stared deeply into Deans' eyes. 'It was all about you. For Babbage, it was all about you!'

Deans heaved a breath and turned away. 'Yeah, well – thanks to that twat Jackson, I guess we'll never know what else Babbage might have said.'

'In any event,' Ranford continued, 'the Crown Prosecution Service decided that there was enough evidence to charge and remand Babbage with murder while the nitty-gritty of the investigation continued.'

Deans thought for a moment and ran a hand through his hair.

'But while Babbage was with you – here in police custody – nothing was asked about Maria's disappearance, even though Babbage was goading me throughout the interview – practically admitting to ruining my life?'

'It took a while for the information about Maria to filter through to us, Andy. We already had a charging decision for Amy Poole's murder.' He shrugged and shook his head. 'The phone, the DNA – all compelling – and Jackson was keen to get a result.'

Deans shut his eyes. 'When was Jackson last here?' he asked.

'Yesterday,' Ranford said rolling his eyes. 'He was here all day. I think he must stay somewhere locally.'

Deans squinted and watched Ranford fiddle with a pen on his desk.

'Did he say when he would be back?'

'Nope. We don't get a warning. He just arrives.'

Deans chewed the inside of his cheek and looked at his watch. 'Okay. I'd quite like to see Jackson if he returns—'

'Are you sure that's a good idea?' Ranford said quickly. 'You two didn't exactly hit it off first time around.'

Deans cast Ranford a stubborn glare. 'I think he's got some answers to give, don't you?'

CHAPTER EIGHTEEN

The underside of Deans' car scraped and clattered against the divots and potholes of the waterlogged track that lead to the pebble ridge slipway. He parked beside two camper vans on a small tufted island of dry terrain, like prime real estate. Anyone else would have to step out into an inch of spring-tide floodwater.

Deans forced the door against the buffeting breeze and planted his feet. He turned into the wind and sniffed in the air, holding the cleansing freshness in the back of his throat. He released his breath after twenty controlled seconds as if expelling all the crap of the past fortnight.

The pebble ridge looked different today – the hut – the life-guard hut, was missing from the slipway. *Must be a seasonal landmark.*

He made his way slowly up the concrete sleepers, set into the large rounded boulders, until he reached the summit. The blast of chilled sea air was now unforgiving as it whipped-up the spray of frothing foam and spattered his skin. He wrapped himself tighter into his coat. Only the competent and foolhardy would challenge these angry waters at the height of winter.

The beige coloured sun was like an artist's impression; veiled by wafer-thin layers of off-white satin clouds, and only inches above the horizon. He held the moment and for the shortest time, everything else was forgotten. Only the cutting bitterness of the strong westerly wind prevented this from being *perfect*.

Deans stood tall and pulled his shoulders back. He cast his gaze across the smooth, rounded faces of the boulders and stopped about fifty metres away where a mound of pebbles stood proud, six feet above the others. He dipped his head. That was the exact spot where several weeks before he had first met Amy Poole, but she was dead and her beautiful, youthful body had been mutilated.

Deans stepped carefully along the ridge until he was alongside the monument. Several of the stones had messages written on them in marker-pen. Others were painted in various different colours.

He reached down to his feet and picked up a fist-sized pebble. He kissed it and rested it on the top of the pile.

Turning his face to the harshness of the wind he said, 'Amy. I need your help. If you can… please help me.'

A blinding flash of light from the headland a mile away snatched his attention. He blinked the black dots away from his vision and focussed on the light source; it was a large dark building, teetering on the cliff edge. Departed and solitary.

Use the light, a voice said in his head.

His hair stood vertically and his skin prickled with electricity. *That voice.* He had heard it just weeks before when it said, *don't give up.*

Deans peered at the monument of stones. That was the deceased voice of Amy Poole.

Warmth swept through his torso and he looked again at the remote house. 'Use the light,' he whispered.

He scuttled down the stones, pebbles clashing and shifting beneath his quick feet.

The village was not large enough to get lost in and soon he

was driving along a narrow dirt track and the same lonesome house was looming large up ahead.

He slowed as he neared and could not pull his eyes away from the crumbling, red-brick exterior of the Victorian structure.

The house was… *would* have been magnificent in its day. As close to the edge of the cliff as would be comfortable, the views out into the bay were extraordinary.

Deans looked across to the pebble ridge, now just a grey smudge in the distance. He stepped out from his car and the door wrenched from his fingers as a sudden gust of wind slammed it tight. He looked up to the steep-angled roof as crows scattered into the sky, crying out with rasping calls of displeasure. He paused – something in the back of his mind reminded him that a group of these birds was called a murder. The skin on the back of Deans' neck began to tighten – he was starting to feel *the chill*. He looked out to sea, beyond the overgrown brambles that skirted the base of the house like a natural fringe of protection. The sun was dipping away. Deans peered up again at the tall boxy chimney stacks and the crows were already settling back in to place.

He walked to the western face of the property, the side to withstand the worst of the weather. Terracotta tiles glowed amber in the twilight and hung vertically from the walls like a colony of bats. Many had fallen away exposing the ladder-like wooden batons from which they had clung and blemishes in the masonry that was more reminiscent of a building found in a war zone.

He moved back to the front. A decrepit wooden door set within a parabolic archway signified a probably once impressive walkway into the home, but now the wildly overgrown vines and creepers had invaded the spaces and engulfed the front of the property like a slow spreading disease.

Deans shut his eyes, dropped his head and mumbled, 'Amy, why have you brought me to this place?'

He waited and listened carefully for a response.

Half a minute went by and with no answer; he looked up to the brine-mottled windows that peered down upon him. The black edges of the structure were now setting an eerie silhouette against the deepening sky. This house would not look out of place in a horror movie.

Deans squatted down bouncing on his heels. Why was he brought here? Maybe the answers he pursued did not exist. Maybe he had *imagined* Amy's voice; crave something enough and your brain will trick you into believing it is possible. Or perhaps Savage was right, and he was *finally* losing his mind.

He stood up with a groan from his aching knees, flicked the fringe from his forehead and stepped backward away from the house. He offered one last lingering look and then made his way to see Denise.

CHAPTER NINETEEN

Food and a bottle of red wine were waiting for Deans when he arrived.

'Did you do everything you wanted?' Denise placed a plate of ham, fried eggs and chunky chips in front of him.

'Mostly,' Deans said. He picked up a chip between his fingers and dipped it in a puddle of ketchup.

Denise sat down opposite him, no food of her own. 'And tomorrow?' she asked.

He rubbed his face. 'I'm heading back to Bath. Need to progress that case,' he grumbled.

'Do you want to talk about it?' she asked as if she already knew he did.

'To be honest it's helping me take my mind off Maria.' He stared into space. 'Is that bad of me?'

Denise smiled. 'We are each different, Andy. But I'd probably do the same.'

Deans noticed her staring. 'What?'

'That house in Bath is waiting to share its secrets with you.'

He twitched a brow and his thoughts turned at once to the house on the cliff edge.

'It's not by chance that you have been selected,' she said.

'Selected?'

'The entity has *chosen* you.'

Half a chip poked out from his mouth.

Denise had a flat expression on her face.

'Okay then,' Deans said. 'Why pick me?'

'That's what you must find out.'

Deans leaned back in his chair, gave Denise a *come on, give me a break* gaze.

'You will find the dead connecting to you on a more frequent basis. You are their conduit to the living. This is *your* gift now,' she responded.

'More like a curse.'

Denise smiled and enlarged her eyes.

'You know this area well?' Deans asked after a couple more mouthfuls of food.

'Reasonably, yes,' Denise replied.

'There's a large house, on the edge of the headland—'

'Ah,' Denise interrupted. 'The locals call that the haunted house.'

Deans placed his knife and fork down onto the plate with a loud clunk. 'Is it,' he asked, 'haunted?'

Denise shrugged dismissively. 'I don't know. I've never been inside.' She cradled her wine glass and fixed her gaze upon him. 'What is it? Why do you ask?'

Deans turned away.

'Andy?' Denise said. 'You can trust me... with anything.'

Deans scratched behind his ear, noticed her *nothing will shock me* smile.

'I went to the pebble ridge,' he said, 'to where Amy Poole's body was found.'

Denise lowered her glass silently onto the table and gestured with her head for Deans to continue.

He licked his lips and looked down.

'It's okay' Denise said, reaching over for his hand.

Deans stared at her hand, on top of his, and knew that he was *safe*. 'I asked Amy to help me find Maria.'

Denise blinked slowly. 'And?'

'It's probably nothing,' Deans shrugged, 'but right at that moment a bright light shone from the windows of that house directly into my eyes.' He shook his head. 'I know it was just the setting sun, but it was like a bloody beacon or something.'

'Hmmm,' Denise murmured, twisting the glass stem between her long slender fingers.

'Was it...' Deans asked urgently, '...a sign?'

She lifted her glass and stared into it before taking a sip. 'Possibly?' she said. 'Remember, nothing happens by chance.'

Deans took a long gulp of his own drink.

'What did you do then?'

'I drove there.'

'And... what did you find?'

Deans paused and shook his head. 'I don't know... but I want to go back.'

'Do you want me to come with you?'

Deans glugged more wine. 'Would you?'

'I can do early tomorrow morning, but nothing later; I've got a full day.'

'Okay,' Deans said. 'Early tomorrow morning it is.'

CHAPTER TWENTY

The air was cold and tacky from a stiff North Westerly breeze and the sky was depressingly heavy. They had driven separately. Deans arrived first and was already outside of his car staring up at the dilapidated house when Denise joined him soon after. He greeted her with a nod and she came alongside his shoulder.

'Let's find a way inside,' he said.

Denise grabbed his arm. 'Isn't that against the law?'

Deans dug into his back pocket and removed his wallet. He lifted a flap to expose his police badge. 'If anyone asks,' he said with a flick of the eyebrow.

'Are you sure you can do that?' Denise said, but Deans had already hurdled the low, vine-covered wall and was clambering through the undergrowth towards the main entrance.

'Come on,' he said in a half-whisper. 'We need to stick together.'

Denise flapped defeated arms and followed in his path.

Deans peered through the nearest window, shielding light from the corners of his face with his hands, but everything was masked by dirty old Louvre shutters on the inside.

Denise was tight on his shoulder. 'What are we looking for?' she asked, brushing dirt and foliage from her clothing.

Deans tugged against an immoveable door handle and took a step back, looking up at the building. 'I dunno,' he said and flashed Denise a determined stare. 'Maybe Amy will show us?'

He made off around the side of the house, trampling wildly overgrown vegetation down with his feet.

Denise followed tentatively, flicking stray twigs away as she went.

Deans stopped at a ground floor window and hurried Denise along with a hand gesture. A diagonal crack ran the entire height of the rectangular-shaped pane. Using the heel of his hand, he pressed against the fault line feeling for movement and the glass shifted. He manipulated the sheet with more force, and the upper section fell out in his hands. He placed the large shard carefully against the side of the house and went to work on the remaining section until the frame was completely free of potential snags. Deans climbed through the open space and used the torch light on his mobile phone to see where he was stepping.

The place was clearly uninhabited – thankfully, and the kitchen area through which he had just entered was a relic of a time long forgotten. He turned to Denise and after a little persuasion he encouraged her through the gap.

They stood side-by-side in the narrow room. Deans illuminated the water damaged and paper-peeling walls with the limited beam of light from his phone. He searched the doorframe and found an old-style brown light relay with three switches, but none of them worked. There had probably been no electricity supply for decades. Deans chuckled to himself, if this had been Bath, a property of this one-time grandeur would have snapped up by developers long ago.

'Stay close,' he said to Denise and shuffled towards a long, dark hallway. The beam of light from his phone highlighted ceiling cobwebs that looked more like flimsy grey hammocks. He felt moisture settling on his top lip and wiped it with a finger.

They came to a side door. Deans pushed it open and saw beads of light streaming in from gaps in the wooden shutters. He told Denise to stay put, entered the room and pulled the shutters wide in a cloud of choking dust. Daylight drenched the floorboards from the large bay windows and Denise stepped into the room and joined him. Deans looked out through the windows into the vast bay. The cliff edge was so close he might just as well have been looking out from a porthole on board ship.

'Are you picking anything up?' Deans asked, turning to Denise.

'Oh, what's that,' she said raising a hand to his face. 'Your nose is bleeding.'

Deans looked at the hand he had used to wipe his lip. It was streaked in blood.

'Here,' Denise said, handing Deans a tissue. 'Why didn't you say something?' she said.

Deans dabbed his face. 'I didn't know,' he replied. 'I think it has stopped,' he said investigating the tissue. 'Has it stopped?'

Denise shook her head and deep creases formed in her brow.

'Don't worry,' Deans said plugging his nostrils. 'We'll be out of here soon. I just want to look upstairs.'

'Go careful,' Denise said. 'There is *something* about this place.'

'Are you coming?' Deans asked, heading for the hallway. Denise groaned and followed in his wake.

Deans stood at the base of the staircase and looked up. Daylight from the upper levels revealed a kinking and winding row of decorative white spindles, and dark mahogany posts and handrails rose up towards the tallest extremities of the house. He stepped gingerly onto the first tread and slowly climbed the steps, each one echoing with a unique creak.

He reached the first floor landing, a wide expansive space. He looked towards the light source – it was a beautiful, yet neglected patchwork of lead-lined-stained-glass running the height of this floor and onto the next. Deans looked around. *Go higher*, his inner voice said, and he climbed the next set of steps and reached the upper level.

It was darker. There were five rooms, one at each apex and three in the middle. Four of the doors were already open, but he was drawn to the closed door on the west-facing side of the building. He zoomed in on the tainted brass doorknob and his chest plummeted into his belly as if he had just sped over a humped-back bridge. The hairs stood rigid on his arms as he leaned forward for the handle. The door pushed open with a reluctant whine of the hinges and his eyes immediately settled on the single most striking feature in the middle of the room, an ancient metal-framed bed with a heavily stained and soiled mattress sagging off one side and the exposed and redundant rusty sprung-metal-coils of the base.

Beside the window, he saw a standalone white basin with a fracture in the wall running diagonally behind it, so large he was amazed the side of the house was still standing. He took in the rest of the room; the peeling and hanging orange-flower wallpaper, and a small fireplace with a dune of grey soot that had blown back into the room over an extended period of time.

He sniffed the air and scowled. It smelt like perfume – familiar perfume. *Can't be.*

He stepped back to the landing and inhaled deeply again, but the smell had completely disappeared. He scrunched up his face and shook his head again.

'Andy,' Denise yelled from below. 'Someone's coming.'

Deans lingered at the doorway. Something was drawing him back into the room, but Denise needed him. He closed the door and scampered down the steps.

Denise was already talking to an old man at the bottom of the stairs when Deans arrived.

'Good morning,' Deans said confidently, bounding down the

final few steps and waving his warrant badge ahead of him. 'We are from the CID. We heard noises from outside. Thought we'd come in and check it out.' He beamed a smile. 'There's nothing to worry about.'

He looked at Denise. Her eyes were on stalks.

'How did you get in?' the little old man asked.

Deans looked down and noticed a long dead bolt key in his hand.

'We discovered an insecure window. So, do you look after this spectacular place?' Deans said, quickly changing the topic.

'Yes,' the man said straightening his age-buckled back. 'I've been watching over this place since Ruby died.' His wrinkles puckered on his cheeks. 'Eleven year now,' he said with melancholy in his voice.

Deans squinted. 'Sorry, who owned it before?'

'It were in the Mansell family for generations,' the man said.

'Ruby Mansell?' Deans asked.

The old boy peered up at Deans through pea-sized eyes. 'Did ee know her?'

'Sadly, no,' Deans said and cast an enthusiastic gaze around the hallway. 'It's a mightily impressive house.'

The old man didn't respond.

'Did you visit when Ruby lived here?' Deans asked.

'I did,' the old man said. 'Frequently.'

'Hmm,' Deans murmured. 'And in that top bedroom looking out towards the lighthouse—'

'Ave ee been up in there?' the old man scowled.

'No,' he said briskly.

'I never went in that room.'

'Why not?' Deans asked.

The old man caught Deans' eye for a short moment. 'Oh… no particular reason,' he said.

Deans looked the gentleman up and down and rubbed his

chin. 'Well,' he said. 'We didn't find anyone that shouldn't be in here. Would you like me to fix that broken window?' he asked.

'No,' the old man said. 'I best take a quick look around the place.' He offered Deans and Denise a cautious glance and off he shuffled.

Deans turned to Denise. 'Come on,' he whispered. 'Let's get out of here.'

CHAPTER TWENTY-ONE

Deans was back in Bath later that afternoon, he was due to start the next set of six shifts the following day. He had a revitalised energy and an aching determination. He had arranged to meet Maria's parents at their place. It had been nine days since they last met properly and Deans was pensive. Graham and Joyce Byrne were lovely parents-in-law and about as loving a couple as you could wish to meet. They were the tightest unit he knew and were always together, always smiling, always happy, always so proud of their daughter.

Graham shook Deans' hand and took him through to the living room where Joyce was sitting in semi-darkness with a tepid cup of tea and a plate of biscuits in front of her. She noticed Deans enter the room and immediately stood up.

'Andrew,' she said. 'We saw DC Aldridge this morning.' DC Aldridge was the FLO (Family Liaison Officer) assigned to Maria's parents as a single point of contact for the police.'

Deans pinched his lip between his teeth, gave himself a couple of seconds to think. 'I saw her too – the other day.' In fact, he had spoken to her several times, including at his most recent visit to the Major Crime Investigation Team in Bristol.

'She told us there has been some progress,' Joyce said.

Deans stared into her despairing eyes. He could see the same hollowness he had witnessed in Amy Poole's mother. He dropped his head and glanced away.

'When did you find out?' Graham asked in a calm voice, moving alongside his wife.

'Couple of days ago,' Deans replied. He looked up and saw their disappointed reactions. 'I had to go to Devon,' he said. 'I didn't want to worry you, or tell you over the phone.'

'Jesus, Andrew,' Joyce snapped. 'Of all the people that can help us and you decide to gallivant off to Devon again.'

'I was working,' Deans replied in a frank voice. He heard Joyce tut and noticed her rolling her eyes. 'I was trying to find Maria,' he said and looked at each of them in turn. 'Not a second passes when I'm not trying to figure out where she is.'

A thorny silence beset the room.

'Well…' Graham said comforting his wife with an arm over her shoulder as she slumped back into her chair. 'Maybe you can fill in the gaps for us, Andrew?'

'What have you been told?'

'Maria visited her bank,' Graham said.

'Yes.'

'But they don't know where she went after that?'

Deans blinked and shuffled his heels. He caught Graham's stare eating into him, and he looked down at his feet again.

'What have you been told?' Graham asked forcefully.

Deans felt his Adams apple rise and drop as he swallowed and considered what he *should* say. Moreover, would it *help* them to know? Deans exhaled slowly, and he looked them both in the eye.

'Maria's been taken,' he said.

Neither of them moved for several seconds.

'W… wha…' Joyce was trying to speak.

'The police aren't having it,' Deans continued, 'but I saw it for myself. That's why I've been in Devon – trying to follow up the leads that the police here won't acknowledge.'

'Why not?' Graham whispered, his voice bereft of energy.

Deans shook his head. He felt his face burning. 'I don't know,' he said. 'But I'm not going sit back and wait for...' He stopped himself.

Graham's mouth dropped open.

'Did you see *that woman*?' Joyce asked.

Deans stood taller and faced her square on. 'Yes,' he replied. '*That woman* is also doing all she can to help find Maria.'

Joyce tutted again and faced the other way. Deans glared at Graham, who mouthed silently, *don't*.

'So what now?' Graham asked, clearly attempting to change the subject from Denise Moon.

'I'm waiting to hear back from Major Crime,' Deans said. 'And in the meantime, I'm going to do whatever it takes to find my wife.' He leaned over, directing his next words at Joyce. 'To find your daughter.'

'Have you heard of a Sergeant Jackson?' Graham asked.

'Why?' Deans snapped, taking a half step backwards.

'We had the strangest phone call from him yesterday,' Graham said, now sitting beside his wife, clutching her hand.

'Jackson phoned you?'

'Well, yes.'

'What did he say?' Deans stepped closer towards them.

'Um... he asked if we'd had any contact from Maria, and general chit-chat—'

'Chit-chat?'

Graham shrugged. 'Maria's work, her social life... her relation-ship with you.'

Deans narrowed his gaze. 'Her relationship with me?'

Graham shrugged. 'Yes.'

'Who did Jackson say he was?' Deans asked.

'Well,' Graham said looking puzzled, 'a senior detective on Maria's case.'

Deans' eyes were now narrow slits and his teeth were clenched tightly.

'Isn't he?' Graham asked now appearing more concerned.

'Is that the first contact you've had from Jackson?' Deans asked.

'Yes, as far as I know.' Graham looked at his wife, pulling her hand into his lap. 'Is there some kind of problem?'

Deans did not answer.

'Andrew.' Graham's voice was hardening.

Deans looked away.

'Is there some kind of issue, Andrew?' Joyce cut in with harsh tones.

Deans bit his lip. Shook his head.

'We don't get along. That's all.'

CHAPTER TWENTY-TWO

Deans awoke with a muzzy groan. He was still on the sofa and still in the clothes from the day before. He brought himself up into a seated position and grabbed the sides of his face. He looked at the whisky bottle on the coffee table. Most of it was gone.

He found his mobile phone on the floor and grumbled his way through to the kitchen, connected a power lead to his dead phone and flicked the switch to the kettle. His breath was stale and his eyes gritty and unforgiving. His phone vibrated, once, and then twice. He looked at the screen through tender eyes. A voicemail and a text message were waiting for him. His hearing needed less effort than his sight, so he dialled in and waited for the voicemail message.

"Deano, stick the kettle on, I'm coming around." It was Mick Savage.

Deans scratched the back of his head and peered at the clock on the microwave. 9:48 a.m. *Shit.*

He took a tall glass of Alka-Seltzer, nailed three painkillers and crashed back onto the sofa.

A loud knock at the door woke him. He shuffled through and

opened it up. It was Savage, complete with a shopping bag held out in front of him.

He looked Deans up and down. 'Thought you might want a fry up and a decent brew, but it looks like you need a damn good kick up the arse instead,' Savage said.

Deans stepped aside without speaking and let Savage through the doorway.

'Didn't make it to bed I see,' Savage commented, lifting up the whisky bottle from the coffee table in the living room.

'Mmm,' Deans grumbled, shaking his head.

'Show me where the pans are and get yourself freshened up,' Savage said.

'Does Sandra know you have another man?' Deans said, trying to make light of his embarrassing situation.

'You wish. Go on. Get showered – you stink,' Savage said, sparking the gas hob.

'Why are you here, Mick?'

'I want to help you. And I can't afford for you to fall apart, Deano.'

Deans moaned and rolled his eyes.

'These past few weeks...' Savage continued. 'Well, they've *changed* you.'

Deans peered at Savage through hooded lids.

'I'm not criticising you, Andy – I'm really not. But I need the old Andy back now... you need the old Andy back.' Savage sniffed the air, sucked his lips and stared at Deans. 'Maria's situation,' he said. 'It's really not looking good.'

'I know.'

'And you are going to need to be firing on all cylinders to get through this,' Savage said raising the bottle of Jameson's whisky from the table and holding it out in front of his face.

Deans glimpsed the bottle and returned his gaze to Savage.

'What did you do with your rest days, Deano?' Savage asked.

It was obvious from his raised brows and glaring eyes that he already knew.

'I went to North Devon,' Deans replied neutrally.

'Do you think that was wise?'

Deans shrugged. 'I can go wherever I like, Mick.'

Savage groaned and spoke with guarded tones; 'Andy, you might hinder any investigation into…' he stopped short.

'Into what, Mick?'

'Well, they are still looking into Maria's disappearance for one—'

'Are they?'

'Oh come on, you know they are.'

Deans huffed and turned away.

'The perception is that you are getting involved when you really shouldn't be.'

'Whose perception?' Deans snapped. 'Come on, whose perception?'

Savage blinked quickly. 'Doesn't matter.'

'Yes it does.' Deans was not about to let it drop. 'Was it Sergeant Jackson?'

He saw enough in Savage's face to know that it was.

'Don't blame him, Deano. He just wants to keep the investigations on track, you get me?'

Deans dismissed Savage with a backhand swipe of his hand. 'He's a twat.'

'Come on, Andy. As a friend I'm just saying – don't make things any harder than they already are.'

Deans scoffed.

Savage smiled for the first time in minutes and stepped towards Deans, embracing him with a backslapping hug. 'We'll get you through this, buddy,' he said. 'You can count on me.'

Deans washed, changed and sat down at the kitchen table opposite Savage, who was tucking into a ketchup-dripping bacon and egg butty.

'I was hoping you'd be free today,' Savage said between obscenely large mouthfuls of food. 'Someone I think we should go and visit.'

'Who?' Deans asked, turning his face up at the slobbish sight of Savage eating.

'I had a call from Nathan Parsons a couple of days ago,' Savage said. 'He was a bit excited – he's only managed to get a DNA hit on that envelope you sent off.'

Envelope?

'Better than that,' Savage continued, wiping a blob of red sauce from his chin. 'The fucking perv only lives in Swindon – we've got an address and everything. Three hours – bish-bash-bosh!'

It took a moment for Deans to register the information and then it struck home. 'Bloody hell,' he said. 'What the baby-cam footage?'

'Yep,' Savage said, sucking grease from his fingers with lip smacking kisses. 'So, fancy a little drive today – unless you don't feel up to it?'

Deans sat bolt upright and blinked comfort back into his eyes. *Bloody hell*, he thought and sank his coffee.

Deans and Savage were in Swindon by twelve twenty-five. The address they had been given was not far from the local football stadium. The perv had pre-cons for exposure; flashed his penis at a bunch of school kids on a bus stop. He had received a community order, but most importantly for Deans and Savage, his DNA was taken while he was in custody, which was how they could identify him now.

The block of flats looked quite swanky, privately owned by the appearance of them. They walked to the communal entrance and discovered from the mailbox names that their target was on the sixth and top floor level.

Savaged buzzed flat number one.

A frail, elderly voice came over the intercom. 'Hello,' she said.

'Good morning, my lovely,' Savage said. 'This is the police. There is nothing to worry about, but we are just trying to enter the building and we can't get a response from the flat we need. Would you be a love and let us in, please?'

'Who are you after?' the reply came.

'You don't need to worry about that, but you can see our identification before we enter, if you like?'

The intercom went silent.

Deans heard the sound of an unlocking door and an elderly woman shuffled out from the nearest flat entrance and came up to the glass of the door.

Savage waved a hand, and they both pressed their warrant cards up against the glass and smiled warmly. The woman was saying something, but neither of them could make it out and in any event, she opened the door.

'Thank you, my love,' Savage said passing her. 'I very much appreciate it.'

The woman mumbled something, but Deans and Savage were already making their way up the first flight of stairs.

They reached flat number twenty-two and Savage knocked loudly on the door, but there was no reply. He knocked again, this time louder – same result.

Deans removed a small torch from his day-bag and used the butt end to tap against the door, being careful not to mark the paint with the metal.

Savage screwed up his face. 'Can you smell that?' he asked.

Deans sniffed the air and looked blankly at Savage. He dropped onto one knee and smelled the air through the crack of the door. Deans nodded. 'We'd better ask the neighbours when they last saw him.'

The result was not for at least a week and his pushbike was still downstairs near to the entrance. According to the neighbours, Gary Coxley, the perv, worked in a nearby factory – regular hours, routine kind of bloke – until this week.

Deans cocked his head. 'It's your call, you're the skipper.'

'Thanks,' Savage replied sarcastically.

'We can justify it,' Deans said. 'Reasonable grounds for suspecting an offence has been committed. We've confirmed Coxley lives here and we've got his DNA.'

'Shit!' Savage cursed. 'What if he just decided to walk to work, or take the bus, or he's on holiday and hasn't told anyone? What if he's got a smelly cat or a dead rat under the floor boards?'

'One way to find out?' Deans said.

Savage whined and shook his head. He pushed his hand against the top, then the middle and finally bottom edges of the door. 'Well it looks like a single Yale lock. Fancy that one?' he asked Deans.

'Why does it have to be me?'

'You're better at the paperwork than me, plus I've got new shoes on.'

Deans dropped Savage a *come on* look.

'Need a run up?'

Deans huffed and shook his head. He pushed his foot against the sweet spot and imagined the strike. He looked over his shoulder.

'Go for it,' Savage said.

Deans smashed the door open with one mighty boot, the frame splintering at the lock.

'Phwaaah!' Savage choked, covering his face with his hand. 'You first then, Deano,' he said.

The smell of death was overwhelming – not so much a matter of if, as where?

Deans edged through the hallway and listened for the beacon

of feasting flies. He found the body, lying face up on the living room floor. The carpet was crimson all around him.

'He's in here,' Deans shouted back to Savage who was still coughing and spluttering in the entrance hallway. 'He's totally drained.'

Savage peered around the doorway. 'Shit,' he said, from behind his finger-mask. 'Looks like an aneurism.'

Deans agreed. He had seen the same thing several times before, but this was clearly an unexpected death and would need forensic opinion. He looked at the face; sure enough, there had been a nosebleed. Deans knelt down at the top end of the body, the crusty tide of claret near to the tips of his shoes. 'Look at his hair,' Deans said.

Savage came over, squatted beside Deans and coughed near his ear. 'What?' he said.

'Look at that grey streak.'

'So,' Savage said.

'You don't think that's unusual?'

'People have grey hair, Deano. And this one now has a little rouge to complement it.'

'People get grey streaks when they've experienced extreme shock. I've seen images…' Deans' voice tailed away.

'Well, we'd better get the local CID on the blower,' Savage said. 'Go and have a look out in the bedroom, I think you'll find something interesting.'

Deans did as he was told and found numerous shoe boxes full of CDs, the same brand as the one he had been sent in the post.

'The bloke was a fucking pervert,' Savage said coming into the bedroom. He pointed back towards the living room. 'And I believe that is called Karma.'

'We're going to need to seize these,' Deans said, lifting one of the shoe boxes full of disks.

'Jesus, Deano. We've got enough on our plate now.'

'There could be more in here to help me,' Deans said, rummaging through the stack of disks.

'Deano?' Savage said, getting Deans to look his way. 'Are you sure you are not a shit magnet?'

Deans puffed air into his cheeks and tilted his head. 'It's certainly starting to look that way.'

CHAPTER TWENTY-THREE

They spent the next five hours at the local CID office. The 'incident' had gone all the way up to the Detective Chief Inspector and District Commander, who were not impressed with Deans and Savage. Not only were they on another constabularies patch 'uninvited', but they had caused damage to a door and discovered a *sudden death*. A headache at the best of times, but not for Savage and Deans, they had the M4 corridor to act as a buffer from the justifiable questions that were sure to follow.

The body had been certified and removed for an autopsy, and the boxes of recorded perv-material had been sifted and it was agreed that Deans could take the three other *murder* disks back to Bath for analysis.

Deans' Team had all gone by seven, and the late shift was working a fresh GBH assault. Although he was beyond tired, he felt compelled to view the footage that night and took the disks to the small video room within the nick, and made sure he was alone by locking the door. These images were for his eyes only.

The first disk whirred and loaded without issue. Deans stared intently at the screen and the couple's bedroom brought light to the video room. Deans rocked in his seat and searched for clues, but instead he faced Mr and Mrs Rose bang at it on top of the sheets.

Out of instinct, Deans checked over his shoulder, even though he knew nobody else was in the room. He felt awkward – watching two people enjoying one another, knowing that in a small flat in Swindon, someone else was most likely deriving similar pleasure from their intimacy.

By the end of the first disk, which appeared to contain footage from several occasions, he did not identify much; apart from the fact the Roses liked their sex doggy-style.

He put that disk to one side and loaded the next. This time the subject was only Mrs Rose.

Deans watched her in various stages of undress. He focussed on her hair and the shape of her body, so similar in many ways to Maria. He did not pause, fast-forward, or stop, he just watched and struggled... struggled to remind himself that he was not watching his wife.

He checked his phone. Nothing.

He loaded the final disk and rubbed his eyes. It was the same bedroom scene, but this time it was empty. Deans sipped his coffee and allowed the footage to continue. The walls were now a different colour – the same as they were when Deans had been in the room himself. His eyes were leaden and gritty and all of a sudden, *white noise* made the image flicker and the sound crackle. Deans moved closer to the screen taking in every minuscule detail.

He snatched his breath and shot back in his seat, his eyes wide as dinner plates.

Did that just...? Nah, couldn't have.

He rewound the footage and pressed play once again. This time his vision was like laser-sighted rods on one spot of the bed. His mouth fell open, and he quickly played it again.

The bed sheets were bowed and crumpled as if an invisible weight had just sat on them.

Deans ran his tongue around his lips, his throat was powder dry. He watched the recordings again in stark dismay. He saw it happen on another day, and then another, and another, and another. Each day cataloguing an entire sequence of poltergeist activity. Deans was spellbound as the final disk began to show Mr and Mrs Rose in the room once again, mostly sleeping, but Deans could see the air moving around them manifesting itself as washed out light – and then it dawned upon him; movement was activating the baby-cam. The final minutes of the disk rolled on and Deans once again witnessed the deaths of the Roses.

It was at least ten minutes before Deans moved from his seat.

His scalp was so energised that if he touched a single strand of hair his skin hurt. He lingered in complete silence and semi-darkness as he digested the material. What the hell was he supposed to do now? The others already thought he was on the edge. Would they even see what he had seen? *It's all that bloody woman's fault*, he heard Savage saying. And how was any of this helping him find Maria? His sight flickered on the twenty-inch screen and he dropped his face into his hands and remained that way for the next half-an-hour.

It was eleven-thirty by the time Deans arrived home. He had stopped off for a bottle of wine in The Bunker, which he polished off in the same time it usually took him to drink a pint of beer.

He dumped his kit bag onto the floor and made straight for the Jameson's. He turned on the TV and used the emanating light to illuminate the room. He half-filled a tall tumbler with whisky and sank into the sofa with only his thoughts for company, and hooked up his feet. He pulled out his mobile phone – there were no new messages, so he scrolled down to Maria's number – and as he had done every night, every morning and several times in between, he tried to call her phone.

He held the mobile to his ear and even though there was an automated voice telling him the other phone was switched off, he repeated the process again.

Deans stared into the whisky glass and wondered how many paracetamols he had in the house. He knew thirty would be enough.

He suddenly stopped and looked up at the ceiling directly above his head.

What was that?

He stood up from the sofa and slammed his tumbler of whisky down onto the coffee table. Still looking up at the ceiling, he licked the spilled spirit from his hand and his heart galloped.

Maria?

He raced out of the room, clattering his shoulder into the door frame, took the stairs, two at a time and burst through the bedroom door.

Maria was on the bed, facing him.

'Maria,' he yelled out.

She did not smile. Her features were wet and ruddy, her makeup smeared across her face.

'Do it!'

There was the voice from behind him, and even though he recognised he was dreaming, Deans knew that he had to take in more of the scene.

'Do it, now,' he predictably heard Babbage's voice say again, but this time Deans remained looking at his wife rather than turning behind him.

Deans leapt forwards hoping Maria would understand that he was taking control. And then he saw it; the flash of the blade beside Maria's ear. He was too late, again.

'No,' Deans yelled, reaching out, but he was still too far away.

He caught Maria's stare and in that split-second moment, her fears transferred to him.

A hand moved swiftly beneath her jawline. Maria's expression changed, her eyes bunched tightly and the sound of ripping sinew filled the air.

Deans could not move. He could not speak and even though he realised he was in a dream, his limbs would not respond.

Maria slumped forwards, her eyes still open and staring into his. Her raven-black hair covered her face as her head hit the duvet.

Deans sensed movement in his peripheral vision on both sides. He flicked left – it was Babbage, he swung right and for the first time he saw the second person, and their eyes locked together. Deans spotted the glint of the dripping blade in the hand and time stopped still.

Everyone froze apart from Deans. His eyes fogged with building emotion and as he slowly approached, he grabbed the blade and threw it far away along the floor. He rushed over to Maria and felt for a pulse, his hands drenched in her blood, but she was already dead.

Deans wiped his eyes with the material of his shirt and turned back to the killer. His limbs fell weak and limp, and he sank to the floor upon his knees.

He mustered the strength to look up through his despairing eyes, and grinning back at him, was his friend.

Deans awoke and sat bolt upright. He had been crying in his sleep. He peered at the television; the display glowed brightly as a still image burned onto the screen. Deans leaned forward, lifted his glass from the coffee table and took a big mouthful of whisky. The DVD controller was under his midriff and he tugged it out from beneath him, and pointed it towards the screen. His hand shook as he held it outstretched before him. He could feel the piece of skin at the corner of his eye twitching as he pondered the decision to press PLAY. Was he simply torturing himself?

Those were happy times, the happiest. He looked at Maria and penetrating warmth filled his chest. He traced the contour of her face – her smiling mouth, nose… the delicate veil lifting from her hairline. His vision flickered and he peered then at himself.

He looked much younger even though their wedding day wasn't so very long ago, but Maria had not really changed, not to him anyway. Deans looked away from the screen and focussed on his trembling finger, poised on the button. His eyes narrowed and he finished the contents of his glass with one determined hit.

He planted the tumbler firmly onto the coffee table, closed his eyes and pressed the button.

The sound of chiming bells, cheers and laughter filled the living room. He kept his eyes bunched until he heard Maria's voice and had no option but to open them again.

Maria had a soft southern Irish lilt; her accent was one of the most endearing traits that first attracted him to her. Deans smiled. There were times when she would enhance it – mostly when she was drunk, or angry, and he loved the way she would tell him to "Feck off" when he teased her about it. What he would do now for one of those flash-tantrums?

He picked up the bottle of whisky by the neck and splashed another large measure into his glass. He paused the DVD player with an image of them both embracing on the steps to the church with confetti on the wind and in their faces. The corners of his mouth lifted and he sank another large mouthful.

"It's all her fault," he heard Savage saying again in his head. *"Her fault."*

He topped up his tumbler and scrolled through his mobile phone until he located Denise Moon on his dialling list.

'Hello,' she said with a groggy, delayed voice.

Deans did not speak. His breathing was laboured.

'Andy?' Denise said. 'It's almost one a.m. What's wrong?'

'Are you playing me?' Deans said.

'Sorry?' Denise responded sharply.

'Are you playing me for some kind of idiot?'

He did not hear a reply, so he continued speaking.

'All this shite about spirits and the bloody *gift*. Well, where has that got me... hey? Hey?'

'Um... Andy, I don't think we should talk about this now—'

'No. This is a terrific time to talk about it. Everything is always on your terms. Always a load of garbled bollocks; "Ooh, let's have a treatment and suddenly you can rule the world",' Deans said in a sarcastic and mimicking tone. 'Well I don't want to rule the sodding world – I want my world – *my world*. Not a world that you think I should have.'

Deans stopped talking and took a loud gulp of his drink.

'You know? I honestly think that you may be full of shit... and I almost thought... pah!' He shook his head. 'Doesn't matter what I almost thought. Well...' he said hesitating, '...I don't want your help and I don't need your sympathy... I'll do just fine on my own... okay? Okay? I don't need your mumbo-jumbo mystic bollocks anymore. I'll be fine...' Deans stopped talking and snorted the remains of his tears away.

Denise was still on the line, but she hadn't spoken a single word. Deans snivelled and breathed heavily into the mouthpiece and then he heard her speak.

'Let's talk properly another time,' Denise said softly. 'Good-night.' And she put the phone down.

CHAPTER TWENTY-FOUR

Deans peeled his body from the sofa and clutched his head. 'Oh, God!' he said and covered his face with his hands. He looked around him, his phone was not there – and then he remembered. He got up from the sofa, walked across to the other side of the room and eventually found his phone beneath the armchair. He stared at the screen – nothing.

'Shit,' he said rocking his head. What was done, was done, there was nothing he could do about that, but now was not the time to put anything right.

He heaved a sigh and groaned with each pulsating surge of pain in the crown of his head. He rubbed the back of his neck and dragged his hand along the front of his face. The more he thought about it, the worse it became.

In the short time that he had slept, he had envisioned a vivid dream. But this was one that he *could* turn into reality, and *needed* to. He figured nine a.m. would be about right and if that was too early, tough luck.

He picked up his phone and sent Mick Savage a text message saying that he had enquiries to follow up and would be taking a pool car for the day, and did not know when he would be back. In fairness, that was as much as Deans knew. This was to be a day of discovery – not least for him.

Ahead of time, he banged loudly and repeatedly on the door giving no choice to the occupier but for it to open.

Samantha Fenwick greeted Deans with a roll of the eyes and an attempt to close the door in his face.

'No fucking around now, Samantha,' Deans snarled, using the toe of his shoe to stop the door from closing. He pushed his way inside and followed close behind Samantha as she retreated swiftly away from the door.

'What now?' she whined.

'Find something warm to wear, we're going out,' Deans said.

'Like fuck we are,' she said turning to Deans, her face like a puckered pink prune.

'Like fuck – WE ARE!' Deans growled. He pushed beyond her and started to rummage through debris on the floor in an effort to find some footwear that she could put on.

'What are you doing? Fuck off, will you,' Samantha squealed, but Deans was not slowing and he did not intend to leave without Samantha.

'You're coming with me and I don't give a shit if I have to drag you out of here in your bare feet,' he said launching empty cider bottles through the air like a man possessed.

'Why are you being so horrible,' Samantha said curling herself into her chair.

Deans leaned in close, his teeth bared. 'Get your shoes on, right now.'

Samantha covered her face with her hands and coiled even tighter.

'Too late for that,' Deans said. 'Holds fuck all weight with me. You're coming. Right now.'

'Where are we going?' Samantha asked from behind her arms.

'Having a little get together… a little *family* time with Pops.' Deans had been stuffing a Co-Op carrier bag with her tobacco,

Rizlas and a three-quarters-full bottle of her cheap and nasty cider.

'No way,' she cried out, 'I haven't been there in ages. Not going now.'

'Yes way. You are coming, and we are leaving right now. Time to take a little drive.'

'I don't want to,' she said in a timid child's voice.

Deans loomed over her. She was a pathetic picture of a human being. Her sobs were the only thing he could now hear. Deans snapped his head and blinked sense back into himself. He wiped the front of his face and looked at the carrier bag in his hand. *Jesus Christ!* He looked towards the doorway and back to Samantha. His face flushed with anxiety, his chest pounded and a trauma boiled from deep within. He panted heavily as if he had just jogged up the stairs. He filled his cheeks with air and blew slowly through a small gap in his lips.

'Samantha... Samantha. I've got everything you'll need.' His voice was now calmer. 'You can drink as much as you like. I really need your help... Please?'

She unfurled her arms and Deans could see her puffy and terrified eyes. A ball of guilt lodged in the back of his throat.

She looked at the carrier bag and Deans lifted the bottle so that she could see it was inside.

'I'll even buy more bottles for you,' he said. 'I'm sorry if I scared you.'

Her eyes scanned the floor – the empty cider bottles scattered all around.

'How long?' she asked.

'Not long,' Deans replied gently.

In reality Deans did not know how long they would be, but her voluntary agreement, more or less, was far more preferable to false imprisonment and kidnap.

Deans helped Samantha to her feet, and she directed him to a pair of manky Adidas trainers that he then helped place onto her feet.

'Do you promise you will buy more cider... and I won't have to pay you back?' she asked.

'Absolutely,' Deans replied. 'Come on, let's get to the shops.'

He assisted her down the stairwell of the flats and into his car. In this proximity, Deans realised how much she needed a bath, or at least a wash and a change of clothes. He opened his window to the fullest extremity, even though drizzle was pitching on his arm.

The care home was no more than five minutes up the hill and ignoring the speed restrictions, Deans brought the car to a sudden halt scattering gravel outside of the care home entrance.

'I don't want to see him,' Samantha said defiantly. Her arms folded and her pout classic *fifteen-year-old.*

'I actually don't give a shit what you want,' Deans said. 'You're coming in with me.'

He stepped out, slammed his door, came around the front of the car and fixed a constant glare onto Samantha.

'Out,' he said holding the door wide open.

Samantha did not move.

Deans stuck his head inside the car. 'Don't test me, Samantha. You are only ten minutes away from being booked into custody for accessory to murder.'

She faced him with pleading eyes. 'But it's got nothing to do with me.'

'It has *everything* to do with you *and* your old man. Now, I'm only going to ask you one last time. Please, get out of the fucking car.'

She unhooked her belt, keeping a watchful eye on Deans and slowly inched her way out of the seat.

Deans shut the door and quickly locked the car. He noticed Samantha staring at the front of the care home building.

'You haven't been here before, have you?' he said buzzing the entrance door.

She shook her dirty matted mop of hair. 'Why are you doing this?' she asked quietly.

The answer was simple. 'Three dead people,' Deans said.

'But we didn't kill them.'

Deans huffed and looked her in the eye. 'I'm giving you the opportunity to do the right thing.'

Following the same procedure as before, Deans was once again face to face with George Fenwick, only this time they were in his private room and Samantha and a carer were also present.

'Hello, George, remember me?' Deans said loudly. 'The policeman.' He knelt down, so that he was the same height as George and beamed a wide smile. 'Look who else has come to see you?'

George blinked moisture to the metallic sheen coating his eyes, his stare falling short of Deans' face.

'He probably doesn't have an idea who you are,' the carer suggested.

'Oh, I think he does,' Deans said and nudged Samantha in front of her father. 'Look George, it's your daughter, Samantha.'

'Peter?' George spluttered with his delicate voice.

'No, George,' the carer said, 'this is your daughter. How special is that?'

Deans noticed George begin to turn but then stop himself.

'Do you know what, George, I'd love to hear all about Peter,' Deans said and dragged a plastic chair from the back wall, placed it directly in front of the old boy and sat down.

The corners of George's eyes pooled with tears. He raised an arm; slow, deliberate, trembling and prodded a handkerchief at his face. His lips were ajar, and the skin pulled tight at the corners of his mouth.

'Peter?' George repeated tamely.

Deans leaned back against the chair, straining the plastic with his weight. He locked his hands behind his head but did not take his eyes away from the old boy. 'Do you know what, George? I have as long as it takes. I'm in no rush.'

'Excuse me,' the carer said abruptly.

'George knows why I'm here, don't you, George?' Deans said still focussed on his subject.

'I'm sorry,' the carer said placing a hand on George's shoulder. 'Why are you talking to George like he is some kind of common criminal?'

Deans smiled but did not break his attention away from George. 'Isn't that the million dollar question?' he said.

'I really have to object to this,' the carer said, sidling in between Deans and George. 'I'm sorry, I don't care where you say you are from,' she said.

'Tell me about Charlie,' Deans said, leaning around the flank of the carer.

'No, no, no. Now that is quite enough. Please leave,' the nurse said using her hands to usher Deans away. 'I think you will need a warrant if you wish to speak to George anymore.'

Deans stood up and pushed the plastic chair over onto the floor with the back of his knees. 'And I think you've been watching too many films, love,' he said.

Samantha stepped forward.

'He knows, Dad,' she mumbled down to her feet. 'He knows about Charlie.'

Deans looked over at Samantha. For the first time he saw real emotion on her face.

She crouched over and grabbed her father around the neck, and hugged him tightly.

George made a strained sound in the back of his throat causing Samantha to let go and step away. All three of them looked at him.

'I think you already know I'm not letting this go, George,' Deans said. 'A man of your experience...'

'Huh!' George muttered. 'Well then... Sammy... the day has

finally come,' George croaked. An unsteady hand moved toward his face and dabbed a wet trickle of tears with a handkerchief.

The carer stood back and looked at George with utter surprise painted across her face.

'You tell the detective what he needs to know, there's a good girl,' George continued, 'Daddy... Daddy can finally be at peace.'

Samantha grabbed her father's trembling hand, she crouched down before him and she began to sob.

The carer was still gaping as she peered between George and Deans, but did not speak.

'Okay, Samantha,' Deans said. 'I think it's time we left and gave George a little time to explain a few things to this lovely lady.'

He encouraged Samantha away from her father with a few gentle tugs of the arm and he thanked the young carer on their way out.

CHAPTER TWENTY-FIVE

'Where are we going?' Samantha asked nervously. 'Are you getting my drink now?'

Deans concentrated on the road ahead; he was doing well over forty within the city limits.

'Where are you taking me?' Samantha's shaking voice asked again.

Deans faced her for the first time since they were back in the car. 'The Willows,' he said.

'No!' Samantha screamed curling herself into a ball against the car door. 'Please, no,' she cried.

Deans accelerated and overtook a car directly into oncoming traffic.

'Please,' Samantha pleaded, her hands gripping her kneecaps. 'Please, no. I can't go back to the house.'

'Why?' Deans yelled, now driving almost twice the legal speed limit.

Samantha tugged at the door handle, but Deans had locked it from his side of the car and there was nothing she could do about it. She cowered further into the seat, legs and knees tucked in against her chin.

'Why, Samantha?' Deans shouted.

'Because…'

'Because?'

'He'll kill me.'

'Who?' Deans bellowed. 'Who will kill you?'

She turned to Deans; her face was a picture of abstract fear. 'Charlie,' she screamed.

Deans ground to a halt at a set of red lights. He reached behind her headrest and leaned in close to Samantha. 'Why will he kill you?'

'Because…'

'Tell me,' Deans shouted.

'Because Dad stole his money.'

A toot from the car behind reminded Deans where he was. He waved a hand in the rear view mirror, pulled away at a normal speed and came to stop again at the next available space at the side of the road. Samantha was bawling.

'What money?' Deans asked calmly.

Samantha looked away out of her window.

'Samantha, what money?'

She dropped her head into her hands and still sobbing said, 'Half of it was Dad's anyway.'

Deans sucked in a deep breath through his teeth and checked outside, looking through each window in turn. Satisfied, he stopped and focussed again on Samantha.

'If you tell me everything I need to know about the money, and the body, I won't take you to the house.'

She glimpsed a look his way. 'Please…' she said, 'don't.'

Deans rummaged through the door pocket and handed Samantha a bunch of tissues. 'So tell me,' he said.

She blew her nose and dabbed her face with the paper for a few moments and then she began to speak. 'Dad… Dad was a banker… in London,' she sniffled and blew her nose again. '… in the sixties.'

'Go on,' Deans said.

'He… he did some favours—'

'For?'

Samantha looked him in the eye. 'For bad people.'

Deans clamped his jaw. 'And?'

'One of them came after the money.'

Deans rubbed his face and sucked in a knowing breath. 'Who?'

Samantha's voice juddered. 'His name… his name was… Peter.'

Peter? That was the name the old man kept saying.

'Peter Charleston,' Samantha continued, her face haunted by the name. 'Don't make me go back in there,' she begged.

'You won't. I promise. Go on,' Deans said, 'tell me about the money.'

Samantha sniffed and pointed to the side pocket of Deans' door. He obliged with another fist full of tissues.

'Dad didn't take all of it,' she whimpered. 'Maybe six.'

'Six what?'

'Hundred,' she replied.

Deans frowned. 'Six hundred quid?'

Samantha faced him. 'Thousand… six hundred thousand pounds.'

Fuck me. 'And you are saying that money is somewhere in that house?'

She did enough to nod and peered out of her window. 'And Charlie,' she said.

CHAPTER TWENTY-SIX

Deans had already dropped Samantha at her home and was interrogating the computer system in the office. Peter Charleston, or 'Charlie-Boy' as he was known to his associates, was a nasty bastard. Born in 1929, he was on the fringe of east London's organised crime in the heady, 'celebrity' days. He had the foresight others in his circle failed to recognise; an ability to drop off the police radar before the heat set in. He was a survivor. But you would not cross him. And you certainly would not antagonise anyone in his extended 'family'.

Deans scrolled down the page; luckily, for him, Charlie-Boy was enough of a 'somebody' that he had his own Wiki page. Charlie-Boy went missing in 1974. The Met police closed the file soon after – missing – presumed living it up somewhere with Costa in the name. He left a wife and three kids to fend for themselves and melded into obscurity, or so it was believed.

Deans took several long slurps from his coffee. Samantha's story was becoming all the more compelling.

A team of detectives, 'The Bravo Squad', had been assigned to build a case against the bit-players – the cannon fodder, and close the net on the big boys, only; Charlie-Boy was ahead of the game

– as he always seemed to be. His reputation as a lackey dwindled just as fast as his status as a 'brain' grew. There had been a job – a big one. A Flying Squad balls up to the tune of eight million by today's prices. Charlie-Boy was instrumental, or so The Bravo Squad understood. But none of the associated shit-bags would finger Charlie-Boy. He was so untouchable the detectives ended up nicknaming him, 'The Prophet.'

Deans read on, but stopped in his tracks by a hyper-linked name written in blue – Chief Inspector George Julian Fenwick.

You are shitting me! He clicked the link.

There were only a few lines of information, but enough. George had headed The Bravo Squad between '65 and '67. He was a detective of the highest order – until the botched job forced him to retire before pensionable age and under a cloud of suspicion and intrigue.

Deans leaned back in his seat and cradled his mug. Lose that amount of cash and someone has to pay. On this occasion, it was poor old George.

Poor old George. You sneaky little bastard. No wonder you did not like me sniffing around.

Deans now had a big problem. The scene at The Willows had been shut down, closed, ended as an evidential avenue. The police had left the scene and locked up behind them. That meant any powers to continue searching the premises had ceased the moment they had turned the key and walked away. The police couldn't just waltz back inside the building willy-nilly. They would need a magistrates' warrant of entry to gain further access, but not only that, Deans would have to justify what he was looking for… and how he came by the information.

He made himself another coffee and found Savage in the Intel department. They found a quiet corner and Deans announced his plan to return to The Willows.

'What are you talking about, Deano? It's finished,' Savage said in an off-hand manner. 'Complete the coroner's file and have done with it.'

'This isn't about the Roses,' Deans said looking over at the other officers behind their desks. He leaned in closer to Savage. 'I've received information regarding...' he looked back towards the rest of the team, '...regarding, the commission of a further serious crime inside that property.'

'What crime?' Savage asked.

Deans scratched behind his ear and whispered his response, 'Another murder.'

Savage stared blankly back at Deans.

'There's another body, buried within the grounds,' Deans continued, 'and a large quantity of cash stashed somewhere inside.'

Savage's face became increasingly knotted. 'What are you talking about?'

Deans grabbed Savage by the arm and pulled him towards the door. 'Probably best we chat privately?'

'I think we had,' Savage said.

They moved to a recently vacated office and Savage stood with his back to the door, arms folded, as Deans spoke.

'Samantha Fenwick disclosed to me this morning that her father, George Fenwick, used to be a London banker. They came into some money, and someone else came looking for it – Peter Charleston, AKA, Charlie-Boy Charleston – a nineteen sixties gangster who went missing forty years ago. Charlie-Boy came to Bath for his money. But he didn't leave.' Deans paused, waiting for Savage to say something, but he didn't and so he continued. 'Somewhere inside The Willows we will find Charlie-Boy... and the rest of the stolen money.'

Savage's mouth was wide and his eyes unblinking.

'Thing is,' Deans said, 'George Fenwick wasn't a banker. He was a Flying Squad Senior Detective.'

Savage finally moved, closing his mouth and stepping towards Deans. 'Fuck me, Deano!'

Deans could see the ridges of muscle flexing in Savage's jaw, and given the considerable padding in that area, that took some doing. Deans needed to jump right to the point.

'If we obtain a warrant, Samantha will show us where we need to look for the body and the money,' Deans said.

Savage put a finger into his mouth and chewed the end off a nail, spitting it out onto the floor. He looked at Deans beneath his brows and shook his head.

'I think...' he sighed. 'I think you should go home, mate.'

'What?' Deans replied.

'You've come back too soon,' Savage said. 'You need to get things straight in your head.'

'Mick,' Deans said striding towards Savage. 'This is *real*. All I need is the warrant. Samantha and Denise—'

'Moon?' Savage barked. 'It's that bloody woman feeding your brain with all this shite that is causing all the problems.'

'What problems?'

'Oh, come on, Deano – ghosts, spirits, hearing voices... what else do you want me to say? I can go on.'

Deans scowled. 'Everything Denise has said has so far come to fruition. And just for the record, she doesn't even know about this... yet.'

Savage pulled a chair from the top of a tall stack at the side of the room. 'Sit down a moment,' he said.

Deans obliged.

Savage was tight-lipped and spoke in secretive tones. 'I can't keep shielding you, Deano.'

'From what?'

'From the bosses who are looking for any excuse to reduce our numbers further.'

'Meaning?'

'You are pushing the boundaries, Deano. You are under a

bloody great microscope right now, and currently people still want to help you. But don't for a second think that those same people won't be the ones after your badge and ready to burn you given half the chance.'

'And if I'm right?' Deans asked.

Savage's stare beat down upon him. 'We are never going to find out, Deano. The case is closed. And so is the door to that sodding house. Do you understand me?'

Deans glared at Savage. 'You don't... you don't believe any of this... do you?'

Savage scuffed his heels against the floor tiles and shook his head. 'It's got nothing to do with belief—'

'It has everything to do with belief. What don't you understand?'

Savage narrowed his large brown eyes and leaned against the stack of tables. 'Andy,' he said drawing breath. 'I'm going to spell it out. I wouldn't be a friend unless I did.'

Deans watched him, unmoving.

'The bosses...' Savage said, hesitating, '...well, they've already approached me. No one else on the team knows this yet, Deano, but we are being disbanded.' He hooked a finger under his collar and pulled the material away from his skin. 'I don't know when, but they are looking...' Savage turned towards the door and then back to Deans. 'They are looking for excuses to get rid of officers. Not re-deploy – get shot of – do you understand me, Deano? I have been trying to warn you, but you really need to start listening—'

'I have been listening,' Deans cut in. 'It's you that refuses to hear.'

Savage grunted and slapped his hands on the side of his thighs. 'I give up,' he said. 'Grab your stuff and go home,' he scowled. 'Please, Deano... just go home.'

Deans rose slowly from the chair and Savage smiled reluctantly.

As Deans reached the door, Savage stopped him with a hand on his arm. 'I'll pop in and see you in a day or two,' he said.

Deans did not answer and continued out of the room.

Deans did not go home. He went direct to see Samantha Fenwick and an hour and a half later he was standing before the DI and Savage in the privacy of the boss's office, with a statement from Samantha detailing the existence of the money, and the body.

'There,' Deans said, tossing the statement sheets onto the DI's desk. He gave Savage a challenging stare. 'Try to ignore the evidence now.'

Savage scooped the statement from the desk and flicked through the pages so quickly, there was no possible way he was reading any of the detail. 'What's this?' he asked, throwing the pages back onto the desk.

Deans stood tall, his shoulders pinned back. 'Evidence of a murder, and the concealment of stolen cash within The Willows, Bathwick.'

The DI shook his head and turned to Savage. 'What? The place where we pulled that couple from?'

'Yes, Sir,' Deans said quickly.

Savage rocked his head and extended Deans a raised brow.

'Let me take a look,' the DI said.

He began reading the first page, shaking his head. 'I'm confused. How has all this come about?'

Savage gave Deans a withering stare.

'It was volunteered, Boss,' Deans said.

The DI looked at Deans over the top of the statement papers. 'Do you believe any of this?' he asked Deans.

'Absolutely, Sir.'

The DI turned to Savage. 'Mick?'

Savage groaned. 'Let me digest it,' he said, taking the papers back from the DI. 'I'll chat to Deano and let you know what I think.'

'Good,' the DI said. 'We had better consider a warrant of entry if we have reasonable grounds to suspect a body is buried somewhere within those grounds.'

Savage dropped his head. Deans smiled.

CHAPTER TWENTY-SEVEN

Deans sat inside the job car at the rear of the station. He played the conversation repeatedly in his head, but it did not improve with repetition and he knew it was down to him to make the peace. He turned the ignition but did not move. The sound of the engine was a useful muffle from any officers who might walk past and hear his conversation. Denise answered with a stony silence.

'I'm sorry,' Deans said immediately. 'I… I need your help.'

'I know,' Denise answered.

'I was wondering if you could come up to Bath, to help me with my job?'

'Help you?'

Deans sniffed. 'I was wrong to question anything about you,' he said. 'And I appreciate everything you have done for me.'

'Okay.'

'But I really need your help now.'

The line went quiet.

Deans scratched the back of his neck.

'I can't do this without you, Denise,' he said after a moment. 'Any of this.'

'What do you need?'

'Can you come to Bath tonight?'

The line fell silent again.

'Denise?' Deans said. 'Please. You are the only person who understands me now.'

'No more questioning?' she asked.

'None.'

'You understand and *believe* what we are – what *you* can do?'

'Let's not push it.'

'Okay,' Denise said.

'Okay?' Deans repeated.

'Okay.'

Denise arrived in Bath and met Deans at the train station. Any thoughts of awkwardness evaporated as she hugged him as if it was the last time they would see each other. 'Thank you,' Deans said taking her bag.

'I wanted to see the house,' she said gazing deeply into his eyes. 'And I needed to see you. Will you take me there now?'

'We can't go inside today,' Deans said. 'An entry warrant is booked from eight a.m. tomorrow. We'll have twenty-four hours to do whatever is necessary from then.'

'Take me there now,' Denise said. She did not appear to be in a negotiating mood.

Deans shrugged and took the lead. The Willows was just a ten-minute stroll from the station, however, today with the mass of Christmas shoppers, it turned out to be at least twice that.

They approached the terraced row of properties, Denise walking between Deans and the building line. He had not told her the address, neither had he indicated where exactly the property was, but as they neared, he noticed Denise begin to fidget. Deans himself shivered as a cold air penetrated the back of his neck. He did not talk, and neither did Denise.

He saw the front door, but instead of indicating that they had arrived, he continued walking beyond the entrance.

'Where are you going?' Denise asked, stopping directly outside of The Willows.

Deans stopped and beamed a smile. 'Forgot where I was for a moment.'

She leered at him. 'Were you testing me?'

Deans grinned and joined her as she looked up at the front of the building. Fingers of energy tickled the back of Deans' neck and he shook away the unwelcome itch.

'Don't step any closer,' Denise said touching Deans' hand. 'He's drawing us in.'

Deans scowled – he did have the strangest of sensations enticing him to walk forwards, like some weird vertigo tempting him to step a little closer to the edge, but it was Denise who walked towards the house.

'No,' she said all of a sudden in a loud and defiant voice.

Deans watched on with interest.

'No we will not,' Denise said angrily, flapping her arms and shaking her body like she was shaking rain from a wet jacket.

She turned to Deans with a serious look. 'This is going to be interesting,' she said.

'Interesting?'

'Oh! He's an angry soul,' Denise said. 'Very angry indeed.'

Deans noticed a pedestrian taking a wide berth of them both.

'Perhaps we should do this once we are inside the house tomorrow,' he said.

She raised an uncompromising brow. 'He will be waiting for us,' she said, her voice guarded. 'This won't be like anything you've experienced before.'

Deans shrugged. 'Bring it on.'

'Oh,' Denise replied. 'He intends to.'

CHAPTER TWENTY-EIGHT

Denise woke him up just after six. He had not made it from the sofa. He strangled the bottle of whisky by the neck and stuffed it away at the back of the cabinet.

'Is that every night?' Denise asked.

Deans ran his tongue along the cracked ridges of his lips and nodded.

'That has to stop. It won't help,' she said.

Deans shuffled over to the kettle and filled it with water.

'How much rest are you getting?' Denise asked.

Deans shrugged. 'The usual.'

'It's not enough,' she said and removed two cups from a cupboard, placed them in front of Deans and then went back inside the unit and pulled out another half-consumed bottle of whisky. 'This won't bring Maria back,' she said holding the bottle in the air between them.

'No,' Deans said. 'It won't. But if it helps me to relax—'

'I heard you *relaxing*, remember?'

Fair comment. He chewed the inside of his lip and watched Denise fussing around the kitchen.

'Maria was abducted,' he said.

Denise stopped what she was doing and stared at him.

'Was it Ash Babbage?' she asked.

Deans shook his head. 'Couldn't have been. He was in police custody. But those things he said to me... practically admitted to ruining my life.'

Denise did not react.

Deans approached and took Denise by the hand. 'I want you to contact Maria.'

Denise placed her cup on the breakfast bar and stared at him intently. 'Are you sure?'

'I need to know... I'm ready to know.'

'Okay,' Denise whispered, 'Okay.'

She patted the bar stool and Deans sat down. He watched her for a moment as she prepared herself. She took a number of deep breaths and appeared to reach a meditative state. He could see her lips moving, but heard no words. She dipped her head and her long dark hair fell forwards.

A vice-like pressure crushed down on Deans' skull, he grabbed the sides of his head, but just as quickly, it went again.

Denise looked up at Deans through her strands of hair.

'What?' he asked at once. The muscles in his stomach tightened and cramped.

'I can't reach her,' Denise said.

'But I felt—'

'You may have felt the presence of the guardians.'

Deans stood up from his stool. 'Then Maria is still alive.'

Denise broke eye contact and nibbled the nail of her thumb.

'Denise?'

She shook her head. 'It means I cannot reach Maria.'

Deans stood beside Denise and grabbed for her hand. 'Denise. Is Maria still alive?'

He felt the pressure release from her grasp and she turned away.

'Denise. What did you pick up?'

She shook her head and pulled her hair away from her face, her eyes faltering.

Deans let go of her hand and took a step backwards.

'I couldn't reach her,' Denise repeated. 'I'm sorry.'

Deans watched Denise for a quiet moment. His eyelids were heavy and sullen as he tracked her movement in the kitchen. She was wiping the surfaces down and tidying the mess on the worktops. His body was saggy and defeated.

She noticed him staring, stopped what she was doing and smiled. 'What?' she asked. 'What?' she said again with a small titter.

'I had the dream again,' he said.

Her smile dimmed. 'The nightmare?' she asked and nibbled the side of a Digestive biscuit.

Deans nodded. He blinked slowly, but did not take his eyes off Denise.

'I know who was holding the knife,' he said.

Her chewing slowed; she leaned against the side of the worktop and peered at him. 'In the dream?'

'I forced myself to view the dream to the end,' he said, 'like you told me to do. I know who was with Ash Babbage.'

Denise swallowed her biscuit and wiped crumbs from her chin. 'In the dream,' she said again.

Deans shrugged. 'I haven't worked that part out yet.'

'Well, come on,' Denise smiled. 'Don't keep it to yourself. Tell me, is it someone I know?'

Deans looked blankly at Denise. He saw her face drop in a heartbeat and her eyes grow wider.

'Me?' she uttered, taking a very subtle slide backwards against the worktop.

Deans didn't move.

Denise blinked feverishly and began to shake her head as she tried to speak.

'You,' Deans said quietly.

'But it wasn't...' Denise spluttered – her voice was now panicked. 'I'm... it... it wasn't me,' she pleaded.

'You said I had an ability,' Deans said calmly, 'so, please explain to me why I can see you in my dream and why you are killing my wife?'

'Yes, I know I said that,' Denise said back-peddling, 'but that doesn't mean you are right about the dream.' She scooped a handful of her hair and pinned it behind an ear. Her eyes were wide and scared, but she refused to look at him. She fiddled with an ornament on the worktop and did all she could to avoid eye contact.

Deans squinted and waited.

Twenty more seconds went by, and then she caught his eye. 'You are lying,' he said.

Denise shook her head and looked down. 'Oh, come on, Andy,' she said down to her feet. 'Do you seriously think I would have anything to do with Ash, or Maria's disappearance?' She looked up at him; her eyes moved quickly around his face.

Deans sized her up and slowly shook his head. 'You're not convincing me,' he said. 'Why wouldn't you have anything to do with Babbage? He was working with you in the shop. He was your apprentice... you were his teacher. It makes obvious sense.'

Her shoulders dropped and she reached for the worktop to prevent herself from falling. She turned sideways to Deans and leaned on the counter. Her hair dropped forwards over her face and she remained in that position.

Deans raised himself from the seat and moved towards her as if his feet were on autopilot. He stood immediately beside her and grabbed her arm.

Denise looked up at him; her eyes were puffy and distant.

'Tell me,' Deans said gripping her arm tightly.

Denise shook her head with short, sharp movements. 'It's not…' she dropped her head again.

'Denise,' Deans shouted, and shook her by the arm.

She faced the other way and began to weep.

Deans sensed his anger building. 'Denise,' he said again through gritted teeth.

She flicked around and faced him. Her features were warped and pained. Deans shook her again and this time she gave in.

Deans let go and took several backwards steps. He gawped at Denise and felt his stomach twist like a knot.

'It wasn't Maria.' Denise whispered, as tears dropped off her chin. 'It was my mother.'

Deans was open mouthed. He looked her up and down. 'What was your mother?'

Denise wiped her face with her sleeve and peered over at the table. 'Can I sit down please? I need to sit down.'

Deans moved aside, allowing Denise to pass him and followed close behind her over to the kitchen table. She scraped one of the chairs out along the stone tiled floor, fell into the chair and sank into her hands.

Deans pulled out the seat opposite and sat down, staring at Denise.

'I've never told a soul,' she whispered beneath her shroud of hair. 'I have carried this silent torment with me for over forty years.' She looked up and stared at Deans.

He didn't move. Didn't speak.

'My mother was sick,' she uttered and looked down at the table, fixing her stare at an imaginary point halfway between them. 'I mentioned to you previously that we used to live together…'

'Your mum was a psychic, she taught you things when you were young. Yes, I remember what you said, but what does this have to do with Maria?'

'It doesn't,' Denise mouthed. She looked Deans in the eye and held her hands together as if in prayer. 'Your ability...' Denise hesitated and shook head. 'Well, it obviously extends beyond your personal loved ones.'

Deans' brow furrowed deeply. 'I don't understand,' he said.

'You have manifested dreams – dreams so powerful that you have somehow identified a secret in me so deep, I was certain it would follow me to the grave.'

'You sliced your mother's throat?' Deans asked in astonishment.

Denise shook her head. 'No. Mother was sick, very sick, but because of her unwavering beliefs she refused to be seen by a traditional doctor and so self-medicated with medicines and potions she created herself.' Denise stopped speaking and her eyes glazed over.

Deans was transfixed.

Denise covered her face with her hands and then swept her hair back off her face. She took a number of deep breaths and looked back at Deans.

'Towards the end,' she said, 'she was too ill to take the medicine herself and had me do it for her.'

Deans studied her kinesic cues – testing to see if her body language was telling him something else.

'How old were you?' he asked.

Denise sucked in a deep breath and held her eyes shut for a long moment.

'Fifteen,' she answered and lowered her head.

'Go on,' Deans said.

Denise was wilting lower into her seat.

'There was a liquid,' she said. 'A vial. Mother had told me about it before she became too ill.' Denise looked away into space. 'She told me to give it to her when things got bad. Said it would take her pain away...' Denise stopped and dabbed a tissue around her eyes. 'I was only young,' she said breathlessly. 'I didn't know what I was giving her. I just wanted Mum to get better.'

'Poison?' Deans said.

'I didn't know,' Denise said, looking up at Deans through rheumy eyes. 'I was fifteen. I couldn't have known she would die.'

Deans watched her; considered her subtle gestures. 'Were the police involved?' he asked.

Denise hunched forwards. 'There was a post mortem. That's when they found all of the cancer—'

Deans blinked and gazed at her. 'And why they didn't look any further.'

He heaved a deep breath and leaned back in his chair. He traced her face and slowly shook his head. He waited twenty, maybe thirty more seconds and then leaned forwards, resting his forehead in the palm of his hands, his elbows drilling into the edge of the table.

'I'm sorry,' Denise said.

Deans held a hand up to stop her talking as he continued to support his heavy head with the other.

'That's why I am in your dream,' Denise pressed. 'I promise… it has nothing to do with Ash Babbage, or Maria.'

Deans sucked in a large breath through his teeth and peered up at Denise. 'Okay,' he said. 'Okay… have you ever told anyone else… family members, best friend whilst drunk… vicar?'

'No one,' she replied without hesitating. 'I'm ashamed of what I have done, but it was mother's wish…' Denise stopped and bowed her head. 'I know you have a duty to do.'

Deans planted his hands flat onto the kitchen table. 'It stays with me… but you must promise never to tell anyone, and if you do – you never told me – alright?' His eyes glared wide.

'I'll take whatever punishment I deserve,' Denise said. 'I have lived with this agony for a very long time.'

'And you will have to live with it for a bit longer. There will be no punishment. There will be no further mention of it, do you understand me? I'm going out on a very large limb here, because without you, there is no Maria.'

Denise stared at Deans for a moment. 'You would do that for me?'

'No… I would do that for Maria.'

CHAPTER TWENTY-NINE

Deans was quiet for the remainder of the morning. Denise gave him space and did not place him under any pressure to talk, which he appreciated. On reflection, it was going to be tough to hear about Maria either way, but at least there was still hope.

They did not say much on their way to the station, each in their own time and zone. Deans decided against telling Denise that she may receive a frosty reception from the rest of his team. He thought she might change her mind about visiting The Willows in the face of a room of disbelievers.

Deans formally introduced Denise to his team and to CSI Parsons, who had been volunteered to join the search party. Deans took a backwards step and watched them interact with Denise, who herself was coping with the situation with impeccable poise and decorum.

Deans briefed his team. 'She doesn't know it yet,' he said, 'but I'm collecting Samantha Fenwick and bringing her to the scene. The rest of you head straight for the property and we'll see you there.'

'Where do we begin?' Nathan Parsons asked.

'Don't worry, Samantha will show us everything we need to

know,' Deans said. He noticed Savage staring at Denise, and it was not a friendly look. 'Denise will be coming with me,' Deans said talking directly at Savage.

'I'm sorry,' Parsons said. 'But why is she here?'

Before Deans had a chance to reply, Denise was already on her feet and responding. 'I am going to keep you all safe,' she said.

Savage made a 'Pfft' noise between his lips and for the first time in five minutes, he spoke. 'From what, exactly?'

Denise faced him and smiled sweetly. 'There is a determined spirit contained within that house. One that has already shown the desire to kill.'

'Pah!' DC Mitchell spluttered and began to giggle, along with several others.

'You lot do not have to believe it,' Deans said standing beside Denise. 'But I'm not prepared to go inside that house without Denise being with us.'

'Come on, you lot,' Savage huffed now also standing up. 'Down your drinks and let's get this friggin freak show over and done with.'

Deans could not get a response from the Travis Street Flats intercom, but had made his way inside the building thanks to a postal worker making a delivery to a different flat. He banged on Samantha's door, but got no reply. He tried again. And again, and shouted through the letterbox but without any answer. He pushed on the door. It was locked.

'She must be inside,' he said to Denise. 'All the bolts are across.'

'We can still do it,' Denise said softly. 'I can find you what you need. I will ask the spirit to show me.'

Deans flapped his arms in frustration. 'Fine,' he said. 'Seems like we have little choice. I'll write her a note. When she wakes up she can make her own way down to us.'

He scribbled on a torn-out sheet of his day-book and pushed it under the door. He smiled at Denise. 'She'll come. I've promised to buy her five more bottles of cider.'

Fifteen minutes later, they were all inside The Willows, minus Samantha Fenwick. Parsons was kitted-out in a white forensic suit and all eyes were on Denise.

'Okay,' Deans said. 'Samantha said in her statement that the body was buried in the back garden.'

'Bit clichéd,' Savage said. 'But we need to start somewhere I suppose. Come on, let's dig it up and get the hell out of here.'

Deans led the way through the hallway and into the kitchen. The further he entered, the chillier he became. He looked over his shoulder; Savage was right on his tail.

'You feeling any colder, Mick?' Deans asked.

'It's a cold day,' Savage said pushing Deans forwards with his hands. 'Let me tell you now, Deano. I'm not wasting all this manpower for very long. One hour tops, and then I'm pulling the troops away. You can stay as long as you like, but I've got proper work to be getting on with.'

Deans nodded. He did not know how long Denise needed, but he realised he was fortunate to have the team there in any event. Deans continued toward the rear of the property, Denise was now alongside him and the others were trailing.

'Can you feel that?' she whispered to Deans.

'Why is it only us?' he replied quietly. Denise shook her head.

Deans unlocked the back door and walked down the dozen or so concrete steps to the rear garden area. Every step he took increased his inner chill.

Denise suddenly hooked her arm around his. 'He's here,' she said.

'I know,' Deans whispered. 'What do we do?'

Denise shook her head. 'We wait for contact.'

Deans walked ahead and scoured the outdoor area. Most of the ground was laid to lawn – albeit tufted and coarse. His eyes rested on a large rectangular section of wooden decking in the corner where a high fence joined to the back of the house. He called Nathan Parsons over and asked him to take snaps of the area with his camera.

'Got your screwdriver?' Parsons asked playfully and began assembling his photographic equipment.

Deans noticed Denise had returned inside the house. He told Parsons to crack on and headed back up the steps into the kitchen.

Savage was now sitting in a chair, looking about as disinterested as he possibly could.

'Where's Denise?' Deans asked.

Savage tittered under his breath. 'Upstairs I think. Looked a bit upset about something.'

Deans jogged up the stairs and found her in the main bedroom. As soon as he entered the room, Denise rushed to him and latched her arms tightly around him.

'I saw it,' she said. 'I saw the murder.'

The hairs lifted on Dean's neck. 'What did you see?' he asked urgently.

'A fight… in the kitchen between two men. A girl… a young girl gave one of them a knife… he… he stabbed the man in the chest, like this—' Denise clenched her fist with an imaginary blade coming out of the bottom of her hand and repeatedly jabbed it forwards through the cool air.

'Her dad?' Deans asked.

'He was just a little man, but full of rage.'

'What happened next?' Deans asked.

Denise rocked her head. 'They… panicked…. dragged the body down the steps and the man dug a large hole.'

'Could you see exactly where the body was dumped?'

Denise was staring into space.

'Denise? Could you show me where the body was buried?'

'Yes,' she whispered.

'What about the money?' Deans asked.

She shook her head. 'I don't know about the money,' she breathed.

Deans helped her back down the stairs and they joined Parsons in the garden. Denise looked around briefly and then pointed towards the decked area.

'Over there?' Deans asked. Denise looked away and nodded.

Half-an-hour later, and the decking was all but removed, exposing a paved area approximately fifteen feet long and six feet wide. Everybody at the scene, including Savage, was now gathered around the aged mossy patio.

'We need to get this up,' Deans said turning to Savage.

'Not a hope,' Savage replied. 'Unless you've got a pneumatic drill?'

'We'll have to call Support Group,' Deans said.

'I'm not doing that,' Savage said. He put a hand on Deans' shoulder. 'Come on; let's just call it a day. We can at least say we gave it a chance.'

Deans turned to Denise. Her face looked as disappointed as his thoughts. A door slammed loudly from inside and everyone turned at the same time to look back towards the house.

Savage scowled and made it obvious he was conducting a head count.

'Are we expecting anyone else?' he asked.

'That wasn't one of us,' Denise said and began walking slowly back towards the house.

Deans jogged up alongside. 'Was it him?'

'That was contact,' she said.

'I'm just going inside with Denise,' Deans shouted back to the others.

Savage waved approval and then deliberately tapped the face of his watch for Deans' benefit.

Denise went first and entered the kitchen. Deans could see the vapour of his breath suspended in front of his nose. He shuddered as a frigid jacket tightened around his body.

'He's here,' Denise said. 'Stay close to me. Don't do anything without telling me first.'

Deans nodded keenly; he did not need telling twice.

They crept through hallway to the base of the stairs and peered up. Denise faced Deans and exaggerated a nod. Her eyes were wide and her pupils as small as pinpricks. She took the first tentative steps of the stairs and Deans followed as close behind as her shadow.

They stopped at the top landing, side-by-side. Denise pointed to the master bedroom. The door was closed.

Deans frowned – he was certain he had left it open. He took several gentle steps forwards. Denise followed. There was no sound – just the suppressed breaths of two nervous people.

Deans reached for the handle but Denise snatched his hand away before he could touch it. She shook her head and bunched her eyes in a display of apparent pain. A thunderous crash sounded the other side of the door and Denise jumped backwards with fear painted across her face.

Deans lunged for the handle and forced it open with all his strength. The door opened a fraction before crashing against a solid object on the other side, causing Deans to slam against the door with the side of his face.

'Sodding hell,' he moaned and rubbed his cheek. He jabbed at the door handle again, but each time he hit something hard on the other side.

Determined to see inside, he lay down on the floor, lined the soles of his shoes up with the sweet spot of the door, and whacked it repeatedly until a gap appeared large enough to look through.

Deans jumped to his feet. He looked for Denise, but she was holding back, he edged towards the gap in the door and stuck his head through the narrow space, but nothing could have prepared him for what he saw.

CHAPTER THIRTY

The others came rushing up the stairs, alerted by the sound of Deans shouting. By the time they had reached him, Deans was sitting in the hallway alongside Denise with her arms wrapped around his shoulders.

'What happened?' Savage asked, out of breath from running – probably for the first time in several years.

'He's okay,' Denise said softly. 'He's just had a shock, that's all.'

The others started paying attention to the gap in the bedroom door.

'Wait,' Denise shouted. 'Not without me.'

Mitchell scowled. 'Who the hell are you, anyway?'

'She's right,' Deans said, raising his head from his knees. 'Don't go inside. Please.'

Savage hesitated; his hand was already on the door knob. 'You look like you've seen a ghost, Deano.'

Deans bumped Denise's arm from his shoulder and pulled himself up from the floor. He noticed Nathan Parsons looking at him with unusual curiosity. Deans went up to the doorway and diverted Savage's fingers from the handle. He turned and faced the others, his back to the door. 'You can come in, but I'm not promising any of us are safe,' he said.

Savage looked at Deans like he had just been knocked around the chops with a wet fish.

Denise stood beside Deans and blocked the open space leading into the room.

'Denise first,' Deans said. 'And anything you see... well, don't say you weren't warned.' He pushed the door to the limit of the toppled wardrobe on the other side and gestured for Denise to walk inside first.

She hovered at the doorway, turned to Deans and whispered, 'He's gone.'

'I know,' Deans replied as warmth began to return to his limbs.

'Come on, Deano,' Savage said. 'Stop pissing around.'

He shoved his way beyond Deans and squeezed his mid-rift into the Savage-sized space created by the partially opened door. Deans and Parsons followed closely behind, but Savage stopped abruptly in the middle of the room. He turned back to face Deans, his face was a picture of bewilderment.

'It was Charlie,' Deans said blankly in response to the question Savage could not get out of his wide open mouth.

Deans looked beyond Savage to the facing wall. The master bed was turned up onto its side and the legs were thrust several inches into the wall, with plasterboard and masonry debris scattered all around the floor. Deans walked up to Savage, tapped him on the shoulder and pointed with a finger directly above their heads. Words were scribed onto the ceiling in masonry dust: *LEAVE IT ALONE... OR YOU WILL DIE.*

Savage covered his mouth.

'It's okay,' Denise said from behind them making them all jump. 'He's gone for now. He has made his point.'

'Just...' Savage stuttered nervously, '... who is this *he* you keep talking about?'

'Charlie-Boy,' Deans said, stepping between Savage and

Denise. 'A sixties hoodlum, who died and is buried somewhere within these grounds.' Deans looked up again at the ceiling. 'And he is terrorising anyone that he thinks is after his money.'

'Come on?' Savage laughed nervously.

'Do you need to look again?' Deans asked pointing towards the upturned bed.

Savage shrugged and rolled his eyes.

'Wait outside, Nate,' Deans said to Parsons, who did not need a second invitation.

Once Parsons was out of earshot, Deans stood directly in front of Savage, inches from his face. 'Maybe now you'll start to believe me?'

'Andy, this is bollocks, come on? I mean… fuck me. I mean… that just can't happen.'

'It can. And it just did,' Denise said unsympathetically.

'You,' Savage said, jabbing a finger above Deans' shoulder in her direction. 'You can shut it.'

'Hey,' Deans shouted, pushing Savage back by the shoulders. 'You're not speaking to Denise like that.'

Savage batted them both away with the back of his hand, mumbled something incoherent and left the room.

'You need him to believe this, or someone is going to get hurt,' Denise said quietly.

Deans held his hands out in a submissive pose and shrugged. 'I'd better check on Mick,' he said. 'He's not open to this kind of stuff.'

Savage was pacing back and forth in the hallway.

'Nobody is asking you to understand,' Deans said stopping Savage in his tracks.

'Fucking ghosts?' Savage said. 'Fucking ghosts?' he shouted louder.

'You give me a better explanation and I'm all ears,' Deans said calmly.

Savage clamped his jaw and stared back at the bedroom. 'Okay,' he said. 'So let's say this *is* a ghost. Why is it here?'

'The money,' Denise said stepping alongside Deans. 'He is here for the money that was stolen from him. He has no other purpose to remain here.'

Savage shook his head. 'Money stolen by?' he asked impatiently.

'George Fenwick,' Deans said.

Savage pulled a face. 'What, the old bugger in the nursing home?' Savage's mobile phone began to ring in his pocket, and then Deans' phone sounded as well.

They looked at each other for a beat and simultaneously dug a hand into their pockets.

Deans looked at his screen, *withheld number.* He glanced over to Savage, who looking at his phone shrugged. 'Withheld,' Savage said.

Deans sneaked a glance at Denise. She acknowledged him with a nod and a look towards the stairs. 'I think it's time we went outside and checked on Nate,' Deans said.

Savage heaved a despairing breath. 'Suppose I'd better see if we've got a Support Group in the area.'

'And a dog,' Denise interjected.

Deans and Savage looked at her.

'Dogs can sense far more than humans,' she said.

As they made for the stairs Deans held Denise back until the others were sufficiently out of hearing range.

'Can't you get rid of the spirit... tell it to bugger off?' Deans asked.

Denise shook her head. 'He is a powerful energy. You've just seen that for yourself.'

'But why is he doing all of this?' Deans whispered.

'He doesn't know he is dead,' Denise replied. 'He is protecting whatever he believes is rightfully his.'

Deans locked his fingers behind his head and huffed.

'You could leave him,' Denise said. 'Walk away. You still can.'

'Two people have died in this house,' Deans said lowering his arms. He spoke down to the floor, 'And I can't allow that to happen again.'

'Does anyone else at your station believe a spirit is responsible for the deaths?' Denise asked.

Deans shook his head and scratched the back of his neck.

'Maybe this is your calling. Your spiritual purpose,' Denise said softly.

Deans drew a deep breath from the cool air and dragged a hand over the front of his face, covering his open mouth. He looked back towards the master bedroom briefly.

'Can I say something?' Denise asked.

Deans dipped his head, still looking towards the partially opened door.

'You will need all of your energy for Maria,' Denise said. 'Why not hand this job over to somebody else?'

Deans laughed through his nostrils. 'Who? Who else can I trust? They already think I'm bloody nuts,' he replied.

Denise formed a down-turned smile. 'That's the curse of our kind,' she murmured quietly.

Our kind? Whatever happened to my boring old life?

CHAPTER THIRTY-ONE

DS Jackson and DC Gold arrived at the prison and made their way through the security checks deeper into the beast. There was always something edgy about being a cop inside prison; a certain vulnerability, even though the inmates were confined. They had to sign over all of their protective equipment at the air lock; their gas, extendable batons and protective vests – all left under lock and key with the first line of prison security. Even though they were wearing suits, they still stood out as *the filth*. Maybe it was the way they held themselves, the way they walked, or maybe the way they looked into the eyes of the shit-bags who were *giving it large* on the other side of the wire fence.

Jackson had led the way, alongside the prison officer as Gold brought up the rear to the innuendo and jeers dished out by the inmates, just feet away.

"I don't mind you gripping me," one prisoner shouted. "Come and see what I've got for you down here," another said, tugging his tracksuit bottoms out at the waist while delving a hand deep inside his trousers.

'Don't look at them,' Jackson said to Gold as they walked on by.

Gold kept her head low and did as she was told, even though a hock of spittle landed on the side of her arm.

They were shown through to a small room with no furniture other than a stainless steel desk bolted to the floor and two stainless chairs on either side.

'Wait here,' the prison officer said. 'I'll just go and get it.'

Gold turned to Jackson with a puzzled expression.

Soon after, Ash Babbage came into the room flanked by two guards. He immediately noticed Gold and began to smile.

'Sit down,' Jackson said to Babbage, who finally looked away from Gold and did as was expected.

Jackson turned to the guards. 'Do you both have to stay in here?'

The guards grunted and gave Jackson a unfriendly glare, but left the room.

Babbage was sitting down facing two empty seats. Jackson was pacing the room and Gold was standing in the corner beside the only door in or out.

'We're just waiting for your brief,' Jackson said to Babbage who did not respond and continued staring at Gold. 'Suddenly decided you need one, eh?' Jackson continued.

Babbage slowly turned his attention onto Jackson.

'You more than anyone should know that I didn't need one. But it seems, thanks to Miss Gold over there, I require one to get me through the red-tape of leaving this place.'

'Enjoyed solitary have you?' Jackson sniped.

'Hmm,' Babbage spluttered. 'Had you done your homework on me properly, you would have known that a gentleman's prison was not appropriate for me in the first place.'

'Ah, yes,' Jackson said. 'Well, had you not impersonated your dead brother and lived a lie for the last twenty years, we wouldn't've had to, would we?'

Babbage smiled and looked back over to Gold who was still leaning against the door.

'Hello, Miss Gold,' Babbage said. 'And how is my second favourite detective doing?'

Gold coughed and tightened her folded arms around her midriff.

Jackson perched himself on the far edge of the table, with his back to Gold, blocking direct line of sight between Gold and Babbage. Jackson was close enough to be imposing, but far enough away to be outside of Babbage's striking range.

Gold shuffled to one side and as she looked on, she noticed Babbage making unusual facial responses to Jackson as he spoke.

'Trouble with London Barristers,' Jackson said, 'they have to travel all the way down here from the big smoke. We could be here a while, just the three of us.'

Babbage blinked, looked towards Gold and then back to Jackson with a half-smile.

'So you will be on electronic curfew, more than likely,' Jackson said. 'That means you will have to stay in your home between the hours that the judge stipulates. Any deviation from that and you could end up back in prison.'

Gold saw Babbage nod vaguely.

'And we don't want that, do we?' Jackson finished.

Gold edged forwards with two tentative steps. Babbage locked eyes with her and leaned back deliberately in the chair. Jackson stopped speaking, coughed and unfurled his body, turning to Gold as she approached.

'Sarah, come and sit down,' Jackson said, patting the back of the shiny metal chair that his feet were occupying. 'The brief was meant to be here ages ago, I'll go and find out what's happening – see if they have an ETA.' He winked at Gold and Babbage, gave Jackson a lasting stare as he rose from the edge of the desk and left the room.

Gold and Babbage were now alone in the room.

'And how is Andrew?' Babbage asked.

Gold turned away in disgust and then finding an inner

resolve, she looked Babbage in the eye. 'How could you ask?' she spat.

She saw Babbage's lips twitch with excitement.

Gold scowled. 'How should Sergeant Jackson have known you didn't need a solicitor before now?' she asked.

Babbage cocked his head and Gold saw creases appear beneath his eyes.

'Can you imagine what it's like to be a woman in a male dominated prison?' Babbage asked. 'They're all *animals*.'

Gold shrugged. 'That's all down to you.'

Babbage squinted and breathed in a purposeful and slow breath. 'Yes. Yes, I suppose it is.'

'Why take your dead brother's identity if you were going to lead this kind of lifestyle?' Gold asked, 'when sooner or later, you could end up in a place like this.'

Babbage grinned. 'But I've got you to thank for getting me out, haven't I, Detective Gold.'

Gold squirmed in the slippery seat and leaned in closer to Babbage. 'I did not destroy those exhibits and I think you know that.'

Babbage shrugged and smiled with a pout. 'Either way.'

The door opened and Jackson walked in with a man wearing a navy blue, pin-striped suit and holding a battered, black leather brief case.

'I do hope you two have been playing nicely,' Jackson said and gestured with his head for Gold to stand up.

'This is your barrister, Mr Samson,' Jackson said to Babbage. 'Play your cards right and you could be out of here in no time.'

Jackson and Gold waited outside in the hallway as the brief spoke privately with Babbage.

'Why are you being so nice to Babbage?' Gold asked Jackson.

Jackson shrugged. 'Our case is screwed without that evidence,' he said. 'For every day that Babbage festers in that cell, we, the force, could be sued for unlawful detention.'

'Bullshit,' Gold said.

'Excuse me?' Jackson snapped.

Gold glared at him and shook her head. 'You know that I didn't destroy those exhibits.'

Jackson peered at Gold with his uncompromising beady eyes and leaned over the top of her.

'I don't think you are in any position to make statements like that, missy. Let's wait and see what Professional Standards makes of it all, shall we?' Jackson turned away and stormed back outside.

CHAPTER THIRTY-TWO

Dog handler, PC Greenwood and his excitable cocker spaniel, Brice, arrived at the scene before the Support Group. Deans greeted them and led the way through to the rear garden.

'So what do you need us to do?' PC Greenwood asked. Deans had not told Comms anything about the purpose for a dog unit.

'I want Brice to have a free range of the property,' Deans said. 'Use the time for some confined training, tracking or whatever you want to do.'

'Okay,' Greenwood answered hesitantly. He had a slightly puzzled expression. Most times, the dog units did not have such a luxury. 'Anything I need to know – places or rooms to avoid?'

Deans shrugged, 'Why not start on the ground level, the rest of us will stay out of your way in the kitchen. Just one thing, though,' Deans said touching Greenwood's arm. 'If you come across anything... unusual, would you let me know right away?'

'Sure,' Greenwood said and started preparing his dog for release.

Deans returned to the kitchen and, ushering Denise away from the earshot of Savage and Parsons, asked her, 'So now what?'

'We'll see what little Brice can find,' she said with a tentative smile. 'I just hope the entity doesn't harm him.'

'What?' Deans said. 'What sort of harm?'

Denise raised an eyelid. 'Well, it's already killed two people hasn't it?'

'Three,' Deans replied. 'It's killed three people.'

Ten minutes went by and Savage was becoming increasingly restless in the kitchen, as he could not sit still for more than thirty seconds before having to pace to the window and back.

Deans could still smell damp masonry in the air. He turned to Denise. 'Do you get anything from here?'

Her eyes lit up. 'It's here,' she said, just as a sudden jolt shook Deans to the soles of his feet. 'He knows what we are up to,' Denise said. 'Andy, this is stupid. We have put ourselves in danger.'

Right at that moment, they all heard a loud yelp from outside in the garden.

'Brice,' Deans shouted and ran out of the kitchen towards the rear garden.

He saw PC Greenwood kneeling on the grass with Brice across his lap.

'What happened?' Deans called out, running up to them.

'I think he stepped on something over there.' Greenwood pointed towards the decking. 'It must be a splinter in his pads, but I can't find anything.'

'Will Brice be okay?' Deans asked.

'Should be,' Greenwood said, standing Brice back onto his feet. Brice was holding his front left paw in the air. 'Strange thing is,' Greenwood said, 'he didn't want to go anywhere near that decking, kept cowering away each time he got close.'

'Is that normal?' Deans asked. 'I mean…'

'No. Brice is one the most experienced dogs we have. He's not usually a sissy.'

Denise joined them outside.

'Did you say it was over there?' she asked Greenwood, who confirmed. 'It's there then,' she said to Deans. 'The body will be somewhere over there.'

'Body?' Greenwood queried. 'What body?'

'Will you show me what Brice did, please?' Denise asked Greenwood.

'I can try,' Greenwood said, 'but he's obviously picked up some kind of injury.'

Greenwood walked towards the decked area and crouched down encouraging Brice to join him, but his dog refused and limped off in the other direction.

'I'm sorry, Deano,' Greenwood said scooping Brice up from the floor with one arm, 'but that looks like the end of our training session.'

Deans shook Greenwood's hand and rubbed the top of Brice's head. 'I hope the little fella is going to be alright.'

'I'll take a proper look back at the kennels. Sorry I couldn't be more help.'

'You were,' Deans said. 'Believe me, you were.'

Sergeant Niamh Freeland and her team of six PCs were on scene before lunchtime. Savage was in luck; they were on a spare shift, kicking their heels, looking for a training opportunity and that was how he Savage had sold the gig.

Interest in the police activity outside, however, was growing – further emphasised by the large Support Group meat-waggon blocking half of the cobbled pavement in front of the terrace. Donald Ellis, the local rag hack, had been hovering in the street for the last hour. He had an uncanny knack of being in the right place at the right time. Deans had previously suspected someone on the inside was feeding him the tip-off – possibly someone in the station, or even a call operative in Comms. Either way, Ellis could be a real pain in the nuts. Parsons said he had seen him arrive and run off a burst of snaps of the police vehicles – more than likely unaware of why they were there. If only he knew!

Sergeant Freeland was with Savage, Deans and Denise Moon in the bedroom as her team broke up lumps of paving and concrete in the back garden. Deans was delighted to hear that she and her husband were thinking of moving house because of the *supernatural problems* they had been experiencing in their home. A call on Sergeant Freeland's radio piqued everyone's interest; the team had broken through to soil and discovered something they wanted to show.

They all stood in a confined circle looking down at the dustbin-lid sized hole in the concrete.

One of the officers handed Savage a fist full of mud. Savage stared down at his hand and then looked back at the officer with a curled lip.

'Look at it,' the officer said.

Savage prodded a finger into the ball of sludge and struck something hard in the middle. He routed another digit inside and pulled out a coin. He looked at the officer who gestured for Savage to take a closer inspection. Savage grabbed a rag from one the others and rubbed the coin. He flipped it back and forth and then peered at Deans, a look of amazement on his face.

'It's a George the Fifth gold Sovereign,' Savage said and handed the coin to Deans. 'Any more?' he asked the officers.

One of the team stepped to one side and showed a mound of soil with many more coins easily visible amongst the dirt.

Denise looked at Deans, wide-eyed. 'These would be worth a small fortune these days,' she said.

'Keep digging, guys,' Deans said. 'And make sure you shout when you come across bone.'

Savage, Deans and Denise went back into the house.

Savage was pacing the kitchen, pinching the bridge of his nose between his fingers.

'So, let me get this straight in my head,' he said. 'We've got a gangster ghost, a pot of money, and an old sod in a nursing home who knows something about all of it?'

'And three dead bodies,' Deans said.

'So far,' Denise butted-in.

Savage dragged a kitchen stool towards him and flopped down onto the seat. He looked at Deans and shook his head. 'Shit magnet.'

Deans smiled for the first time in days. 'Yep. Certainly looks that way.'

'Are you sure about those coins?' Savage asked Denise. 'I mean the value? Shit – this could be a media circus a few hours from now.'

'As sure as I can be,' Denise replied. 'Take a look.' She handed Savage her mobile phone with information about gold sovereigns on the screen.

Savage scrolled through the pages and, for moment, nobody spoke.

Savage looked up at Deans. 'Right,' he said. 'I need you to figure out what we are to do with George Fenwick, and I'm going to head back to the office, before the headless fucking horseman stampedes through this kitchen.'

Deans chuckled. 'I'll start with Samantha. See if I can *encourage* her some more.'

'Good,' Savage said moving to the window. 'I'll leave Support Group here to do their thing.' He puffed air into his cheeks. 'Let's hope they don't dig anyone up. That would just about top off my day.'

He turned back to Deans. 'Shit magnet.'

CHAPTER THIRTY-THREE

Deans and Denise were back outside Samantha's flat and following repeated attempts to bring her to the door, Deans was growing increasingly concerned for her wellbeing.

'I'm going to give her one last chance and then we'll have to bust the door,' he said to Denise.

'How can you do that?'

'We'll need a door opening team for this one; too many locks.'

Deans faced Denise. 'I know she's inside... and so is Christ knows how much heroin?'

Denise took a step backwards. 'Well, come on.' She waved her hands. 'Do whatever you do.'

Deans knelt down and lifted the metal flap to the post box. 'Samantha. I know you are in there. Just give me a noise to show you can hear me...' He turned an ear to the small slot in the door. He waited a moment and then pulled a face to Denise.

He dug his phone from his pocket and called Savage.

'Mick, I'm at the Travis flats. I need the big red key.'

'What for,' Savage asked.

'I think Samantha's topped herself.'

'Oh Shit! Are you sure?'

'I can't get a response at the door and all the sliding bolts are across. She's definitely inside.'

'Deano... you really don't need this... but the boss wants you to see you urgently.'

'I can't leave, Mick.'

'Alright, alright, I'll speak to the uniform team and get someone up to you with the door ram. You are absolutely certain she's inside?'

'Yep. Hundred percent.'

'Fine,' Savage huffed. 'I'll get a lift up with them. See you shortly.'

They waited no more than ten minutes before a PC from the day shift approached them cradling the bright red door opener in his arms. He lowered the weighty lump of metal onto the floor with a reverberating clang. Sweat dripped from his face and he needed a few seconds before he could speak.

'The... the others... are... are just coming,' he said.

Deans looked along the hallway and saw Savage flanked by two other officers, carrying protective headgear.

'Right, is this it?' Savage asked Deans in a hurry.

'This is the flat. The bolts are across at the top, middle and bottom. It won't be easy,' Deans said.

'We'll keep going until the frame gives in,' one of the PCs said. 'Have you given the appropriate warnings?'

'Yep,' Deans said. 'There are no pets and if you look through the letterbox, you can see a light on in the living room.'

'Just do it,' Savage said. 'I need to get Deano away from here as soon as.'

Deans' brows met and he stared at Savage.

'Come on,' Savage said. 'Hurry up.'

The PCs prepared themselves and lined up the flat head of the ram against the main lock of the door. The PC at the front turned to Savage, who nodded permission for them to damage the door.

'This is the police, we are forcing entry through this door, please step away,' the lead PC shouted through the letterbox as other residents hovered in their doorways muttering about the "Fucking pigs".

The doorframe gave way after the sixth whack of the ram. Deans was first through and went directly into the living room. Samantha was slumped in her chair; an arm draped over the side, her eyes closed and her lips a grey pastel shade. Deans quickly scanned the floor beneath her arm, and he saw the needle.

'It's an OD,' he shouted. 'Someone get an ambulance.'

He pressed his fingers against her neck and felt for a pulse, there was nothing. 'Shit!'

'I'm a first responder,' one of the other PCs said coming alongside Deans and instantly went to work on resuscitating Samantha.

Deans stepped back. His mouth wide open. 'No,' he mumbled. 'Please, not another?'

The PC turned to Deans and shook her head.

Deans covered his face with his hands and crouched down to the floor.

'We need to leave uniform to sort this out, Deano,' Savage said. 'We have to go.'

Deans slowly stood up and gripped the sides of his head. *Did I push her too far?*

Savage grabbed Deans' arm and encouraged him away. 'You stay here,' Savage said to the PC. 'Wait for the medics and update us.'

The PC agreed and Savage, Deans and Denise headed back to the station in Deans' car.

On the return journey, Savage updated them that the Support Group had excavated all the concrete and found considerably more gold sovereigns, and what Nate Parsons and the Crime

Scene Manager suggested to be the skeletal remains of an adult human, minus the skull.

Deans could tell something was amiss, even though Savage wasn't letting on, so he told Denise to wait for him in town while he returned to the nick.

The DI sipped from a mug and gestured for Deans to take a seat. He kept a watchful eye on Deans and placed his drink down gently onto the desk. He stared intently, unnervingly for a long moment.

Deans knew what he was doing – killing time, giving himself thinking space, or an opportunity to sound the words in his head before they came out of his mouth.

'Boss?' Deans said standing back up to his feet.

The DI looked away slightly, only momentarily, but enough. Deans' body sagged, and he dropped to the seat.

The DI faced him again.

'Andy,' he said drawing breath, 'I need you to go to Bristol. We…' he hesitated. '…we've had word from Devon.' His eyes flickered and he looked downwards. He shielded his mouth with the back of his hand and stared at Deans. 'They…' he stopped and coughed into his fist several times before regaining his composure. '… They have located an item of jewellery.' The DI leaned over his desk and picked up a sheet of paper.

He held it out towards Deans who looked at the page quivering gently in the DI's grasp.

Deans' arms were like stiff metal bars by his side and no matter how much he needed to see and hear the information, his body simply would not allow it.

The DI waited a moment and then spoke. 'These are the details I took over the phone.'

Deans peered at the paper but he could not read the words through his misted eyes.

'Okay,' the DI muttered and summarised the information for Deans' benefit. 'An off-duty officer in Devon located the item in a pawn shop, North of Torworthy, in a small harbour town. DI Thornton has been fully briefed and DC Gold and DC Ranford are already on their way to Bristol with the exhibit.' The DI bunched his lips together. 'Andy, it's exactly as you described on the MISPER report: a black coral chain and a black stone pendant in the shape of an elephant.'

The DI shook his head and pinched his top lip between his teeth.

'It's the same size... same everything. And we need you to formally identify it.'

Deans' vision blurred. There was one piece of jewellery unique to Maria – a black moon stone elephant on a long black coral linkage, which he had bought in the Caribbean. Maria was never without it. The woman in the market who sold him the pendant said it would bring Maria abundant luck, and what they craved most – fertility.

'There's a crisis meeting at five with the Op Engage team,' the DI said and leaned forward, touching Deans' arm. 'I want you to be there too.' He offered Deans a painful smile.

Deans blinked a slow wet puddle and nodded.

The DI reached forward with a tissue and gestured for Deans to wipe his face. 'I don't want you to drive over,' the DI said. 'I'll ask one of the team to take you.'

Deans shook his head. 'No... I want to be alone.'

'Okay,' the DI said. 'In that case I'll arrange a rail warrant from admin. I don't want you anywhere near a car.'

Deans accepted and gulped away his rising emotion.

The DI stood up and hugged Deans with a tight embrace.

'You take all the time you need, that's not an issue. But keep me updated and let me know if there is anything I can do.'

CHAPTER THIRTY-FOUR

Bath to Bristol by train would take no more than fifteen minutes, but it might as well be eternity on this day. Deans found a front-facing seat next to the window and placed his go-bag on the floor beside him. He was wearing sunglasses even though it was practically dark outside. He rested his forehead against the cool misted window, shut his eyes and pictured Maria.

Several solitary minutes passed by. The clattering pane against his skin was almost therapeutic, but soon he began to sense that somebody was watching him.

He raised his head and looked around. Nobody was next to him and a couple of office workers in the adjoining aisle seats were fully engrossed in their laptops. Then Deans noticed a woman staring directly at him – four rows ahead, on the opposite side, in a backward facing seat.

The glasses. He looked back out of his window. The tree-lined River Avon on the other side of the train reflected on his window as the sped by, but he still had *that feeling* and again glanced four seats ahead. The woman was still looking, but this time smiling as if she knew him.

Fuck off, lady. I'm having a bad day.

Her smile grew wider, and he saw her laugh as if she had just heard his thoughts.

Seriously, Deans silently sneered. *Just fuck off.*

The woman's eyes opened wide and she lifted an arm above her head and brought it down past her ear like a front crawl-swimming stroke. And then she ducked away from view behind the seats.

The carriage suddenly juddered and slewed and Deans' face slammed into the hard plastic seat-back in front of him like a swatted insect, as a shrill metallic sound screeched through the entire train and the floor rumbled beneath his feet. Deans was thrown against the window, his back pinned against the glass. Luggage and smaller items flew through the air, crashing into him on their forward trajectory. A boy, just a toddler, somersaulted from somewhere behind him like a rag doll, his body smashing into the seat in front of Deans and his legs cartwheeling over the top, taking him further away from Deans' despairing reach.

Move away from the glass, Deans heard, over the sickening din of the carriage grinding along the floor.

It was as if time had stopped and the voice soothed and reassured him.

He clawed at the aisle seat, his fingers tearing into the fabric as his body weight dragged him in the other direction. He reached a metal armrest and linked his elbow around the post, hauling himself away from the window with all his strength. He secured his hold, kept his head tight in against the seat-upright and held on for all his might. Then the realisation of the situation and the cacophony of noise invaded his every sense. His body slammed, shook, bent, and buckled, but he still managed to cling on.

Deans opened his eyes but all he saw was the blue and orange fabric of the seat in front of his face.

For an eerie moment, there was nothing but a still acrid

silence; a delayed reaction to the inevitable cries of anguish, pain, hurt and possibly loss.

He waited. Prepared for the suffering – but it did not come.

A cold air whipped around his ankles and a strange, sparkler-like odour came and went in waves. Deans flexed his fingers, and then moved his arms, his head, and then finally his legs. He slowly unfurled his fingers, blood seeped from deep cuts in his hands, but he felt no pain. He twisted his head and looked around.

The carriage was now on its side and he was more or less in an upright position, but was pinned at the waist by something from below.

He wriggled to adjust his body so that he could look down. The window was now completely gone, replaced by the broad branch of a tree that to his horror had impaled the seat that he had been occupying. The 'V' shape of a smaller branch, the thickness of his arm, was keeping him in place and he could see blood seeping out through his torn work shirt.

The staring lady, he thought, and tried to move, but failed.

He looked beyond the thick branch to his legs. His trousers were shredded and one shoe was missing. Blood was everywhere – his blood, but he still felt no pain.

He took a moment to take in the situation and then the over-whelming realisation sank in that he could hear nothing other than his own groans and attempts at movement.

He bounced his body and found a little leeway. The abrasive bark of the tree sliced the skin on his waist like a cheese grater. He drew deep breaths and tugged himself up again. This time he felt pain and cried out in agony as the wooden captor finally relin-quished its grip.

He used the side of the twisted seat in front to steady himself and he stepped onto the tree branch. Pain surged upwards through his entire body and he crumpled into a heap on top of the tree, screaming uncontrollably. He gasped several sharp breaths and lifted the flap of his trouser leg – his ankle resembled a pork chop, blooded and splintered with the bone exposed. A deep emotion spewed from the pit of his stomach and he began to weep, but instead of salty tears, he tasted warm metallic liquid. He touched the top of his head. It was hot and tacky. He brought his hand down in front of his face. It was drenched with his blood. He began to panic, his breathing raced away from him and his hands started to claw tightly as his body shut down protecting all but the most important organs. His vision wobbled, his throat filled with vomit, but then he noticed movement up ahead.

'Hello,' he cried, doing his best to lift an arm above head height. 'Over... here,' his fractured voice called out. He saw the person ahead, stop and turn. It was the smiling woman. She appeared unharmed and was *still* smiling.

Deans heard a woman's voice, but the woman's lips did not move. *You will be fine now,* she said.

Deans' eyes closed under the unbearable weight of his lids. He could no longer speak and as he fought to keep his sight focussed, the smiling woman turned, walked away from him and was lost to sight.

CHAPTER THIRTY-FIVE

Mick Savage paced the corridor as DI Feather and a doctor conversed just beyond earshot. Savage had been at the hospital for nearly ten hours and to say he was irritated would be a drastic understatement. Perhaps the seven machine-dispensed coffees had something to do with that.

Deans was inside the adjoining room. He had been out of surgery for almost two hours, but the hospital staff were still refusing to let Savage and DI Feather through to see him, and that was griping Savage more than anything.

DI Feather walked over to Savage and spoke close in to his ear.

'Okay, he's going to let us through to see Deano. It's not good though…' the DI paused and Savage could see he was struggling to hold back his emotion and so did not interrupt.

'Deano's on life support,' the DI said. 'They don't know if he is going to make it through.'

The DI looked away and wiped his eyes. Savage didn't move.

'I feel responsible,' the DI continued. 'I made him take the train. If I hadn't done that…'

Savage broke his silence. 'No one could have envisaged any of this.'

'I guess he's in the best place,' the DI said. 'Are there any next of kin we haven't yet informed?'

'Is it that bad?' Savage asked.

The DI nodded ruefully.

Savage shook his head. 'Maria's all he's got left, apart from her parents.'

They both looked at each other and fell silent for a moment.

Savage was next to speak. 'That woman, Denise keeps pestering me to see him.'

'Miss Moon?'

'Yeah.'

'That's fine,' the DI said. 'Where is she now?'

Savage shrugged. 'Somewhere here in the hospital. Probably with all the other relatives at the major incident desk.'

'The doctor told me they lost another one during surgery,' the DI said.

'How many is that now?' Savage asked.

The DI's lips tightened and he frowned. 'Must be over sixty.'

Savage shook his head. 'Unbelievable.'

'I know the transport investigators want to speak to Deano,' the DI said diverting the conversation away from the fatalities.

Savage raised his brows. 'Don't we all. They can wait their turn.'

'It happened on our patch, Mick. We are going to need to work together on this, and if that means they get to talk to Deans first, then so be it. On that note, the Major Crime Team are asking for support. They want us to lend them ten DCs for the investigation.'

'That's nearly half of the office—'

'Just until the statements are taken. You know how these things run.'

'What about the district jobs?' Savage asked.

The DI glowered at Savage. 'Mick. It doesn't get much bigger than this and one our own is involved.'

The door opened and the doctor's face appeared in the gap. 'Okay,' he said. 'You have five minutes.'

Savage and DI Feather followed the doctor through a large dark room with electronic equipment resonating loudly in all directions. They continued on to a side room with glass walls.

Savage could see a heavily bandaged person in the bed connected to half a dozen tubes.

'Is that Deano?' he whispered.

'You have five minutes,' the doctor repeated and held a finger to his ear. 'Just so you know – he can't hear you.'

Savage looked at the bank of equipment around Deans and focussed on some sort of pump that was moving up and down in a steady, repetitive sucking motion.

'Is that machine helping him breathe?' Savage asked.

The doctor smiled.

'Your colleague is in a dire condition. We can offer him the support to breathe, we can drain away the build-up of fluid, but ultimately, it will come down to his desire to fight. The next few hours are critical.'

'When will he wake up?' Savage asked softly.

The doctor smiled with thin lips. 'I can't answer that.'

CHAPTER THIRTY-SIX

The short, sharp, electronic rhythm of the equipment was the first thing that Deans heard, followed by the muted sound of people talking. It was dark. He wanted to open his eyes, but they refused. He attempted to raise a hand, but it would not respond. He tried his legs – same result. His mouth and throat were unbearably dry. He went to lick his lips but something prevented his tongue from moving, and all the while, the steady, rhythmical beat continued behind his head.

He picked out one of the voices at the back of the room; it was Savage.

'But how long?' Savage asked.

He sounded stressed. Deans usually avoided Savage when he was *on one*. Today though, he clearly had little choice but to listen to Mick's rant.

There was another voice, but one he did not recognise, one with slow southern drawl.

'We don't know how long,' the American woman said.

'Come on,' Savage shouted. 'This is beginning to fuck me off.'

Mick, don't. Wind your bloody neck in and come over here.

'Okay,' came another, gentler voice. 'Let's just all keep calm. None of this will be helping Andy.'

It was Denise.

What do I need help with? Deans attempted to grab someone's attention.

'This is a critical time,' the American said. Her voice was becoming sharper. 'The consultant is concerned about the increased GCS.'

GCS?

Deans knew that medical terminology. It referred to the Glasgow Coma Scale; the degree to which a person is able to respond to stimulus.

The beeping behind his head began to increase in speed.

He felt someone touch the back of his hand and hold on.

I'm awake, he tried to say. *I can hear you. Can you hear me?*

He battled to move the fingers of the hand that was being held.

Why can't somebody see that I'm awake?

Panic gripped him. He wanted to shout. Cry. Do anything to be seen.

'I need to call the consultant,' the American said. 'It's probably best that we continue this conversation at the desk.'

No, Deans shouted in his head. *No, please don't go. I'm here. I can hear you. I just can't see you.*

Savage's voice was the loudest in the room once more.

'I want to speak to the consultant?' he demanded aggressively.

'Yes, of course. But she may not have the answers you seek,' the American said doing well to keep calm.

Deans could feel a downward pressure on the top of his forearm and he heard a sniffle near his ear. It was Savage, but he did not speak. The force upon his arm gently released and the sound of leather-soled shoes on a hard surface moved away from his bed.

Five or ten more seconds went by, and he felt warmth on his

cheek, as if being kissed by soft heated pillows.

'You're not leaving us, Andy.'

It was Denise.

A drop of liquid splashed on his face and his hand was wrapped in an other's. It was soft and comforting.

'I know you can hear me,' Denise said softly into his ear.

I can. I can. Please help me, Denise.

'I'm going to help you,' she said. 'Don't be scared.'

Deans wanted to cry out, but his body would not allow it. He felt the warmth of Denise's lips again on his forehead.

Don't leave me, he screamed out. *Please, don't go.* But nobody responded to his appeals.

Denise whispered again. 'We have to go. The consultant is going to see you now. She is a good woman. You are in a safe place.'

The echo of solemn feet moved slowly away from his bedside.

'Thank you,' the American said and then hesitated. 'Well… okay,' she continued, '… but literally one minute, that's all you have.'

The talking stopped.

Deans sensed that someone else was in the room.

A door closed with the suck of a gas mechanism and a tight solid clunk.

Deans waited, his hearing finely tuned to his surroundings.

Maria? Maria? Please, please, please be Maria!

Footsteps approached, slowly at first, and then with more purpose until they were directly beside him.

Deans could hear breathing. He waited for a voice and felt air moving across his face. Someone was leaning in close.

He heard an intake of air and sensed a smiling face.

He tried to turn his head, but nothing happened, and then he heard a voice. A voice that he recognised.

'Your eyes tell you what you want them to believe. Die you fucker.'

CHAPTER THIRTY-SEVEN

Light poured into Deans' eyes and he blinked away the burning discomfort. He rolled his head and saw Denise sitting beside him. She immediately rose to her feet and grabbed for his hand. Her face was a mixture of relief and pain.

Deans tried to speak, but his voice rasped with dryness.

'I'll grab the nurses,' Denise said urgently, giving his hand a gentle squeeze.

As focus gradually returned, Deans took in his surroundings: the narrow bed with side railings, a glass wall and door that Denise had just walked through, and a bank of electronic equipment somewhere behind his head, sounding and bleeping that familiar beat. A mask hissed air onto his face. He lowered his chin to his chest and saw a weave of plastic tubes sticking out of the back of his hands. He blinked slowly, looked again and his eyes widened.

Fuck me.

Denise came back into the room followed swiftly by two nurses, who scurried either side of the bed. One nurse studied the monitors while the other leaned over Deans' bed and talked to him as if he was a child.

Denise found a space between one nurse and the IV lines and brushed hair away from Deans' forehead with her hand.

Deans looked into her eyes – it appeared that she had not slept for about a week.

A thought galloped into his head – *Maria!*

Deans raised his shoulders from the pillows but a nurse forced him back down with a gentle persuasion.

'Now, we're not quite ready for that,' she said. 'You must stay still. Rest is all you need right now.'

She fussed with the sheets, tucking him tighter into the mattress like a babe in swaddling clothes.

Deans hurriedly looked for Denise. She was back on the plastic chair beside his bed.

She forced a downwards smile.

Deans shut his eyes and rolled his head back into position.

The *bleep, bleep, bleep* of the monitoring equipment was deafening. He tried to speak, but failed to produce enough energy to be heard above the hiss of the facemask.

A nurse leaned over and spoke close to his face. She had a caring smile.

'That's all looking really nice,' she beamed. 'We will notify the doctor that you are awake and you'll see her soon.' She touched his shoulder and again smiled.

Deans did his best to nod.

Denise stood up and held his hand once more.

Deans ushered her hand toward his face.

'No,' Denise said. 'You should keep that on.'

Deans pleaded with his eyes.

She looked over her shoulder, smiled a nod, and gently lifted the plastic shroud from his face.

'Just for a moment then, okay?' she said. 'I don't want to get into trouble.'

'Maria?' Deans asked with sandpaper abrasiveness.

He saw her face change and she shook her head.

'I don't know anything. Nobody has said a thing to me,' Denise whispered.

Deans bunched his eyes.

'You have generated a lot of attention,' Denise said. 'That was a terrible accident... one of the worst...' She paused and raked her hair to one side of her face. 'Andy,' she said. 'You were the only survivor in your carriage.'

Those final moments on the train all of a sudden saturated his mind.

'No,' he mumbled. 'The lady.'

Denise lifted one of his hands and stroked it with loving softness.

'No, flower,' she said. 'Nobody else made it out.'

A pain raced behind his eyes and jabbed like hot needles. He winced as he croaked, 'Lady... she saved me.'

Denise frowned for a moment or two.

'What lady?' she asked, searching his face.

Deans could picture her clearly in his mind, but he lacked the energy to answer.

For a long minute Denise said nothing. Just watched him and held his hand.

Deans could tell that Denise was deep in thought.

'Some of us,' she said eventually, checking over her shoulder, 'well, some of us are fortunate enough to have seen our Earth Angels.' She smiled warily and came within inches of his face.

'I'm not saying that's who you saw, but if you did, then that is why you are still alive... and that makes you very special, indeed.'

Deans stared up at the ceiling. Moisture came to his eyes.

'How many?' he asked.

Denise squeezed his hand a little tighter.

Deans rolled his head and looked at her. 'How many?' he repeated.

'Sixty-three,' Denise replied to the floor.

'Dead?' Deans asked.

She confirmed this without having to say a word.

Deans closed his eyes and rolled his head back the other way.

'The majority made it out from the other carriages,' Denise said. 'But yours…' her voice tailed away.

Deans recalled the little boy tumbling through the air, and his chest ached with sorrow. He did not move for a long while and then he turned back to Denise.

'My injuries?' he asked.

Denise leaned back in the chair, not missed by Deans who saw the symbolic distancing from the question.

'I'm sure the doctor will give you the full details,' she said quietly.

'Tell me,' Deans demanded. He was not prepared to wait for the medical bumph.

Deans saw her watching him warily. He reached out with his hand. 'Tell me.'

'You have been in a coma,' she said.

'Coma?'

Denise cupped his hand. 'Four days.'

His head felt suddenly as heavy as a boulder and sank further into the pillow. Tears formed and ran down the sides of his cheeks but he made no attempt to wipe them away.

'There was a large impact to your head,' Denise said after a quiet moment. Her hand was grasping tightly onto his. 'Your brain swelled… They… *We…*' she hesitated. 'We didn't know what was going to happen. They put you into an induced coma.'

Deans stared up at the ceiling. 'Voices,' he said breathlessly.

'Voices?' Denise repeated. 'Well, I think that's entirely possible, especially when you're coming out of the coma.'

Deans shook his head. 'Dream,' he said. 'Bad dream.'

'It's not a dream, sweetheart,' Denise said stroking his hand. 'This is really happening.'

'No,' Deans said, struggling to lift his upper torso from the mattress. 'I keep getting… dream.'

'You keep having a dream?'

Deans nodded the best he could. His eyelids were becoming heavy.

'I don't know,' Denise shrugged. 'I didn't think you could dream during a coma. Come on,' she said putting his arm down alongside his thigh. 'Rest now. Let's pop this mask back on before the nurse tells me off.'

Denise replaced the oxygen mask and within minutes Deans was sleeping.

Denise observed Deans for a long while. She monitored his chest rising and falling in time with the sound of the equipment. She could see his eyes flickering beneath his lids; he *was* dreaming, or at least, that was how it appeared.

She noticed the time, seven-twelve p.m.

The journey back home to North Devon felt long at the best of times, let alone in the dark, when she was feeling completely exhausted. She had not let go of Deans' hand for the last two hours as her thumb softly carved an arc on the top of his knuckle.

She sniffed and looked back towards the nurses and smiled as she caught one of them looking back at her.

Deans was remarkable. In all her years of alternative therapy and exploring *the gift*, she had never come across someone of Deans' potential, and the best bit was, he did not realise it. If he had seen an Earth Angel, then the guardians had truly selected him.

She heaved a deep sigh. If he was not so bloody-minded and reticent, she could help him develop his skills. If he could recover enough from his injuries, then perhaps being alive would be all the evidence he needed.

DS Savage shattered her thoughts as he bounded through the doorway with a nurse in his wake trying to slow him down.

'He's sleeping,' Denise said, letting go of Deans' hand for the first time, '…but he's fine.'

'What did he say?' Savage asked impatiently.

He had asked the same thing when Denise called him to say Deans had woken.

She gave the same answer. 'Not much. He's still very weak.'

A different spluttering noise came from beneath Deans' mask. They all looked towards the bed.

'He might be coming around again,' the nurse said. She looked at Savage. 'Please don't pressurise him to talk.'

Savage held his hands up in a *why are you saying that to me* way.

'No problem. Thank you,' Denise said.

Savage moved closer to the bed.

'He can hear us,' Denise said to Savage's back.

'What?' Savage gasped, facing her with a horrified glare.

'He said he heard talking in the room – voices,' Denise beamed.

'What… everything?' Savage glared.

'I don't know,' Denise said.

'Is that possible?' Savage asked, 'I mean… how much could he hear?'

'I don't know,' Denise repeated.

Savage pinched his nose and turned his back to Denise. 'Shit,' he shrieked.

Deans gurgled something incoherently from beneath the mask.

Savage and Denise rushed to either side of the bed. Deans' eyes were rolling frantically beneath his closed lids.

Denise lifted his hand from the mattress and spoke. 'I'm still here, flower. You are safe. Your friend Mick is here now too.'

Deans' breathing became more urgent and his upper body began to jerk in a violent juddering motion.

'What's happening?' Savage yelled anxiously.

'I don't know,' Denise replied. 'He said he was having dreams of some kind. Some sort of nightmare.'

'Is this alright... should we get a nurse?' Savage asked more urgently, but before Denise could answer, Savage was already running out of the room and calling for help.

Deans was now thrashing his arms wildly. A loud buzz sounded from the equipment and a nurse came rushing into the room.

'Please move aside,' she said.

'He's having a bloody fit,' Savage said, gripping the sides of his face.

'It's okay, this happens,' the nurse said in a vain attempt to reassure the others.

'He said he's been having bad dreams,' Denise said.

'I doubt it,' the nurse replied, fiddling with the control box behind Deans' head. 'His brain activity has been controlled by these machines.'

Denise looked at Savage and shook her head behind the nurse's back.

The nurse pressed something on the control panel and the machine stopped buzzing. She turned around with her arms outstretched to the side and walking back towards the door, scooped up Denise and Savage.

'I think that will be it for the night, thank you,' she said. 'You can come back again tomorrow. But for now he must have total rest.'

'But I've only just got here,' Savage implored.

'Mr Deans needs complete rest,' the nurse insisted using her arms to usher Savage backwards.

'Come on,' Denise said. 'Let's leave Andy alone.'

CHAPTER THIRTY-EIGHT

The guard's keys rattled and clanked and all eyes turned to the secure dock.

A burly prison officer walked into the courtroom trailing an arm from which Ash Babbage was connected.

DC Sarah Gold saw Babbage's grin and faced forwards once again with a taste of disgust in her mouth.

'Court rise,' the usher called out, and everyone stood to their feet as the judge entered the room and took his seat behind the raised bench.

DC Gold returned to her chair and DS Jackson hovered just a moment longer on his feet, before following suit.

'Your Honour,' the Court Clerk said. 'This is the mention hearing of Mr Ash Babbage, currently remanded at her Majesty's pleasure awaiting trial for the murder of Miss Amy Poole.'

The judge looked over the top of his glasses at Babbage sitting fifty feet away in the secure dock.

'Yes,' the judge said.

The defence barrister stood to her feet.

'Your Honour,' she said with a slight bow. 'The defence call this case for the immediate release of Ash Babbage—'

'On what grounds?' the judge interceded.

'On the grounds that the prosecution have a catastrophic failing with their case and a questionable ability to see it through to trial,' the defence barrister continued.

The judge removed his glasses, placed them down onto the bench in front of him and peered at the Crown Prosecution Service barrister.

'Is that so, Mr Gardner?' the judge asked.

Mr Gardner, for the prosecution, stood gingerly from his seat and said with a bowed head. 'Quite possibly, Your Honour.'

'Quite possibly?' Judge Meeks repeated. 'Need I remind you of the tax payer's finance funding this and any subsequent hearing? I do not wish to hear "quite possibly", I *need* to hear factual and educated reasoning to enable me to deliver swift and fair justice, Mr Gardner.'

The CPS barrister clamped his jaw. 'Yes, Your Honour.'

'So, would you like to address me again with the pertinent issues that affect this case, that may well influence any decisions I am minded to make.'

Mr Gardner turned to the long table behind him – to where Gold and Jackson were sitting.

He looked first at Gold and then at Jackson, who held his stare.

'Your Honour,' Mr Gardner said. 'It came to my attention very recently that crucial evidence in favour of the police and crown prosecution case had...' he paused and looked at Jackson again.

Jackson gestured with a subtle wave, encouraging Mr Gardner to continue.

Mr Gardner coughed into his hand.

'Yes, Mr Gardner,' the judge said impatiently. 'I am eager to hear about this *missing* crucial evidence.'

'Of course, Your Honour.'

Mr Gardner took several sips from a plastic cup of water and steadied himself by his fingertips on the lip of the desk.

'It would appear that the evidence has been destroyed, Your Honour,' Mr Gardener said guardedly.

Judge Meeks stared down his nose at the barrister.

'You had better furnish me with more detail, Mr Gardner,' the judge said placing his pen down upon his note pad.

The CPS barrister turned behind him again and glared at Sarah Gold who quickly looked away.

'It would seem,' Mr Gardner said, 'that the police have suffered a monumental failing with their detained property system, resulting in the release and destruction of several key exhibits.'

The judge frowned and directed his attention onto DC Gold and DS Jackson.

'It is not the police bringing this case to trial, Mr Gardner; it is the Crown Prosecution Service. So what is to be done with regard to this missing evidence?'

'A detailed investigation is underway, Your Honour and we hope—'

'I am not interested in hope, Mr Gardner,' the judge said in a firm voice. 'Facts. Facts and evidence, Mr Gardener. When is the trial listed to go ahead?' Judge Meeks requested to the court clerk sitting at a desk immediately in front of the judge's bench.

'June, next year, Your Honour,' the Clerk said in response.

'Very well,' the judge said. 'Ash Babbage, please stand.'

The cell officer and Babbage both rose to their feet.

'You have heard the application made by your defence barrister,' the judge said, staring at Babbage above the top of his glasses. 'On hearing the facts presented to me today, I agree that you should be released from remand with immediate effect, pending a review of the prosecution case no later than ninety days from today. In that time, you will remain on bail to return here for your trial. You will be subjected to a strict curfew of residence and any failure to abide by the conditions of this bail will render you liable to a further incarceration. Do you understand?'

'Thank you, Your Honour,' Babbage said compliantly from the back of the room.

'Very well,' Judge Meeks said. 'Is that everything?'

'Thank you, Your Honour,' the clerk said and Judge Meeks stood.

'Court rise,' the clerk called out and everybody stood as the judge disappeared through a door behind the bench.

DC Gold noticed Jackson nodding to the defence barrister. She continued watching as Jackson turned and looked back towards the dock.

Babbage beamed a wide grin and shared a joke with the cell officer who also laughed.

Gold peered at Jackson again, who unaware she was looking, smiled at Babbage who was led away from the court by the dock officer.

CHAPTER THIRTY-NINE

The light of the room seared the back of his eyes. Deans blinked with discomfort and lifted his head from the hot, sticky pillow.

'Hello, mate,' he heard from nearby. It was the unmistakable voice of Mick Savage.

'They said you would probably come around this morning.'

Deans lifted his hand and dropped it onto his face. He was no longer wearing the mask, and there were no sounds of beeping machinery anywhere near him. Apart from Savage's tones, the room was blissfully quiet.

'Aargh!' Deans screamed. 'What the hell is that?'

'That'll be your busted ankle, mate,' Savage said.

'What the…' Deans squirmed and wriggled in the bed. He was in a stiff and heavy cast right up to and beyond his knee.

'You needed an op,' Savage said. 'Six pins and enough metal to drag you to the bottom of a swimming pool,' he grinned.

'Hello, Andy.' There was another, female voice in the room.

Deans turned his head towards the voice. It was DC Gold.

'Sarah! Hi,' Deans said.

She smiled and Deans stared for a moment too long at her full, pouting lips.

'Deano,' Savage said, coming alongside the bed. 'Good to see you my friend.' He leaned over the rails and gave Deans a solid hug. 'So, did you see the light and all that?' Savage jested.

Deans frowned.

'No angels then, pearly gates?' Savage continued.

Deans' eyes widened and he looked anxiously around the room. 'Where is Denise?' he asked.

'I think she is back in Devon,' Sarah Gold said.

Deans groaned and shuffled himself higher up the pillow and into a more comfortable position.

'Don't worry about her, Deano, not when you've got Miss Gold sitting here next to you,' Savage said, brushing invisible fluff from the lapel of his suit jacket.

Deans turned to Sarah and considered her for a moment.

'Why are you here, Sarah?' he asked.

She fidgeted and broke eye contact.

'I wanted to see you?' she said coyly.

Deans stared at her and shook his head. 'Come on?'

Sarah quickly looked away. Something was wrong.

'Do you need to speak to me privately?'

Sarah quickly caught his eye once more.

Deans glanced towards the door. 'Mick, give us a few minutes, would you, please?'

'Yeah, suppose,' Savage replied as if he were a spare part at a party. He shuffled over to the door, stopped and looked back.

Deans signalled for Savage to leave with a backwards swat of the hand and waited until he had closed the door.

'What's up, Sarah?' Deans asked, offering her his hand.

Her face puckered and twitched, causing a little dimple to appear in her cheek which he had never noticed before.

She edged forward and took his hand but did not speak.

Deans waited.

'Sarah?'

'It's gone,' she said quietly.

Deans blinked. 'Sorry, what has gone?' he asked screwing his face up.

Her eyes darted down to the left.

Deans scowled. Whatever it was, it was not going to be good.

Come on, Sarah, I'm feeling like shit.

She pulled away from him a little, but Deans still holding her hand, encouraged her back toward the rail of his bed.

'Sarah?'

She dipped her head and peered at him for ten seconds before she answered.

'The evidence,' she said quietly. 'The case.'

Deans glared at her. She surely did not mean…?

She looked down at her feet and continued speaking.

'The phone… the photos… forensics…'

Deans sat bolt upright. His jaw was on his chest.

'H… how?' he struggled to say.

Sarah shook her head and looked up at him.

'I'm being investigated by Professional Standards for gross misconduct.'

'What?'

'The exhibits were authorised for destruction.'

Deans noticed her eyes were pink and watery.

'I didn't do it, Andy. I'm being made a scapegoat—'

'Bu… but…' Deans spluttered. '…everything?'

She nodded. 'More or less,' she said. 'Enough to destroy the case against Babbage, anyway.'

Deans' eyes bored into Sarah.

Her grip tightened upon his hand.

Deans' mind was working for the first time since the accident. He shook his head, 'But—'

'I've played it over and again,' Sarah said. 'I've checked what I was doing at the time the evidence was authorised for destruction. I was not even there. But they just say that I have created an alibi.'

Deans let go of her hand and clutched his head.

Holy shit.

He stared at Sarah wild-eyed.

'What about Babbage… what's happened to him?'

Sarah coughed and shuffled her feet.

Deans looked on in disbelief.

'Sarah,' he said with more purpose and volume. 'What has happened to Babbage?'

She wiped her hands over her nose and mouth and finished in a praying pose, her chin resting on the tips of her fingers. Her eyes bounced around Deans' face.

'Released on bail,' she said finally.

Oh my God! Deans flopped back onto the pillow and covered his face with his fingers.

'Aargh!' he cried out from beneath his hands and pressed them firmly into his face. *Shit, Babbage is back out.*

He released his shroud of fingers and sat upright again.

'You were OIC on the Amy Poole investigation for a specific reason,' he said. 'That reason being that you were inexperienced… fallible.'

He grabbed her hand again.

'…But mostly because you were expendable.'

He saw her swallow. She was crying.

'Sarah, you are a brilliant detective. Don't let this put you off. As soon as I'm back on my feet, we'll take them on – you and me.'

He squeezed her hand. 'I know it wasn't you.'

Savage burst back into the room.

'That's enough, you too,' he said excitedly. 'You ought to take a look outside. We've got SKY News, BBC, ITN… everyone wants a piece of you, my friend.'

Deans and Sarah stared at Savage in silence.

Deans squeezed her hand again and softly asked, 'Can you give me a moment with my skipper, please Sarah?'

She did not reply, but clutched his hand a little tighter.

'It's alright, Sarah,' Deans said and twitched his lips.

Sarah let go of his hand and silently walked out of the room.

Savage bounded over to Deans. 'She's bloody gorgeous, mate,' he said like a hormonal adolescent. 'You kept that quiet, you tiger.'

Deans stared at Savage with a poker face. He did not even blink.

'Sorry, Andy,' Savage said quickly. 'I was just trying to make you smile.'

Deans watched Savage bounce uncomfortably from one foot to the other.

'Maria?' Deans asked. 'Mick, what about Maria?'

Savage looked away towards the window.

'Maria?' Deans said again, but this time louder.

Savage licked his lips, looked at the floor for a brief moment, moved slowly to the side of the bed and leaned his body against the metal railings, causing them to strain and angle inwards.

'Well, you don't need to worry about The Willows any longer,' he said, 'The Major Crime Cold Case team have taken it on as a historic murder enquiry. They will deal with the lot; the skeleton; the old man... even Samantha.'

Deans watched him, his eyes burning wide.

Savage slowly raised his head, looked at Deans square on, and then quickly looked away again.

'Mick?' Deans whispered. 'Maria?'

Savage closed his eyes and slowly shook his head.

CHAPTER FORTY

DI Thornton arrived within the hour.

He handed Deans a small exhibits bag; the kind used during any investigation to keep items of evidential value protected and secure.

Deans stared through the clear plastic bag at the object contained within. He lifted it up in front of his eyes and stroked the item between his fingers. Tears began to well, and he lowered the bag into his lap still holding it tightly. Maria habitually wore the exact same elephant pendant and Deans had no doubts this one belonged to his wife.

Nobody spoke until Thornton decided Deans was ready to listen.

'It was recovered from a pawn shop in Barnstaple,' Thornton said. His chest heaved as he sucked in a lungful of air. 'Apparently a woman cashed it in over a week ago now. She has been spoken to, but according to our colleagues at Devon & Cornwall the transaction was made in good faith and they haven't pursued it any further.'

Barnstaple was only ten short miles away from where Amy

Poole's body was discovered on Sandymere Bay, and therefore not much further from where Ash Babbage lived.

Thornton said the store owner was still helping with inquiries, and one of the DCs from the Operation Engage team had dug a little deeper and uncovered all sorts of undesirable activity that he was going to put on a plate to Trading Standards.

'Do you recognise it?' Thornton asked. 'Is it the item of jewellery you described on the MISPER report?'

Deans blinked and turned to Savage who looked away.

Thornton coughed behind closed lips.

'There is more I'm afraid, Andy,' he said.

Deans looked at him; his jaw, slack and heavy.

The DI began to speak, 'I'm afraid,' he said, but then stopped himself and licked moisture to his lips. He peered at Deans for an inordinate amount of time.

'I'm afraid…' he said again. 'A body has been discovered.'

Deans did not move.

'It's a female.'

The DI cleared his throat again. 'Unfortunately, we haven't been able to… identify the body.'

Deans frowned. 'Why?' he whimpered and noticed Savage turn to Thornton and take a half step backwards.

Thornton scratched the back of his head and the corner of his mouth twitched.

'Every… *standard* option of ID has been… impossible to carry out.'

'Impossible?'

Thornton fixed his stare at Deans.

'The only option we have is DNA comparison, and that is still ongoing.'

The ruts in Deans' forehead were now as deep as corrugated iron. He looked to Savage, but he refused to make eye contact with Deans.

'Dental?' Deans whispered.

The DI shook his head.

'But Maria had…'

This time, the DI was more purposeful in the shake of his head.

Time stopped still. All the voices blended into white noise.

Deans looked at Thornton and Savage in turn. Their mouths were moving, but Deans could hear no words.

'How long?' Deans uttered. 'How long for the DNA results?'

'Soon,' Thornton said. 'Very soon.'

Deans snatched a pillow and covered his face, pulling the foam tighter and tighter across his mouth and nose. Maria's face filled his mind. He did not need the DNA result to tell him what, deep inside, his heart already knew to be the truth. And for a moment, a brief, fleeting moment, he considered how long he would have to keep the pillow over his face before he could join her.

Deans heard Savage's muted voice. 'We're going to leave you alone for a bit, Deano. Unless you would prefer that we stay?'

Deans rocked his head beneath the pillow.

'You know you can call either of us at any time,' Thornton said. 'Take care of yourself.'

A nurse came into the room and removed the pillow from Deans' face.

'What are you doing with that, Mr Deans?' she said. 'Come on, there is no need to be upset, you'll be back on your feet before you know it.'

She took the pillow away from his face and he watched, numb, as she left the room.

Right at that moment, Deans felt completely alone in the world.

Maria and their unborn child were dead, and no DNA result was going to tell him otherwise.

CHAPTER FORTY-ONE

He used the phone connected to the long adjustable arm suspended over his bed to call Denise.

'You need to get me out of here,' Deans told her.

'Andy, you are there for a reason,' Denise replied. 'I'm not going to help you hurt yourself.'

'I'll be fine. I feel fine. But I can't do this without your help.'

'Andy—'

'Denise, let me stay at your place. You can look after me. I *have* to do this.'

'It's not that simple. You were in a coma. You need proper care.'

'I *need* to find where Maria went. And I know where to start.'

Denise fell silent.

'Denise, I simply cannot do this without you and I don't trust anyone else enough to ask.'

He heard her groan in the earpiece and he smiled. 'Denise?' he prompted.

'Okay, okay. But the moment you need specialist help I'm taking you back to hospital.'

'Deal,' Deans said. 'Now, get yourself up here and get me the hell out of this place.'

The hospital staff put up a half-hearted attempt to keep Deans with them. There was most likely a fine line between duty of care and needing the bed space.

He looked up at the heavy grey sky and sucked in the cool city air as the thrum of passing pedestrians hurried about their business – cramming in their Christmas shopping. He stood, supported by his walking sticks, but even then, the desperate and damn right ignorant still bustled and barged him as he stood planted to the spot – Maria's spot.

He watched them flow around him like a stream meandering relentlessly towards its goal, the train station. He squinted. *The train station.* He knew Maria had not taken a train – that line of enquiry had been exhausted, or so he had been told.

He looked up to the CCTV cameras – the ones from which he had watched Maria. He imagined them staring down upon him right then. How would he vanish from view?

He locked his arms inside the crutches and clomped his way slowly forwards. *Maria was going this way.*

He looked around him.

A narrow side street only led back towards the road that ran in front of the police station. He took the diversion, causing shoppers in his path to stop suddenly, back up, and alter direction. He may not have seen where Maria went, but that was the exact same result on the CCTV footage.

It took him about a minute to reach the other side of the alleyway, but for others not hindered by a busted leg, it would more likely take a matter of seconds – twenty maximum, he estimated.

He looked both ways along the road. Buses, minicabs and the emergency services were the only vehicles allowed to use this route during the day. Maria vanished shortly after two p.m.

A covert unit from the station's burglary squad tooted him as they passed by in an unmarked car. Deans raised a stick to acknowledge them and watched as they drove on, out of sight. The corner of his eye twitched, and he quickly scanned the nearby buildings. He was standing in a camera blind spot.

He snatched for his mobile phone and called DI Thornton. The phone rang and rang.

'Come on,' Deans shouted into the phone.

'DI Thornton,' the response eventually came.

'It's Andy Deans,' he said hurriedly. 'Did you say you checked ANPR in Bath?'

'What was the point in trying Automatic Number Plate Recognition?' Thornton replied dismissively. 'Ash Babbage was already in custody and his vehicle was being dissected by CSI—'

'We have a time that Maria was last seen,' Deans interrupted.

Thornton huffed and groaned. 'But we don't have a subject vehicle to cross reference,' he said.

Deans looked over towards the front of his station and saw the response vehicles parked and ready to roll.

'We do,' he said and terminated the call.

He made good time back to the police station and took a lift up to the Intelligence Department. Sergeant Adrian Otto was at his desk.

'Adge, can I talk to you privately, please?' an out of breath Deans asked.

Sergeant Otto gave Deans a long and considered look.

'Shouldn't you be in hospital?' he asked.

'Yeah, yeah. I need your help, but it's sensitive,' Deans said hastily.

Otto laughed. 'Look around you, Deano. Everything in this domain is sensitive. What's on your mind, buddy?'

'Maria was abducted.'

Otto nodded.

Deans checked over his shoulder and leaned over Otto's desk, so that he was only inches from his face.

'In a police car,' Deans said.

Otto did not move. Did not even blink, just carried on staring at Deans.

'I've traced her steps,' Deans said. 'It's the only plausible explanation.'

Otto turned in his chair, swung his knees out from under the desk, stood up, moved slowly to the door and closed it.

'Go on,' he said, returning to his seat.

'Maria wasn't snatched,' Deans said. 'She went willingly.'

Otto leaned back in his seat and considered Deans momentarily.

'What do you want from me, Deano?' he asked.

'ANPR authorisation at the bus gates, on the day Maria vanished. Three hours either side should do it.' The bus gates were a camera operated system that recorded the registration numbers of all passing vehicles. The owners of any unauthorised vehicles received a nasty surprise in the post within a couple of weeks with demands for payment of fines.

Otto scratched his beard with a crackle of ginger bristles.

'Big ask, Deano. I mean, how many times do you suppose our police vehicles pass through those cameras each day?'

Deans shook his head. 'Not ours.'

Otto frowned and twirled a Bic biro between his teeth.

'I really want to help you, Andy—'

'But?'

Otto did not answer and sucked on the end of the pen as if it was a cigarette. He had been a heavy smoker until the station management forced him to indulge his addiction in an uncovered part of the rear car park.

'Would the system easily differentiate between police and other civilian vehicles?' Deans asked.

He noticed Otto looking at a small framed photograph on the side of his desk.

'It would,' Otto said quietly.

'And between constabularies?' Deans asked.

Otto smiled. 'So long as they were registered to the police force. We would probably even know which station used them.'

Deans' eyes widened. 'And camera images?' he asked.

'Some have cameras.'

Deans gazed out into the council car park below them.

'What do the Major Crime Team make of this suggested line of enquiry?' Otto asked after a moment's silence.

Deans did not answer, just gave Otto a knowing look.

Deans saw the smallest of smiles begin to curl in the corner of Otto's lips.

'I'd be glad to help you, Deano,' Otto said. 'Twenty-four hours – you'll have your answer in twenty-four hours.'

Deans reached over the table and shook Otto by the hand.

'Call me on my mobile with the result,' Deans said, because he knew twenty-four hours from then, he would not be in Bath – by that time he would be hunting down Maria's killers…in Devon.

CHAPTER FORTY-TWO

Denise drove Deans to Devon. The North Devon link road seemed quicker this time. Deans had a quiet resolve he had not experienced to this point. This was his time to make a symbolic gesture of intent; a planting of the flag, a sword in the air, and it felt good. He had told Denise about the MCIT update, but did not mention that he was going to take matters in his own hands and find Maria's killers.

They were in Torworthy – back at the place where it all began two months earlier. Deans was in the treatment room of Rayon Vert, Denise's therapy studio. He was determined, if a little fuzzy from his head injury.

'I want you to help me,' he said to Denise. 'I'm ready for you to do whatever it is you do.'

Denise grinned, walked over to Deans and gently embraced him.

'Good,' she said. 'You won't regret this. Would you like to start now?'

Without another word, Deans kicked his shoe off and heaved his body and leg cast onto the treatment couch. Denise pulled a towel up over his body and chest and told him to relax for a few minutes while she left the room.

Deans stared up at the ceiling, lost in his thoughts. His stomach gargled loudly, and he became aware that Denise was now standing behind him.

'You are very unbalanced,' she announced.

No shit.

'I can change that for you,' she said and her hands were moving in his peripheral vision.

'Close your eyes,' she said. 'Think of something sad.'

That's easy.

'Good. Now something happy.'

Deans frowned.

'Wow!' she said.

She came alongside him so that he could see her face. 'I'm not sure how far to take this during the first session,' she said. 'Your chakras are so muddled.'

'Okay,' Deans said.

'But my God! You have amazing energy.'

Deans sniffed. It certainly did not feel that way to him.

Denise smiled. 'If you allow me, I can train you.'

'For what?'

Her face beamed brightly. 'Spiritual enlightenment.'

He blinked and turned his head away slightly. All he was interested in were answers… about Maria.

'I'll just give you a tune up today, make you feel more balanced. But seriously, consider what I say. You could become… extraordinary.'

'I'll chew it over.'

'Okay,' Denise said. 'Now this is important. Ask yourself what you need?' she said walking to the curtains and pulling them closed. 'What you *really* need.'

Deans followed the swirled pattern in the Artex ceiling and deliberated on the question. *What did he really need?* He needed

Maria, and he needed his old life back – the long and late shifts, the uncertainty of conception, a wife in need of his support, a life lacking time and energy – his life – not the life of a pseudo-psychic detective, bouncing from one disaster to the next.

Denise was walking around his prone body and every now and then making eye contact with a smile, her hands waving in small flat circles.

'You said Amy had connected to you,' Deans said.

Denise continued around him slowly wafting her hands six inches above his torso.

'I need her back,' Deans said. 'I need to speak to Amy Poole.'

'You need repairing,' Denise said, not responding to his requests. 'Your energy channels are haywire. You are like a tight ball of rubber bands. You need to loosen up.' She walked behind his head and placed her hands gently onto his shoulders.

He could feel a light tingling pressure through the material of his shirt.

She breathed through her nose with long, slow, deliberate uniformity. Her fingertips pressed into his muscles with increasing firmness. She placed her hands above the centre of his chest.

He caught her eye, and she smiled a *bless you*. He could feel penetrating bodily warmth, even though her hands were inches away from touching him.

'Don't fight it,' she said softly. 'Let the energy flow.'

Her hands were sending rods of tenderness deep into his body. His eyes grew heavy, the muscles of his jaw slackened and the sound of her rhythmic breath close to his face sent him into a near-hypnotic state of consciousness.

His thoughts raked from Maria's face to the streets of Bath where she went missing, to Babbage, and finally to the pebble ridge at Sandymere Bay where he was now looking out onto the incoming tide and a warm dipping sunset above the horizon.

'Good,' Denise said quietly. 'Now, concentrate on nothing else.'

The sound of rolling waves filled his mind. It was as if he was there, back on the ridge. His trance deepened and he could feel himself slipping into a comforting sleep.

He steadied his feet on the pebbles and became aware of someone else beside him. He turned and saw Amy Poole. She was looking out into the fading light of the sunset. Her skin emitted a radiant hue and her long platinum hair billowed gently in the breeze. Deans reached out and touched the side of her face. She was beautiful. *Amy,* he thought.

She turned and smiled with angelic reassurance.

Deans heard his voice talking. *I need you.* But he knew he was not speaking.

Her face was magnificently serene and her blue eyes, spell-binding.

I wish I could have saved you, his voice said.

Amy's smile widened, and he heard her voice, but her lips did not move. *You did,* she said and reached out and took his hand.

Suddenly Deans was in darkness. They glided silently forward and came to a door, which opened of its own accord before they reached it.

Let the truth in, Amy's voice said.

Deans looked beyond the open door. A vertical shaft of light cut through the centre of the room. He stopped moving and fell completely rigid. He was looking at Ruby Mansell's bedroom, and lying blooded and motionless on the mattress, he saw Maria.

Deans opened his eyes with a jolt, his chest heaved and he struggled for breath. He was staring at the familiar Artex ceiling of the treatment room. An intense pain scorched his temples and pulsed down the side of his face. He swung his legs from the couch and slumped forwards, cradling his head in his hands. He did not feel any different, just more exhausted. Denise was no longer in the room and a tall glass of water was waiting for him on the side. He grabbed the drink and downed it in one.

He caught his breath, pulled on his shoe, shuffled out to the shop front and saw Denise sitting at her desk reading a thick book.

'Okay?' she smiled. 'I thought I'd leave you to rest. Your body needed that.'

Deans rubbed his eyes. He had a dull drum banging inside his head.

'Any chance of a coffee?'

'Ah! No coffee,' Denise said, closing the covers of her novel. 'Only water for you.'

'What? You never told me that.'

'Have water first, and then you can have one coffee.' She grinned. 'How do you feel?'

Deans rolled his neck and groaned quietly. 'Fine,' he replied. 'I'm fine.'

Denise stood up and handed Deans a bottle of spring water. 'See how you are tomorrow, we could take you the next stage if you are up to it?' she said.

Deans gulped from the bottle.

'It's getting late,' Denise said.

Deans looked out of the window. It was dark outside. 'What time is it?' he asked rubbing his eyes.

'Coming up to seven. I didn't want to disturb your rest.'

Deans looked down at his hands and rotated them back to front. He clenched his fists and released them again as if he was squeezing a stress ball in each hand. He wanted to speak but stopped himself.

Denise raised a brow as if she was reading his mind and was already answering his question.

'Did I just… I mean. Was that…real?'

Denise did not answer. She simply smiled.

'What does it mean?'

Denise looked away for a short moment and then stood up.

'You must work that out for yourself, flower,' she said.

Deans rolled his neck and breathed in the dream. He looked around the room as Denise watched him with a sympathetic smile. He moved towards the door and looked out into the black, still air. He stretched his shoulders and brought his hands together above his head before resting them on top of his crown.

'I think,' he said. 'I think I need some local constabulary help.'

CHAPTER FORTY-THREE

DC Ranford was at his desk working a fresh overnight case. It was clear from his gob-smacked expression that he was surprised to see Deans hobbling in to the office on his sticks, accompanied by a member of staff from the front of house reception team.

'Andy? You're back,' Ranford said and quickly stood to help Deans to a nearby chair. 'My God! Look at you,' he said. 'I was told about...' his voice tailed away. 'My God! You were lucky to escape that crash.'

'I need your help, Paul,' Deans said.

Ranford shrugged. 'Of course, anything, but I'm a bit stuffed at the moment with these overnight prisoners. Can Mansfield help? He's just popped out for something.'

'No,' Deans replied blankly. 'It has to be you.'

Ranford dropped his pen onto the desk and dragged his chair closer to Deans. 'Okay,' he said, 'I'm listening.'

'Maria's dead,' Deans said bluntly.

At first Ranford did not react. He simply looked at Deans and blinked. Then his face creased in the middle and a look of dismay replaced his professional exterior cladding. 'Oh my God!' he said, his eyes wide open. 'Andy. I am so sorry.' He leaned in closer towards Deans.

'They are waiting on a formal ID from the DNA,' Deans said. 'Should be any time now.'

'Hold on,' Ranford said. 'Is this the body pulled from Sandymere Bay?'

Deans closed his eyes and dropped his head.

'Holy shit! I heard about that. But she was decap—' Ranford stopped himself from saying the rest.

'I know where she was killed,' Deans said.

Ranford's mouth opened, showing his bottom row of teeth. 'What?'

Deans moistened his lips and peered at Ranford. 'I know where she was killed.' He held Ranford's gaze until Ranford glanced away.

'Where?' Ranford whispered, after Deans made it obvious he was waiting for Ranford to respond next.

Deans looked back toward the door. They were still alone.

'There's a house,' he said, 'overlooking Sandymere Bay.' He saw that Ranford was completely immersed in his every word. 'It's known as the haunted house—'

'Yes, I know it… everyone knows it,' Ranford said.

'Maria was killed in the haunted house.'

Ranford sat back in his chair and stared at Deans for a moment.

'Are you sure?' Ranford asked. 'That place is derelict, isn't it?'

'And I need your help to get me inside.'

Ranford blinked and shook his head. 'But… uh… are you certain?'

'Deadly.'

Ranford's inquisitive eyes were working overtime.

'I've already been there once,' Deans said.

Ranford's curious stare turned to shock. 'What? When?' he asked.

'A week before my accident.'

'What did you find?' Ranford breathed.

Deans pursed his lips, looked over at the Post-It notes stuck around the edge of DC Mansfield's computer screen and shook his head. 'Nothing.'

'So then, why do you want to go back?'

'I *have* to.'

'Well, who let you in the last time?'

'I found a way inside—'

'Fuck's sake, Andy,' Ranford said with muted tones. 'You can't do that. It still belongs to *somebody*.'

'And that's why I need your help,' Deans said lifting his leg cast from the floor, as if he really needed to explain.

Ranford dropped his chin to his chest and chuckled. 'Yeah... okay. I said I'd do anything, but I have to finish these interviews first.'

'Good,' Deans said. 'I'll see you later. And make sure you bring Mansfield.'

Ranford allowed Deans to use a job computer for ten minutes. He was searching Google for Ruby Mansell's house to see if anything showed. He was in luck; there was a report from the local *Herald* regarding her death. Ruby Mansell had succumbed to a sudden and ultimately unexplained death by asphyxiation in her bedroom. Her long-time friend, and neighbour, Ivan Greene, had found her days later, deceased in her bed. The family bloodline ended with her demise.

Deans' thoughts immediately raced to Maria and their attempts to have a family. He clamped his jaw and continued reading. Ruby's death was eleven years ago. He pictured the house in his mind and tried to imagine how it must have looked in its heyday. The news article displayed a grainy picture of the house from the outside. Deans leaned in closer. The porch, roof and walls were still perfectly intact. As he scanned the image, his eyes diverted to a piece of text and to a name that shot out of the page at him:

Police Constable Stephen Jackson said, "Any loss of life is tragic, but especially when someone so influential within our community is taken from us in such devastating circumstances."

Deans scrolled down the report and found another image, this time of PC Jackson. He was skeletal even as a younger man, in fact he looked unchanged from today. He was in full dress uniform. The image appeared to have been taken during an award ceremony.

Deans jotted the date of the article in the back of his day-book, circled it and read on. Ruby Mansell was the heir to a small fortune. She lived alone in the grand old property for many years after her husband was killed fighting in the Second World War. Her wealth after death was distributed between charitable organisations she supported, but not her home. Deans checked his watch; he needed to press-on. He checked Ranford was not paying attention to him and took a photo of the screen on his phone.

CHAPTER FORTY-FOUR

Deans left the station and scrolled through his phone until he found DC Sarah Gold's number. Ranford said she was in town, paying Babbage a home visit. Deans arranged to meet her at a coffee house in Torworthy.

Sarah came through the door and picked him out straight away, which was not difficult; he was one of only three people in the café and the only person battered and bruised, and on crutches. She waved and bounced over to him. Sarah was wearing a chocolate brown knee-length trench coat, tailored to the waist. Her blonde hair was caught at the collar and bunched up like ear muffs. Deans grabbed a stick and heaved himself up from his chair.

'Sit down, silly,' Sarah said helping Deans back into his seat. 'Have you ordered anything?'

'I've already had a coffee, but if you're offering, I'd love another?'

Sarah walked to the counter and spoke to the waiter who seemed to know her. Deans heard him call her by her name. Their interaction seemed more than simple acquaintances.

'It's fantastic to see you,' she said coming back to the table.

'When did the hospital release you?'

'They didn't,' Deans said.

Sarah's face dropped. 'What do you mean? You self-discharged?'

'Yep.'

'Why?'

'Things I need to do,' Deans said casually.

'But… you should still be looked after.'

'I am,' Deans said. 'Denise Moon is taking care of me for a few days.' He noticed a flicker in Sarah's eyes.

'Is that wise?'

'It's the wisest thing I've done in my entire life.'

The waiter came over to the table. 'One Grande latte for Madame and a large Americano for sir.'

Deans nodded. Sarah looked back over her shoulder as the waiter returned to the counter. 'Thanks, Dan,' she said.

Deans watched her closely and sipped from his mug. 'So what are you doing back here?' he asked. 'You are still based in Exeter, aren't you?'

'Yeah, yeah,' she sighed. 'They haven't sacked me yet.'

Deans looked around the room at the two other occupied tables and shrugged, 'So?'

'Oh, Sergeant Jackson asked me to do a welfare check on Babbage. He's on electronic curfew, but the sarge seems to think we also need doorstep presentation.'

'Why would he want that?' Deans asked.

Sarah shrugged. 'I don't know.'

'So,' Deans said after a couple of sips of his coffee. 'How was his… *welfare?*'

Sarah scratched the side of her neck and instead of answering the question, removed her coat and placed it on the chair next to her. She was wearing an undersized suit jacket that was straining at the button beneath her chest. Deans looked over to Dan, who was staring back at him.

'Does Babbage still bother you?' Deans asked.

She fiddled with the spoon on her saucer but did not answer.

'Were you alone?'

She lifted her cup with both hands, taking a frothy slurp from the latte and nodded.

'Jackson didn't suggest you should go with someone else?'

'He did,' Sarah said quickly. 'I did ask in Torworthy CID, but no one could help me, so I went alone.' Sarah made it obvious what she thought of that with a raise of her eyebrow and a momentary glance up to the ceiling.

Deans took a long drawn out sip from his mug and waited a few moments.

'I was meaning to ask before,' he said. 'How is it that you live so near, yet work all the way over in Exeter – why not work in Torworthy?'

'I'd love to, it would be so convenient. But I had to go where the detective post was offered.'

'Jackson... did he have anything to do with that?' Deans asked.

Sarah's eyes wavered slightly. 'Yes,' she said.

'Did you know him before you joined the job?' Deans asked.

She looked down and away.

Deans cocked his head. 'It's okay,' he said. 'You don't need to answer. I'm sorry if I'm prying.'

Still looking down towards her lap, Sarah began to speak, 'My mother was beaten by my father. One day she was so badly hurt that I called the police.' She looked up and stared Deans in the eye. 'But Mum didn't want me to.' Sarah blinked slowly. 'Sergeant Jackson was one of the officers to attend. He was kind to Mum... and caring towards me.'

Deans did not interrupt and allowed Sarah free recall.

'I was fifteen,' she smiled sadly. 'Eleven years ago. I've grown up a lot since then.'

As she took another drink, Deans asked her, 'That was here?'

Sarah placed her cup gently back down onto the saucer. 'Yeah, my mum still lives in Torworthy...' She hesitated and shifted in her seat. 'Dad upped and left once the investigation was over.'

'What happened to him?' Deans asked.

Sarah frowned and pouted her rounded lips. 'Nothing. Mum retracted any complaint. Those were the days before victimless prosecutions.' She scratched the side of her nose and hid her face behind her cup once again.

Deans could tell she was embarrassed to be talking about it. 'Has Mum found anyone else?' he asked.

'No,' Sarah replied without taking breath. 'She still blames me for wrecking their marriage by calling the police that night.'

Deans scowled. 'What does she think about you being an officer now... a detective?'

'She is fine – talks about me when it suits her.' Sarah looked away again.

'And Dad?'

Sarah shook her head.

'So how did you find Jackson, or was it the other way around?' Deans asked.

Sarah scratched at her ear. 'I saw him at my initial interview. He was one of the assessors. He just always seemed to be wherever I ended up, like it was fate or something.'

Deans smiled and created a minute of silence to consider his thoughts as he took another drink.

'How was Babbage?' he asked eventually.

'Eww,' Sarah responded, screwing up her face. 'Still gives me the willies.' She quickly checked left, then right and leaned in towards Deans.

He reciprocated.

'Did you know that Babbage is female?' Sarah said.

Deans gave a half shake of his head but did not reply.

'Turns out her brother died in a boat accident when he was

only seven and her parents both died together in a car accident a few years later.'

Deans rutted his brow and dipped his head.

'Ash, or Donna as she was originally named, was orphaned away from the area and returned as an adult with a new male identity and a name changed by deed-poll.'

Deans took several long sips from his mug.

'Babbage should have told us from the start,' Sarah said. 'Might not have ended up in a bloke's prison... but you'd never tell, looking at him, I mean her...'

Deans wiped froth from his top lip. 'Well, if that's the life that he chose, who are we to say otherwise?'

Sarah gave an exaggerated jerk of her shoulders and groaned again.

'Are the Crown Prosecution making all the right noises, now that Babbage is out?' Deans asked.

'Seem to be and obviously a bit shocked to have him released the way that he was.' Sarah rubbed the side of her nose and looked away furtively.

'What?' Deans asked, leaning closer towards her. 'What else, Sarah?'

She blinked and glanced down.

'Sarah?'

She covered her mouth with the back of a hand and peered at Deans. He gestured for her to continue. Her eyes had pity etched into them.

'Sarah?'

'We intercepted one of Babbage's phone calls from prison,' she said and shook her head. 'Not a full transcript, but one-way CCTV footage of Babbage speaking.' She paused and drew a deep breath. 'He was...' she hesitated, 'he appeared to be asking whoever else was on the end of the line *"if it was done. If everything was arranged and sorted."'*

Deans placed his mug down in front of him and leaned on the

table with his elbows. 'Who was on the other end of the phone?'

'We don't know. We weren't permitted authority to check.'

Deans sat back in his chair and grabbed his mouth.

'We did try,' Sarah said. 'But the prison governor said it didn't prove a thing… could have been talking about lottery tickets.'

'Did Jackson challenge that?' Deans asked.

Sarah nodded, 'I think so.'

Deans watched Sarah for a moment and then leaned in close again. 'Why didn't Jackson authorise any questions about Maria while we still had Babbage in custody?'

Sarah lowered her head. 'I don't know.'

Deans studied her face; watched her drink from the cup. DC Gold had been set up for failure from the start of the Amy Poole investigation. She had been selected for a reason, and now, this brilliant young detective was being made the scapegoat.

'None of this was your fault, you know that don't you?' Deans said.

She pouted and flicked hair over her shoulder with a hand.

'Jackson is at the root of everything that has gone wrong,' Deans continued.

Sarah caught his eye and looked away again.

'Was Jackson a PC in Torworthy?' Deans asked.

'Yes. He was still a PC when I first met him.'

'When did he move across to Exeter?'

'He was promoted into position about six years ago…'

'But he still comes back?'

Sarah nodded.

Deans heaved a deep breath and looked out of the window.

'Have you ever seen Jackson and Babbage together at any time during this investigation?' he asked, still looking outside.

Deans turned back when Sarah didn't answer.

'Well yes,' she said. 'At the final interview and when Babbage was released from prison.'

Deans smiled. 'Thanks for the coffee, Sarah.'

CHAPTER FORTY-FIVE

Deans and Denise waited in the small car park beside the haunted house. They had been sitting there for almost two hours. Deans checked his phone, five fifty-three p.m. Ranford said he would be there just after four. He must have become tied up with a job, but he could have let Deans know. Beautiful as the view had been, Deans was now freezing his nuts off. He stared up at the walls; the silhouette against the darkening sky was classic *Hammer House of Horrors*. The steady growl of waves reminded him of the nights he had slept nearby in his car.

He clambered out of the passenger side and looked around him. The only sign of life was the glowing windows from a property further back towards the village – probably the caretaker's home. Deans smiled inwardly – it was looking like they would not be disturbed tonight.

The sound of an approaching vehicle caught Deans' attention and bright headlights dazzled in his face. It was a marked police unit.

The squad car pulled up alongside and Ranford and Mansfield stepped out.

'Thought using one of these might help,' Ranford said.

Deans extended Mansfield a reluctant nod. Mansfield returned the gesture and removed several large Dragon Lamps from the boot of his vehicle as Denise stepped out of the car.

'What's she doing here?' Mansfield asked abruptly.

'We don't go inside unless Denise is with us,' Deans replied. 'You got a problem with that; you can sit outside in your car, in the cold.'

'Okay you two,' Ranford said, grabbing two of the lamps from Mansfield and handing one to Deans. He grasped Deans by the elbow and turned him to the side, with his back on the others. 'Seriously?' he asked quietly in Deans' ear.

'Same goes for you,' Deans said and gave Ranford a fierce look.

Ranford scowled but agreed.

'So what are we after?' Mansfield asked, hurdling the low, crumbling boundary wall and lighting up the front of the house with the brilliant whiteness of a million candle lights from his lamp.

'Why did you ask me to bring him?' Ranford whispered to Deans as they walked shoulder-to-shoulder toward the house.

'Sometimes it's better the devil you know…you know?' Deans muttered under his breath.

Mansfield was already out of sight. Ranford helped Denise over the wall and then assisted Deans with his stiff leg and crutches.

'What are we looking for anyway, Andy?' Ranford asked as they neared the side entrance.

'I'll know when I see it,' Deans replied.

'I don't understand,' Ranford said, 'Why would this place have anything to do with Maria?'

Deans shrugged. 'I guess we are all going to find out.'

Ranford went ahead of Deans and joined Mansfield at the decaying side door.

'Shall we boot it in?' Mansfield asked, his voice full of excitement.

'God, no,' Ranford answered quickly. 'Look in the boot of the car,' he said. 'We should have a jemmy.' Mansfield grinned and raced back to the car.

Ranford stood between Deans and the door. 'I really don't know what you hope to achieve other than potentially dropping us all in the shit with this stunt.'

'Just wait and see,' Deans said.

Mansfield returned and went straight to work on the door lock, springing the latch with one firm shove of the bar. 'Awesome,' Mansfield chuckled. 'What a shit-hole, I've been dying to see this place since I was a kid.'

'Careful,' Ranford said, handing Mansfield a dragon lamp. 'Think about squatters and other hazards.'

'No one is going to live in this dump, not even squatters,' Mansfield said, directing the bright beam of light around the internal walls and ceilings, before charging off into the building with complete disregard for his own safety.

'I need to go upstairs,' Deans said to Ranford as they moved through the doorway.

The three of them traipsed through the hallway. Deans' heavy cast clunking loudly on the exposed wooden floorboards every other step. They reached the base of the stairs, Ranford at the lead. A brittle chill filled Deans' spine, neck and head. He faced Denise who was already wide-eyed and staring back at him.

Mansfield rejoined them and raced to the front. 'Let me go first,' he said, his lamp already illuminating the rungs and handrails of the stairway.

Deans glanced at Ranford who shrugged and shook his head. Deans looked back at Denise; she was hugging herself with her coat wrapped tightly around her body. Mansfield was providing an expletive commentary as he raced ahead up the stairs.

When they all reached the second level, Deans saw Mansfield

shining his light through a large hole in the floorboards and giggling like an excitable teen.

'Can you have a look over there?' Deans asked Mansfield, pointing in the opposite direction to where Deans really needed to be. Mansfield darted off as directed; still expressing his apparent surprise at each new room he entered.

Deans noticed Ranford was staring at him. 'What?' Deans asked.

'Your nose is bleeding,' Ranford said.

Deans wiped his face and saw a smear of blood on the back of his hand. Ranford passed him a tissue from his pocket and Deans staunched the flow. He glanced over at Denise. She acknowledged and came alongside him at the doorway to Ruby Mansell's room.

Deans turned away from Ranford, closed his eyes and said to himself, *Amy, show me what I need to see.*

He took a deep breath, twisted the handle and the door creaked open.

Ranford grabbed the crook of Deans' arm. 'Oh! Come on, Andy, this is minging.'

'Just one minute,' Deans said, tugging his arm back. 'I just need one minute.'

'What have you guys got over there?' Mansfield shouted from across the landing and came bounding over to the room. 'Wow! Look at that old thing,' Mansfield enthused. 'That's seen a bit of action by the looks of it.'

Deans peered at the bed. Something about it had to be significant? He stepped slowly inside and directed his lamp around the room. The razor sharp edges of the light picked up every individual particle of dust thrown into the air from the opening door. Deans hesitated and looked back at the others. Ranford and Mansfield were staying outside. Deans slowly rounded the bed, taking everything in.

'Come on then, Andy,' Ranford said impatiently. 'We'd better get going. There's nothing in this old place.'

As Deans reached the opposite side of the bed frame he noticed something on the floor and knelt down – as much as his leg cast would allow.

'What is it?' Mansfield asked stepping forwards.

Deans took out his mobile phone and snapped a quick sequence of pictures, tracing the lamp light up and around the metal bed frame. He scanned the floor and took another burst of shots.

'I'm going back downstairs,' Ranford said. 'We've been in here too long. Somebody is going to notice sooner or later.'

'Okay,' Deans replied. 'I just need another thirty seconds and I'll be there.' He studied the upright of the bed frame again and gently blew air onto the floorboards – just enough to shift the top layer of dust.

He paused, stood up again and sniffed the air.

'Anything?' Mansfield asked.

Deans shook his head. 'No. Come on.'

CHAPTER FORTY-SIX

Deans hung back with Denise. 'Did you see that?' he asked.

'It's not real, Andy. It wasn't really there.'

'The others couldn't see it, could they?'

She shook her head. 'No. Only those of us with the gift can see beyond reality.'

'So what does it mean?' he asked, ensuring his words were not overheard by the others.

'The guardians will make that clear to you in time.'

'Okay,' he said, stopping her at the top of the stairs. 'How do *you* interpret it?'

Denise let out a controlled exhalation of breath. 'It's Maria. She was here. But not necessarily in that room. We saw the marks on the bedframe and the spots of blood on the floor. But they weren't really there. It was a sign—'

'But I've taken photos,' Deans said, urgently swiping the screen of his phone. 'Eh?' he questioned, bringing the screen closer to his face. 'It's gone. It's not there.'

'That was a message for you in the moment, not to be kept for prosperity,' Denise said.

'So what now?' he asked. 'How do I move forward?'

Denise touched his hand. 'I don't know the answer to that, flower. You are way more connected to this than I am.'

They walked side-by-side down the steps and met Ranford and Mansfield at the bottom. The lower they descended, the colder Deans became. He recalled seeing Denise wrap herself in her coat before moving upstairs.

'Wait here a moment,' he said to the others and walked slowly along the hallway, sensing the changing air temperature.

He stopped outside of a closed door, opened it and shone his lamp; it was just another empty reception room at the back of the house, but a surge of energy plummeted into the pit of his stomach.

It was here, he thought and looked back for Denise. She was behind Ranford and Mansfield who had blocked her way through the narrow hallway.

Deans clomped slowly into the room. His head was becoming light and dizzy. He moved closer to the window and suddenly stopped. He took several paces backwards and then moved forwards once again.

In the hallway, Mansfield was chuntering something incoherent.

'Everyone shut up,' Deans shouted and repeated the steps backwards and forwards. He shone the light around his feet. There was a dirty old sheet covering a large section of the floor. He used the end of his walking stick to pull the sheet to one side and he repeated his steps again, but this time stamped down with the base of his leg cast. 'In here,' he shouted.

The others joined him inside the room.

'There's some kind of false floor, or trap door, under my feet,' Deans said and stomped on the floor again. The change in tone was now more obvious.

'Cool,' Mansfield said eagerly, and dropped to his knees, almost at once locating a moveable edge within the floorboards and lifting it.

The floor sucked and a cold torrent of air billowed into the room from below them.

'Come on,' Mansfield said, 'bring over the lamps, this is well spooky.'

They all stood around and watched Mansfield lift and remove the five-square-feet of shutter door from the floorboards.

'Wow!' Mansfield said. 'This place is even better than I imagined.' He stuck his head into the hole and shone his lamp around the void. Deans saw light escaping through the gaps in the floorboards. It was clearly quite a sizeable space below their feet.

'I'm going in,' Mansfield said. 'I can see a ladder.'

'Hold on,' Ranford said quickly. 'We don't know how safe that is. I don't think it's a good idea.'

'I'm going down,' Deans said, moving beyond Ranford.

'Andy – you can't go down there,' Ranford said. 'Your leg – if something happens to you, how the hell would we get you back out?'

Deans ignored Ranford and sat on the edge of the trap door entrance, his legs dangling into the pit. Mansfield had already dropped down and brought a metal three-step ladder beneath Deans' legs.

'I'll help you in,' Mansfield's echoing voice sounded from beneath the floorboards. Deans felt hands around the bottom of his legs and gentle tugs of encouragement from Mansfield. He manoeuvred his body and slowly dropped down into the hole.

The floor was rough concrete, and the air was freezer-cold with a strong draught biting around their feet. The ceiling was just high enough for Deans to stand with his head slightly bent forwards.

Ranford and then Denise followed into the cellar. Denise was noticeably quieter and tucked herself close in to Deans, looping an arm through his. Deans instinctively lit up the back wall with light.

'What's that?' Ranford said, and they all edged closer.

Attached to the wall were three chained shackles. The central one positioned higher and with a larger diameter.

'It's only a bloody torture chamber,' Mansfield grinned and stepped towards the restraints with Ranford close behind him.

'Don't touch them,' Deans shouted.

'Come on, Andy, these have been here for ages,' Ranford said, grabbing and tugging each of the thick steel bracelets in turn. They were clearly well secured to the wall. The two outer shackles had shorter chains than the one in the middle. Deans calculated a visual measurement from the floor; they were at kneeling height. Deans dropped to his knees as a strong surge of light-headedness overcame him. He reached forward to break his fall and planted his hands onto the damp and sticky floor.

'Shine a light,' Deans shouted as Denise came to his aid. The strobe from Mansfield's lamp illuminated Deans' hands. They were red.

'You're bleeding again,' Denise said.

'No,' Deans replied. 'It's not mine.'

Deans grabbed the lamp from Mansfield and shone it around the floor. There was a large damp patch between him and the shackles. Deans followed the line of the wall with his light and saw a deep gutter carved into the concrete floor. He followed the channel around the square shaped cellar to the wall behind them – the external wall. There was a large square hole in the base of the wall, big enough to crawl through. Denise helped Deans to his feet and they moved towards the gap in the wall. He shone the lamp and saw the jagged rocks of the cliff edge and the pulsing waters below. He quickly looked back to the others. *Oh no.*

'Look over here,' Mansfield said further along the wall. He twisted a tap and water poured out of a short length of hosepipe. 'Why would this place have a water supply?' Mansfield asked.

'We need to seal this off,' Deans said to Ranford. 'We need to test this blood and prove it is human.'

'Hang on everyone… Please,' Ranford said. 'I think we have

all got a little carried away with the legend of this place. Andy, that could be rat blood, or anything. The local cats or foxes might bring their kills in through that gap—'

'And then use the taps to wash the mess away?' Mansfield joked.

'You should wash that blood off, you could get a nasty disease,' Ranford said to Deans.

'Yeah, you're right,' Deans said, swilling his hands beneath the running tap, but only after placing one hand into his trouser pocket and wiping it into the material.

'I'm beginning to feel a little claustrophobic,' Ranford said. 'Anyone joining me up top?'

'Yeah, too bloody right,' Mansfield said.

Deans looked over at Denise and even though there was low light, he could tell her eyes were popping out from her head.

Deans was silent during the entire journey back with Denise. The CID officers had already gone, clearly keen to knock-off.

Deans always carried at least one swab kit in his day-bag and the moment he had a chance, he wiped one of the sticks inside his trouser pocket and re-sealed it inside the tube.

They arrived at Denise's home and she opened a bottle of merlot, handing Deans a large glass with the best part of half the bottle inside. They sat at the kitchen table in introspective silence. Deans stared deeply into the burgundy coloured liquid, his thoughts tangled and barbed. He placed the glass down onto the table and looked at the palms of his hands, prodding the remnants of the faded stain.

'The officer was right,' Denise said watching him. 'You should give those a really good scrub.'

Deans shook his head and carried on looking at his palms.

Denise followed-suit and placed her glass onto the table. 'We don't know she was there,' she said.

Deans looked up at her and held eye contact for the first time since they had arrived back at the house. 'We do,' he said. 'She was.'

They stared at each other until Denise spoke. 'What are you going to do?' she asked.

Deans took a long sup from his glass. 'I don't know,' he said. 'But there's one thing I am now sure about – I know who killed my wife and child.'

CHAPTER FORTY-SEVEN

Deans woke from a disturbed night. Maria had been in every thought, dream and conscious wakening. He imagined her horror; being trapped and chained in the dark and dingy cellar. He knew this was the day he would most likely hear about the DNA result from the body dragged from the depths of Sandymere Bay, and finally have to come to terms with his unspeakable reality.

He joined Denise in the kitchen. She offered him toast, but he only accepted coffee. He sensed her studying his every movement.

'So?' she said finally. 'Have you decided anything?'

Deans nodded and kept the mug of coffee close to his mouth.

'Do you need me today?' she asked.

He looked her in the eye and nodded again.

She came over to the table but did not sit down. 'Andy, the guardians have spoken to me. There is grave danger ahead for you.'

Deans blew the steam from the top of his drink and returned the mug to his lips.

'Andy, this is serious,' Denise continued.

'Yep,' he said. 'It is.'

'What are you going to do?' Denise asked, her voice full of concern.

'Unfinished business.'

'Where are we going?' she asked.

'Torworthy CID.'

Denise shrugged. 'But they said they couldn't help anymore.'

Deans' eyes moved from the dead space on the table in front of him and settled on to her troubled face.

'They will,' he said.

The journey to Torworthy took far too long for Deans, only to be informed at the front desk that no one from the CID department was in the office. Deans looked at the police cars parked in a neat row, noses facing outward for a quick response. His eyes settled on a gap. One of the unmarked vehicles was out.

He rummaged through his day-bag, removed a lightweight stab vest and proceeded to put it on beneath his jacket.

'Take me to Babbage,' he said to Denise.

'You can't can you?' she asked.

'I can,' he said, giving her an unyielding stare. 'Please, will you take me?'

Denise stared wide-eyed at Deans and raked hair from her face. 'What are you going to do?' she asked.

'Confront my wife's killer.'

'What about me?' she asked.

Deans paused and considered his answer.

'You need to be there too.'

Denise remained open mouthed for a moment, but then gave in when she realised Deans was not going to take no for an answer.

. . .

They parked short of the address but close enough to see the front door.

'Are you sure this is wise?' Denise asked.

'Probably not,' Deans said, looking all around the car through the windows. 'But what else have I got left to lose?'

Denise pulled the keys from the ignition and tightened her long raincoat around the waist. 'I'm not letting you go in there alone,' she said. 'I feel partly responsible for that monster and I'm not prepared to let anything else happen to you.'

Deans half-smiled. 'That's up to you. I am not asking and I am not making you come with me... but thanks.'

They both stood outside in the fine drizzle and Deans hobbled his way towards Ash Babbage's property.

'What are you going to say?' Denise asked under her breath.

'I haven't thought about it,' Deans said, and as they neared the front door, Deans turned to Denise with apprehensive urgency. 'You do have your phone on you?' he asked.

'Yes,' Denise said.

'If this gets messy call 999, okay? Tell them where we are and say an officer needs urgent assistance. Alright... alright, Denise?'

Denise nodded. Her face was ashen grey.

Deans banged on the door with the ball of his fist. His breathing was fast and heavy, and he could feel his chest beating against his stab vest.

He waited thirty seconds and banged again.

This time the door unlatched and was jerked open with one swift motion. Detective Ranford stood in the doorway. He peered at Deans, then Denise, and then back to Deans.

'Andy!' he said. 'What... What are you doing here? I thought you were the CSI.'

Deans looked down at Ranford's hands. He was wearing forensic gloves. Deans noticed the recognition in Ranford's face and he moved his hands behind his back.

'I've come to speak to Babbage,' Deans said. 'Don't try to

stop me.'

Ranford stepped out into the rain but kept one hand on the edge of the door. He checked left and then right and grinned. 'Mate,' he said, putting a hand on Deans' shoulder. 'You may have a problem there. Babbage has killed himself.'

Deans rocked backwards. 'What?' he spluttered. 'Where is he?' He shoved Ranford to one side.

'Hold up,' Ranford said grabbing Deans' arm. His smile waned. 'This is a crime scene.'

He gave Denise a considered look and then whispered in Deans' ear. 'He's inside, only just done it. I found him about twenty minutes ago. I thought you were the CSI.'

'Let me in,' Deans said jerking his arm back.

'Andy, I can't,' Ranford laughed. 'It's the scene of an incident. We need a full forensic examination.'

'Paul,' Deans said standing as tall as his buggered leg would allow him. 'Let me the fuck inside now. I want to see that bastard – dead, or alive.'

Ranford's face broke into a smile. 'Of course, Andy, I completely understand.'

He pushed the door open but again gripped Deans firmly by the arm. 'Just, please be mindful of evidence.'

Deans glared at him and then turned to Denise. 'Do you want to come in?' he asked.

Denise shook her head.

'Come on,' Ranford said to Denise. 'At least step in out of the rain.'

Denise succumbed but remained on the doormat as Deans followed Ranford into the kitchen diner.

Babbage was at the table. His head flopped back and a huge puddle of blood encircled his chair.

Deans circumnavigated the claret until he was on the opposite side of the table and facing Babbage. There was no mistake; he was definitely dead, and by the looks of it, as a result of several deep slices to his throat. Deans looked to Ranford whose brow twitched as he smiled.

Deans examined the surroundings. There were two place settings. He gazed at the plate of food and coffee cup in front of Babbage, and then the blooded stainless steel carving knife lying on the table immediately in front of him.

'Did a good job on himself,' Ranford commented.

'Looks that way.'

'Suppose that's one less shit to worry about.' Ranford slowly made his way around the table towards Deans.

Deans did not speak, but took in the rest of the area. He sniffed a lungful of the room. A smell of cooking was still in the air. He peered in closer to Babbage, ensuring the toes of his feet remained clear of the blood.

'When did you say you arrived?' Deans asked Ranford.

Ranford shrugged. 'Twenty, maybe thirty minutes ago? I called it in straight away. I don't know why the others are taking so long to arrive.' He smiled. 'Like I said...' his voice tailed away.

Deans nodded and hobbled over into the kitchen area.

'Careful where you plonk that cast,' Ranford joked while keeping a watchful eye on Deans.

'Don't worry about me,' Deans said and continued looking around the kitchen. Cooking pans were still on the hob. He wandered over and looked inside one of them. Scrambled eggs. He touched the outside of the pan – it was warm. Deans sucked in a deep breath; the odour of breakfast was so far overcoming the stench of death. Everything else was as clean and tidy as he remembered it to be when he was last inside the house. *Showroom tidy*, he recalled, and then he saw it – a second steaming mug of coffee.

He quickly turned to Ranford, who was also looking at the hot drink, and they locked eyes.

'It wasn't a dream,' Deans said. 'You did visit me in hospital.'

Ranford cocked his head and grinned. He was now standing

just the other side of Babbage with his gaping neck between them. Deans dragged his leg along the floor and rushed towards Ranford. 'Why did you have to involve my wife, you bastard?'

Ranford stepped back and lashed out, swatting a debilitated Deans away with ease.

Deans headed straight through the tacky tide of Babbage's blood. His teeth bared, and with single-minded determination, he grabbed Ranford by the lapel of his jacket. 'You have played me from the start, you bastard,' Deans seethed.

'She's dead,' Ranford laughed playfully. 'Maria is dead and I *really* enjoyed cutting up her body parts and feeding them to the fish.'

Deans' stomach juddered and convulsed, but before he could do anything, Ranford pushed him hard in the chest causing Deans to slip to the floor, his face splattering in the pool of tepid blood.

Deans scrabbled, slipped, and did his utmost to stand up from the slimy gloop, but struggled with his leg cast to come back to his feet.

Ranford rounded him like a cat toying with an injured prey. 'How convenient,' he said. 'It doesn't have to be suicide anymore.' His gloved hand reached over Babbage and he placed the handle of the kitchen knife into Deans' struggling grasp. 'There,' Ranford said happily. 'That should do it.'

Deans gripped the knife and thrust it in Ranford's direction, but only jabbed at air.

'Now, now, Andrew, one murder should be enough for anyone.'

Ranford pressed the transmit button on his Airwave radio as Deans struggled to lift himself clear of the slippery floor.

'Priority,' Ranford shouted, putting on a breathless and animated voice. 'Immediate backup required – all available units.' He coughed, spluttered, and put on a struggling whimper. 'Murder suspect has returned to the scene. He's... Oh my God! He's got a knife... No!' Ranford screamed and then instantly ended the transmission with a smirk and a wink. 'That should get the troops going,' he said.

Deans knew that the Airwave radio would provide Comms with their exact location thanks to its internal GPS system.

Deans made it up onto a knee, coated in Babbage's blood. 'You fucker, you won't get away with this!'

Ranford drew his extendable steel baton from his utility belt, racked it fully open and held it in a textbook 'strike' pose on his shoulder.

'Do you really want some?' he asked. 'I'd say you were in enough shit as it is.' He stepped closer towards Deans and beamed a wide smile. 'You know it's a shame, I kind of liked you. But I have to say, your wife was pretty fucking hot... considering she was up the duff.'

Deans slid and as Ranford drew the baton up from his shoulder to strike, Deans closed his eyes and curled up into a ball, but instead of feeling pain he heard a loud crash and scattering of objects onto the floor. He opened his eyes and saw Denise clinging on to the back of Ranford's neck.

'Get off me you fucking freak,' Ranford shouted, lashing out wildly with his hands, clattering into the table and into Babbage who dropped sideways off the chair into his own sea of blood.

'Keep him there,' Deans yelled and crawled his way along the floor until he was lying on the back of Ranford's legs. He grabbed Denise who was crying and looking horrified at the blood on her hands and clothing. 'Call the cops,' Deans said. 'Do it now.' He used his body weight to keep Ranford pinned to the floor and squeezed his neck angrily with both hands. There was nothing he wanted more than to end Ranford's life – an eye for an eye – but he stopped himself from strangling Ranford and removed his hands.

The reverberation of howling sirens grew louder in the narrowing distance. It sounded like the entire fleet was approaching from the station. Deans flipped Ranford onto his back so that he was now looking up at Deans. 'Paul Ranford,' Deans said breathlessly, 'I am arresting you on suspicion of murdering Ash Babbage. Conspiracy to murder Amy Poole...' He swallowed and gritted his teeth, '...and the murder of Maria Deans.'

Urgent voices sounded and the front door burst open with a loud crash. Before he could do anything else, Deans was smashed in his back and folded in half from the rear as he was jumped on by a number uniformed officers. His face was pile-driven into the floor, his arms wrenched from beneath him into an agonising position behind his back and his wrists manhandled roughly into handcuffs. He could hear Denise doing her best to complain, but she then began to scream and her voice became frantic. Deans tried to wriggle free of his captors but the pain increased with each attempt to move.

Deans listened to Ranford's voice somewhere above him. 'You little fucker,' Ranford said. 'You're going to rot for what you've done to Ash Babbage... and for what you just tried to do to me.'

'Leave him,' a firm voice shouted above all the commotion.

Deans scraped his face along the floor and looked towards the hallway. It was Sergeant Jackson.

'Ranford. Over here!'

Ranford looked at Deans with ardent hatred and turned towards Jackson as instructed.

'What's going on?' Jackson demanded of Ranford.

'That fucker just killed Babbage. I practically caught him in the act.'

Jackson looked at Deans, lying face down on the floor with four uniformed officers kneeling on his thighs and shoulder blades. Deans caught his eye and saw Jackson staring at the leg cast.

Jackson frowned and turned back to Ranford. 'No he didn't,' he said. His lips were thin and his stare was fierce. He looked down at Ranford's hands. 'Had enough time to put those on though I see?' He suddenly launched out an arm and gripped Ranford by the throat, pushing him up against the wall. 'Ranford,' he said, 'I've been watching you for some time, now.' Jackson bared his teeth and leaned in within centimetres of Ranford's face. 'You must think I'm some kind of blind idiot?'

'Let him go,' Jackson shouted. He turned to the officers restraining Deans. 'I said let Detective Deans go.'

Deans felt the pressure ease from his body and he fought to regain his breath from his crushed rib cage. He looked over towards Denise who was still being restrained against a wall. 'And Denise,' Deans gasped, pushing himself up from the floor.

'Let the woman go too,' Jackson ordered.

Deans dragged himself alongside Jackson, who was still holding a breathless Ranford by the trachea.

'Do you want the honours,' Jackson asked Deans.

'Already done it, Sarge,' Deans said. 'Before the goons shoved me off him.'

'Good,' Jackson said. 'I call that poetic. Now, someone take this piece of shit away from me and book him into custody.'

Two PCs hesitantly came over and half-heartedly took Ranford, choking and coughing, away.

Deans walked over to Babbage and stared at his corpse. He had seen enough death in recent weeks to last him a lifetime, but he felt no sympathy.

DS Jackson joined him beside the mess on the floor. 'We need to talk,' he said, 'but first I feel I must formally introduce myself. I am Detective Sergeant Stephen Jackson of Professional Standards.'

Deans turned to him with abrupt surprise. 'Professional Standards?'

'Well, a covert limb of it,' Jackson replied.

'Have you been spying on me?'

Jackson chortled. 'No. Not you, but you didn't half make my job bloody difficult. Come on, let's follow the others to custody and get you cleaned up.'

CHAPTER FORTY-EIGHT

As they drove through the slow Torworthy traffic, Jackson told Deans and Denise that he was a local lad, but on making promotion through the ranks of the police he was approached by a covert limb of Professional Standards to be secreted within the constabulary. His role was to act just like any other departmental officer, but to also keep detailed dossiers on individuals identified as potential problems to the organisation. Ranford had only recently appeared on his radar. He had displayed an overwhelming desire to be involved with missing person investigations involving young women, until Deans had come along and scuppered their snooping.

As Jackson spoke, Deans thought about the early stages of the Amy Poole investigation; the CCTV and the post mortem – each eagerly lapped up by Ranford.

Jackson said that Ranford's existence was somewhat of a dichotomy; outwardly, his appearance was smart, his actions thorough – verging on the OCD, yet he lived a nomadic lifestyle with little luxury and few friends, apart from, it would seem, Ash Babbage.

'Turns out they knew one another in their youth,' Jackson said. 'Had one thing in common: they were both orphaned.'

Deans did not interrupt and remembered what Sarah had told him in the café.

Jackson continued, 'When Babbage lost all his family members in separate accidents he was carted off by Social Services, ending up somewhere near Weymouth in a home with three other children... one of them being Paul Ranford.' Jackson stopped speaking and negotiated a set of lights.

'It transpires one of the other kids was killed playing train chicken with Babbage and Ranford. They were never investigated and from what I can find out, it was closed down as a tragic accident with lessons to be learned.'

He turned to Deans. 'Appears the only lesson they did learn was how to kill.'

Deans continued staring ahead at the car in front. Denise sitting in the rear appeared transfixed on what she was hearing.

'Did you know Babbage took his brother's name, but was born Donna...' Jackson hesitated, '... a female?'

Deans looked out through the side window and saw his partial reflection in the wing mirror. 'Yes, I knew that,' he said.

'So, when pretty girls began to vanish several years ago without any detection, someone in the force became suspicious and asked me to monitor the investigations. It turns out Ranford was a key player in all of them. He had prime opportunity to cover his tracks or divert attention away from Babbage and himself.'

Jackson nudged Deans with the back of his hand. 'And then you came along.'

'Who was the leader?' Deans asked.

'Hard to tell,' Jackson replied. 'We don't know if they always worked together. Maybe we are about to find out.'

· · ·

They entered the county custody suite. Denise remained outside in the car.

Ranford was waiting his turn in the air lock with the uniformed officers. He was sitting on the bench, motionless and silent, his hands still cuffed behind him. He saw Deans and immediately straightened his back and smiled broadly.

'Are you okay to book him in?' Jackson asked Deans.

There was nothing he wanted more, maybe apart from seeing Ranford suffer in agonising pain.

The secure door to the custody room buzzed. 'On your feet,' Jackson barked at Ranford.

Ranford stared at him but did not move.

Jackson lunged over and hooked his arm through the loop created by Ranford's cuffed hands. 'I said on your feet.' He heaved his arm upwards and Ranford rose reluctantly from the bench with a silent grimace.

'Uncuff him,' Jackson said to one the PCs and kept a tight hold of Ranford's arm.

Ranford shook his hands free and stood nose-to-nose with Jackson.

Deans scowled; this was a completely different Ranford to the one he had experienced… up until now.

'Andy, you go in first,' Jackson said.

Deans entered the charge room and saw a sergeant standing behind the desk with a miserable expression, tapping his fingers impatiently on the counter top.

'Come on,' the custody sergeant called out, 'I've got a chilli waiting for me in the microwave.'

He stared at Deans, giving him a once over, obviously attracted by the blood-smeared clothing, legs, arms and face, as well as his walking aids.

The custody sergeant turned behind him and gesticulated to someone out of Deans' view.

Almost immediately two detention officers burst out of a side door and flanked Deans, one of them whipping the sticks away.

The sergeant looked at Ranford. 'Okay, Paul, you had better tell me what he is in here for.'

'Not him,' Jackson said coming into the room behind Ranford, 'this piece of shit,' he said, shoving Ranford in the back and forcing him towards the charge desk.

The custody sergeant dragged his specs to the end of his nose and looked over the top of them at Ranford and then at Deans for an extended moment. He pushed his glasses back up his nose and turned to one of the detention officers.

'Looks like I'm having cold chilli for lunch again boys.'

The sergeant looked at Deans and then to Jackson. 'And who might you gentlemen be then?'

Jackson stepped towards the desk. 'This is Detective Andrew Deans from Falcon Road CID in Bath.'

The custody sergeant gave Deans an extended once over.

'And I am Detective Sergeant Stephen Jackson, Professional Standards and Major Crime Investigation Team Leader, Exeter.'

The custody sergeant looked at Deans again. 'You've had an interesting morning by the looks of it, detective,' he said.

'You could say that.'

'Right, who is going to tell me why Detective Ranford is standing before me now?' the sergeant asked, nodding for the detention officer to return Deans' sticks to him.

Jackson faced Deans and held out his hand in a, *be my guest* gesture.

'Paul Ranford was arrested by myself this morning on suspicion of murdering Ash Babbage. Conspiracy to murder Amy Poole...' Deans stopped and looked down. He coughed into his hand and swivelled so that he was now facing a smiling Ranford. 'And the abduction and murder of Maria Deans... my beautiful wife and mother to my unborn child.'

Everyone in the room apart from Ranford and Deans were motionless.

The custody sergeant cleared his throat and peered at Jackson who slowly nodded.

'Okay,' the sergeant said. 'Sounds like we have a lot to talk about. How recent was the latest alleged murder?'

Deans pouted and looked at his watch. 'About an hour ago,' he said.

'Right,' the sergeant said to Ranford. 'You know your rights better than anyone. Do you want a brief?'

Ranford grinned and shook his head.

'Are you sure?'

Ranford did not reply and continued staring at Deans.

'Alright,' the sergeant said. 'Take him straight into cell one, strip him and stick him in a forensic suit... and somebody please get me the duty superintendant.'

The detention officers led the way through the narrow cell complex corridors with Deans following slowly behind on his crutches. They reached the open door to cell one and the detention officers encouraged Ranford inside with a gentle hand on the back.

Deans stood in the entrance to the cell, just as he had done following Babbage's arrest for Amy Poole's murder.

Ranford stared continuously at Deans as the DOs removed his belt, clothing and placed him into a white paper forensic suit.

The DOs left the cell, leaving Ranford standing front and centre facing Deans.

The corner of Ranford's mouth lifted, but before he had an opportunity to say anything, Deans curled his hand around the edge of the door and slammed it shut with a solid engagement of the latches.

CHAPTER FORTY-NINE

An hour and a half later, and Deans and Jackson were back on the road with Denise Moon. Ranford was going nowhere, and the DI had authorised Section 18 PACE search warrants at all the relevant properties – including Ruby Mansell's place – allowing the officers to search for all evidence relating to any of the alleged murders. *The balloon had just gone up,* as the police had a habit of saying when things got interesting.

'Where are we going?' Deans asked Jackson who was driving with a purpose in the opposite direction to Sandymere Bay.

'I hope you like boats,' Jackson said. 'We are starting with Ranford's accommodation.'

'Ranford lives on a boat?'

'It appears that Mr Ranford is full of surprises.'

They arrived in Mullacombe, an attractive tourist trap with a small harbour and thriving fishing fleet, just half-an-hour north of Torworthy.

Jackson spoke with the harbour master, flashed his ID and led the way down to the sheltered shingle beach. A picture perfect post-card fleet of fishing vessels, tethered by long seaweed encrusted ropes waited worthlessly in the dry for the incoming tide. The harbour master showed them to a small inflatable boat and pointed out toward the far side of the harbour and in the direction of a large solitary boat tied up against the sheer rock face of the headland.

'Christ!' Deans said. 'He lives on that?'

'Yep,' Jackson said, taking the controls of the small boat as the harbour master pushed them off the shingle bed.

Jackson directed the rib and within moments they were alongside Ranford's vessel.

The water bobbed and chopped as the wake they had created caught up and passed beneath them. Ranford's boat looked imposing from their small craft; at least fifty feet in length and seemingly just as tall. The grey painted hull appeared tired and forgotten, and although it was clearly afloat, Deans guessed this boat had not seen action in open water for a while.

'Shall we?' Jackson asked, tying their boat to the side of the rusting hull.

'I can't get up there,' Deans said, 'not with my leg.'

Jackson raised a finger. 'One moment,' he said and scaled a rope ladder that hung from the side.

He reached the top and then called down to Deans. 'Try this. I guessed he'd have something to hoist larger objects aboard.'

A large wooden platform with thick ropes on each corner clanked its way down the side of the steel barge. Deans turned to Denise and pulled a face.

'Don't expect me to get in that,' she said.

Deans chuckled and climbed on top of the level platform. He looked over at Denise again.

'Good luck,' she said.

Deans raised his thumb to Jackson, and he slowly jolted his way up the side of the boat.

If the hull looked un-seaworthy, then the top was barely habitable with crudely erected tarpaulin sheets positioned to divert rainfall, or capture it in large black plastic water butts. Arm sized logs were stacked neatly against the cabin wall and covered with a taught sheet. Disused tyres were dotted about the deck and filled with soil, a couple of which were sheltered by plastic sheeting like mini-greenhouses.

If nothing else, Ranford was resourceful.

Deans approached the main doorway and found an axe, chainsaw and a large shiny machete knife inside a makeshift storage box to the side of the entrance.

'We'd better take those,' Jackson said.

Deans looked closer at the teeth of the chainsaw and scowled.

They moved inside the cabin and discovered a chaotic mess of tools and kitchen utensils scattered on any available surface. Clothing and bed linen hung from a wire, suspended throughout the entire length of the compartment.

They dropped down three narrow steps into the sleeping quarters and walked into the first room on the left, quite obviously Ranford's bedroom. It was a simple affair and probably the tidiest part of the boat, so far. Opposite, Deans found the confined shower and toilet area.

Deans continued further in toward the bow and a larger space opened out. He saw mobile clothing racks and Ranford's clothes, including work shirts and several suits hanging neatly in a row. The hairs on the back of Deans' neck lifted and he sniffed the air.

His eyes narrowed. *She was here*. As the scent of perfume strengthened, he came across a small bedside unit next to a wooden wardrobe.

He pulled the drawer and found an old-style SLR camera and many rolls of old school sealed film.

He stood against the wardrobe, that was almost as tall as he was, and tugged on the door but found it to be locked.

Why would you need to lock a wardrobe?

He drove a hand deeper inside the small cabinet drawer and located a key dangling from a hook at the back.

Schoolboy error, Paul. He stuck the key in the lock and opened the wardrobe door.

'Come over and see this,' Deans called out to Jackson.

Jackson joined him in front of the opened unit. 'What is it?' Jackson asked.

'Tell me what you see,' Deans said.

Jackson shrugged. 'A cupboard full of coats.'

'Three coats,' Deans said. 'And this door was locked.'

Jackson pulled a face.

Deans swept the coats to one side and stuck his head inside. There was nothing else.

He patted down the jacket pockets – there was nothing inside of them.

'This was locked for a reason,' he said to Jackson and stepped inside the unit. He tapped the rear wooden panel and immediately stopped, turning to Jackson.

Deans had found a sliding door made to look like the back panel of the wardrobe.

He opened it up and illuminated the torch on his phone. He threw his crutches to the floor and crawled through into another open space at the bow of the boat.

Jackson followed behind and helped Deans back to his feet.

Daylight streamed in through small blisters in the steel, and narrow rods of bright light criss-crossed like laser beam trip-wires.

Deans shone his light around the entire space and Jackson did the same. They were standing amongst strings of hanging photographs, apparently developed the old-fashioned way. There must have been dozens of strings and hundreds of photographs.

Deans edged to the nearest string and directed his light onto the photographs. He straight away recognised Amy Poole, and she was in the makeshift photo-studio at Babbage's house.

Ranford was leaning across her, thumbs up to the camera, as she lay slumped in the chair, her face sliced and blooded.

Deans carried on down the line, shining his light on each image, and then he stopped abruptly. He recognised the scenery; it was Bath. It was his driveway and front garden, and it was Ranford's vomit inducing joyful face.

Deans sucked in a juddering breath and dropped to his knees clutching his head.

'Don't look at any more,' Jackson said from behind. 'Come on, Andy. We had better call a search team to recover all of this evidence.'

Jackson lifted Deans to his feet and helped him outside into the mist and cold.

'It's probably best you don't see any more for now,' Jackson said.

'Yeah,' Deans sighed. 'You're probably right. Not here anyway.'

Jackson waved to Denise in the inflatable boat. 'I'm lowering him down to you,' he said and helped Deans onto the platform.

Deans grabbed Jackson's arm. 'Sarah Gold,' he said.

Jackson frowned. Deep creases appeared in his brow.

'She's a good kid,' Deans said. 'She doesn't deserve the treatment she's getting.'

'I know,' Jackson said. 'I'm going to make sure the investigation into her goes away.' He heaved a big sigh. 'It's obvious now that Ranford had a major part to play in the exhibits going astray.'

The wrinkles in the corners of Jackson's eyes lengthened. 'You like her – don't you?'

Deans turned away and blinked. He did.

He shook his head and looked back at Jackson. 'I don't think that is proper for either of us to discuss, given the circumstances.'

'Just so you know,' Jackson said. 'If the time ever comes in the future… she likes you too.' He smiled with his tight lips and readied the winch.

. . .

They rejoined Denise in the inflatable and Jackson called for additional units on his Airwave radio.

'What do we do now?' Denise asked.

'We wait for the troops to arrive and then you and Andy need to go back to Torworthy nick. We need your statements about what happened with Ranford at Babbage's house.'

'What will happen to Ash?' Denise asked.

Deans looked at her, realising that he wasn't the only one to lose someone close to him during this entire mess.

'He will go to the mortuary,' Deans said.

'The Independent Police and Complaints Commission will be all over this,' Jackson said with his head in his hands.

'Nothing we or anyone else could have done to prevent any of this,' Denise said.

Deans noticed Jackson lift his head slightly and stare reflectively at Denise. Their eyes met for a moment and Jackson looked away again.

CHAPTER FIFTY

Six-twenty p.m. and Deans was still with Denise at Torworthy police station. He had updated DI Thornton and Mick Savage with the events of the day and suffered a heart-breaking conversation with Maria's father. The small coastal station was now a hive of activity. The narrow CID office was once again a hub of productivity and Jackson was running the show.

Sarah Gold came into the room and ran across to Deans, hugging him. 'Are you okay?' she asked with a tear in her eye. 'Are you hurt?'

'I'm fine, Sarah thanks. Are you back in the fold?' Deans asked.

'Yes, Sergeant Jackson reinstated me this afternoon and he even apologised to me.'

Deans smiled. 'Good. I wouldn't want anyone else taking your position in the investigation. What can you tell me?'

'All the scenes have been forensically searched and still locked down. Paul Ranford is apparently behaving himself in custody and we have a meeting at seven to discuss the next steps. Your colleagues from Bristol are coming down to interview Ranford because we can't get involved, as he is one of ours. Are you joining us?'

Deans shrugged. 'I haven't been asked. I think I may be too close to the action this time.'

Sarah faced Denise and smiled. 'You must be exhausted,' she said.

Denise nodded. 'We are okay. You have all been looking after us, but I would quite like to go home soon.'

'There's nothing else we can do,' Deans said. 'It's a waiting game now. Jackson has to decide how he plays it. Ranford is looking at three murders, that we know of, and I'm just praying Jackson's not going to mess this one up.'

'Why don't you both go home now,' Sarah said. 'I'll call you if anything happens.'

Deans checked the time. 'That's a good idea,' he said. 'It'll be tomorrow before any questions are put to Ranford, and in any case, I need a drink.'

'Come on,' Denise said standing. 'I think we've all had enough excitement for the day and I need a drink too.'

Denise stared at Deans. He knew what she was doing, but he still downed a triple whisky in one satisfying gulp.

'What are you going to do?' she asked. 'Once tomorrow is over, or whenever that may be… What are you going to do?'

Deans rolled the remaining dribble of whisky around his tumbler, closely inspecting the film of liquid as it became ever thinner.

'I dunno.'

He peered at Denise briefly and then looked back into his glass.

'Will you carry on in CID?' Denise asked.

Deans shrugged and leaned forward for the bottle of Jameson's. He saw Denise out of the corner of his eye as he poured another oversized measure.

'I've got a lot to think about,' he said and took a large swig. 'I've got a funeral to organise.'

Denise sipped from her tea and studied him.

Deans sank back in his chair holding his glass in front of his face. 'Got a funeral to organise,' he repeated, beneath his breath.

Denise did not speak, and they sat in silence until Deans finished his drink and then announced that he needed to sleep.

CHAPTER FIFTY-ONE

Deans stomped back and forth in the living room and checked his phone for the umpteenth time that morning.

'Sarah said she would call,' Denise said. 'Don't get yourself so worked up.'

Deans clenched his jaw, glared at Denise for a second, and then continued to clomp with the hard cast of his leg on the laminated flooring.

'Do you want to go out somewhere?' Denise asked. 'Would that help?'

Deans glowered again and removed his phone from deep inside his trouser pocket… again.

'Why doesn't one of them let me know what is happening?' he said through gritted teeth. He looked at his phone a further time. Eleven twelve a.m. Just less than three hours of the twenty-four-hour custody time limit left.

'Come on,' Denise said. 'Let's grab some air.'

'It's pissing down,' Deans said. 'I don't want to go out until I have to.'

Denise sank her head and turned away.

Deans' phone rang in his pocket. He dived inside and answered it without looking at the screen. 'Yes,' he said.

Denise watched him, saw his eyes moving from side to side, in response to the other person talking.

'We can be there in twenty,' Deans said flashing his lids at Denise, searching for her agreement, which she did.

He ended the call and looked at Denise with purpose in his eyes and fire in his belly.

'The team from Bristol are ready to go,' Deans said. 'Jackson wants me to see them before they go in for the first interview. We need to get going.'

Denise did not talk much on their way to Torworthy CID. Deans was doing enough for the both of them.

They entered the car park and Sarah Gold met them and took them inside the station.

'Everyone is here,' she said as they walked through the security doors.

'Jackson?' Deans asked.

Sarah nodded. 'Yeah. It was his idea that you came. Your Bristol colleagues didn't agree, but here you are.' She looked up at him and gave a soft smile.

They went up to the first floor and the CID office that Deans was now almost as familiar with as his own back in Bath.

Deans immediately saw DI Thornton who came over and shook his hand.

'Andrew,' Thornton said. 'It sounds like you had a lucky escape.' He looked down at Deans' leg; 'Again,' he said and winked.

'Yeah, well, I guess I'm lucky,' Deans replied dryly.

Jackson came into the room and people spread out of his way, like a bow of a ship parting water.

'Andy,' he said, slapping a firm hand down on Deans' shoulder. 'Do you have a minute for an update?

Deans followed Jackson out into the corridor and into the same small room that Jackson had used to give Deans a bollocking those short weeks before.

'Forensics are back,' Jackson said. He focussed on Deans and sucked air in through his nostrils. His mouth was bound tightly together, his lips thin and tense.

'Go on,' Deans replied in a low voice.

Jackson filled his lungs with air and held it in.

'The haunted house… Ruby Mansell's place… well… Maria was there—'

'I know,' Deans said. 'In the cellar.'

'That's right,' Jackson said. He peered away for a beat and then looked Deans square on. 'They found numerous traces of Maria's DNA.'

Deans shut his eyes and imagined Maria's face. 'I knew they would.'

'I'm not sure if you'll want to hear this?' Jackson said screwing his face into a wrinkly prune.

Deans stared at him, permitting the information to pass.

'Okay,' Jackson said taking breath. 'The chainsaw—'

Deans raised a hand and stopped Jackson going any further. His mouth began to quiver, his eyes blurring.

Jackson reached out and planted a hand onto the table in front of Deans, welcoming Deans to take it.

Deans blinked and droplets of tears splashed onto the table and onto Jackson's wrist.

He brought a hand slowly up from his lap and dropped it into Jackson's grasp.

'We are going to get this bastard for everything that he has done,' Jackson pitched. 'And I am going to do this personally… for you.'

Deans saw the hatred in Jackson's face and he squeezed Deans' hand before letting go.

'Are you staying close by?' Jackson asked.

Deans swallowed deeply. 'Yeah,' he whispered. 'I guess.'

Jackson stood up. 'Is there anything specific you want us to ask Ranford?'

Deans lifted his head. His eyes were glazed and reddened, and he simply replied, 'Why?'

CHAPTER FIFTY-TWO

Jackson woke Deans from the sofa in the custody sergeant's rest room. Denise was with him, but she had not slept. Deans sat bolt upright, his mouth open, but no sound came out.

'Have you had a good rest?' Jackson asked.

'What time is it?'

'Twenty-past-eleven,' Denise said.

Deans wiped his face and dug a knuckle into his gummy eyes.

'I'm sorry,' he said. How long have I been—'

'You don't have anything to apologise for,' Jackson said.

Deans groaned in the back of his throat and, as he ran a hand through his hair, he sensed a heightened energy in Jackson.

Deans froze.

Denise leaned over, grabbing his hand.

'Ranford has coughed the lot,' Jackson said. 'Babbage, Amy Poole… Maria.'

Deans' jaw slackened.

'Of course, there's still a hell of a long way to go,' Jackson continued, 'but the hardest part is done. We didn't even have to break him. He blurted the lot – quite proud of the fact, if anything.

I wouldn't be surprised if there are others that come out in due time.'

Deans frowned. 'Don't you think that's unusual? Why would he admit so freely to three murders?'

Jackson rocked his head backwards and looked to the ceiling. 'Ranford might have been a cop, but first and foremost he was a psychopath, as was Babbage. We may never get to know the real reason why he did these horrific acts,' Jackson shrugged and looked back at Deans. 'Anger – hatred – jealously – opportunity? But we must concentrate on the significant steps that have been taken today and make a cast iron case against him so that he never again has an opportunity to do these heinous crimes.'

'Can I see him?' Deans asked.

Jackson jerked his head back and frowned at Deans.

'Not in person,' Deans said. 'Can I watch him on the charge room CCTV?'

Jackson shrugged. 'I don't see why not, but you absolutely must not have any contact with him. Do you understand?'

Deans' bottom lip wavered, so obviously that he was under no doubt that Jackson and Denise noticed.

Jackson held the door open and Deans and Denise walked through to the charge desk and booking in area.

A different sergeant was behind it now. Deans recognised him from when Babbage had been locked up a couple of weeks before.

'This is Andy Deans,' Jackson said to the custody sergeant.

'We've met,' the sergeant said, holding an outstretched hand for Deans to take. 'My sincere condolences,' he said giving Deans a firm handshake.

'Can I see him on the screen?' Deans asked.

'Be my guest,' the sergeant said, directing Deans' attention to a TV monitor and one of the camera cells – the same one that Babbage had occupied those weeks before.

Deans peered at the screen. Ranford was tucked beneath a thin blue blanket, his feet nearest the camera.

'How long has he been out of interview?' Deans asked.

The custody sergeant looked at his computer screen. 'About fifteen minutes now,' he said. 'He's having a compulsory rest.'

'What did his brief say?' Deans asked in a deadpan voice.

Jackson shook his head. 'He just let Ranford speak, didn't try to stop him.'

Deans nodded. 'Good,' he said. 'And the team from Bristol?'

'They're in for the long haul,' Jackson replied. 'They think they might stick another interview into him before the night is out and we still have a bag of time left on the superintendent's extension. They'll be at it all tomorrow as well.'

'Why don't we head off?' Denise said.

Deans heaved a juddering breath and his vision flickered as he stared at Ranford's feet.

'She's right,' Jackson said. 'No point being here. Get off to bed, safe in the knowledge that we caught your wife's killer.'

Deans slowly drew a deep breath. 'Yeah,' he sighed. 'We did.'

Denise walked over to him, wrapped her arms around his waist and gave him a long, firm hug.

Jackson watched them for a quiet moment.

'You two have a potent alchemy,' he said. 'I don't know how you do half the things you... *do*, but you would be a very useful asset to someone, somewhere.'

Jackson's bony features softened. 'And I'd be delighted to have you both on my squad.'

Deans looked up at Jackson, and Jackson smiled back at him.

'I don't know what my future holds, anymore,' Deans said. 'But I've got some serious thinking to do.'

'That is totally understandable, and you must take your time,' Jackson replied. 'Don't make any rash decisions.'

He walked over and touched Deans on the back of the arm.

'You are an extraordinary detective,' Jackson said.

Deans smiled a little and locked eyes with Jackson.

'And you are still an arsehole.'

CHAPTER FIFTY-THREE

'Okay,' the pathologist said to his assistant, 'wheel her in, but give me a moment; I need to tell Jen that I'm going to be late.'

The assistant nodded and smiled as the pathologist walked out of the examination room into the scrubs area, delved into his opened locker and removed his phone.

'Hi, honey,' his wife said breezily after several rings. 'Are you on your way?'

'I'm really sorry, Jen. I've got to work late tonight.'

'Archie, you promised!'

'It shouldn't take too long, sweetheart. The police want this one fast-tracked – something to do with a high-profile case.'

'But we arranged to meet the others at eight. Can't it wait until the morning?'

The pathologist huffed and looked back through the glass wall into the examination room, to where the assistant was just walking away from the body. 'I'm afraid not,' he sighed. 'This is apparently something unusual, and they need the results.'

'Don't they always?'

The pathologist rolled his eyes. 'This doesn't happen all that often, Jen—'

'After thirty-two years of loyal service you would think they could let you enjoy your wedding anniversary?'

'Yes, well, this is the last one that will be affected – by this job, anyway.'

'And it can't come soon enough,' his wife sniped. 'Alright, be quick and I'll see you at home. Make sure you let me know if you are going to be any later than seven, I don't want to let the children down... again.'

'I will,' the pathologist said. 'Just remember Jen, I love you – always have, always will.'

'Love you too,' his wife said. 'And be quick!'

Archie half-smiled and blew a double kiss down the phone.

He looked back at the stainless steel slab and the lawn-green hospital sheet covering the body. 'Okay,' he said. 'Let's get this show on the road.'

He walked over to an ancient but reliable music system and pressed play on the CD stack.

Archie Rowland had a set routine that he followed each time he examined a body. He was old school, and despite the modern-day powers-that-be frowning upon his quirky nuances, that was as far they took it. With only two months before retirement, he was probably in the *"too difficult to handle"* box and best left to his ways.

The London Philharmonic filled the silence of the room as Archie rolled up his latex gloves without looking down at his hands. He hummed along to the opening piece – Saint-Saens La Danse Macabre, and flicked the switch to start the extractor fan above the slab. He donned his mask, entered the examination room and walked over to the counter top housing the electronic weighing equipment and the 'subject' notes.

'So,' he said, opening the file cover. 'Welcome... Mrs Maria Deans.' He hummed along to the music and peeled back the sheet from the top of the slab. 'Oh!' he said taking a partial backwards step. 'Oh dear!'

The assistant came into the room. 'Do you need me any longer, Archie? Only, it's Friday and I was hoping—'

Archie covered the body quickly with the sheet. 'No, that's fine, Annie. I will clean up afterwards. You go and enjoy your youth. Have a wonderful weekend.'

'Thank you,' Annie said. 'I'll see you next week.'

Archie waved a hand as Annie closed the door. This was an autopsy that she didn't need to view.

The county's most revered and knowledgeable pathologist walked back over to the file and read the opening pages. He returned to the body and took a deep breath.

'So, you are the wife of a detective, eh? No wonder they were persistent.' He slowly peeled the sheet back exposing the upper torso once again. He stopped, looked and sighed deeply. 'Well then, Mrs Deans,' he said, 'what has happened to your head?' He leaned in closer to her body and looked at the cauterised folds where her head was once connected to the remaining stump.

'Interesting,' he muttered.

He took his index finger and slowly followed the contour of the seal, five centimetres above the clavicle. 'Hmm,' he muttered, 'very neat.' He pinched the seam of the hospital sheet and walked backwards with it, exposing more of Maria's body. He stopped just below the waist and dropped the material. He stared at her torso and frowned. For a moment, he did not move and then he returned to the notes. He studied them with more detail and pursed his lips.

'*Very* interesting,' he said and turned back to Maria.

He walked slowly counter-clockwise staring at her body. He came alongside her stomach and crouched down so that his eye-line was at the same height as her tummy. He leaned across and gently manipulated the skin around her abdomen.

'Hmmm,' he murmured, stood up and leaned in closer. 'When did you get this?' he said looking at a perfectly straight and expertly stitched wound up the centre of her belly.

He reached for a measure. 'Seventeen centimetres exactly,' he said aloud. He paused, chewed the inside of his cheek, and looked back to where Maria's head should be.

'I'm sorry, Mrs Deans, but I'm going to have disturb this exquisite piece of surgery.'

He took a fresh Swann Morton scalpel from the stainless steel tray beside the slab, moved the large round lamp directly above his head, and slowly sliced and picked the stitches apart, until the skin was free from the sutures. He frowned and coughed behind his mask. He was now completely unaware of the dramatic music playing in the background. He took his index finger and gently pulled one side of the skin flap away. He held it open with a slightly trembling finger and leaned closer in to the body. He could see a small but easily identifiable pair of feet. He sucked in deeply through his nostrils and shook his head.

'Where's the amniotic fluid?' he whispered to himself.

He reached behind him and selected a shoehorn shaped metal implement and edged back towards the body. He took a clamp, parted the incision area and manoeuvred the light above his head so that he could see clearer. He lowered the implement into the wound and slowly lifted it back out. He reached down, hooked the umbilical cord beneath his index finger, and gently unravelled it towards him until the tiny feet were visible. He carefully reached in with his fingers and pulled out the unborn baby.

'Oh God!' He dropped the foetus onto his mother's belly and the tool that he had been holding bounced and clanked on the hard examination room floor.

Archie stood back. He stared at the child's body, his eyes wide and disbelieving. He did not move or blink for at least a minute, and then he quickly checked around the room that nobody was present.

He stepped in closer and peered down again at the foetus.

The little boy – just fourteen weeks old – had suffered the

same hideous fate as his mother. His head had been removed… and the wound had been cauterised with the same exacting intent.

Archie covered his mouth with the other hand through the mask. His eyes burned wide and bewildered. He leaned in close to Maria's body once again and tilted his head. He fumbled for a pair of tweezers from the tray and gently picked at an object from her torso. He held it up to the light and peered closer; it was one of the sutures.

Archie shook his head.

'Can't be, can't be,' he muttered softly and brought it closer towards his face. He peered back at Maria, the surgical wound, and then took time to stare at the tiny strand suspended in his grasp. He leaned in closer still. 'I haven't seen sutures like that since…' His bottom lip quivered and he flashed a glance towards the door.

TO BE CONTINUED…

THE BONE HILL
Available now!

If you enjoyed my writing, I would be grateful if you could leave a review.

I love to hear feedback and reviews help other readers take a chance on a new author for the first time.

It need only take a moment of your time and be as short as you like.

Visit my goodreads page at James D. Mortain,
or my Amazon page at James D Mortain.

Thank you!

BOOKS BY JAMES D MORTAIN

THE DETECTIVE DEANS MYSTERY COLLECTION

A mutilated student. A house with haunting secrets. Sacred ground beset by evil.
Books 1 - 3

Book 1
STORM LOG-0505

This detective's best lead could be a voice from beyond the grave...
When Deans discovers horrific truths in a missing person case, his inquiry takes a turn when he receives impossible-to-deny evidence from a psychic. Despite his lack of belief in the paranormal, following the ghostly thread escalates his case into a murder investigation. To put the killer behind bars, just how much will Deans have to sacrifice in the name of justice?

Book 2
DEAD BY DESIGN

How far would you go to save the lives you love most?
When a married couple is found entwined in death, his colleagues
assume a double suicide, but Deans senses darker forces at work.
He is facing an awakening – *a spiritual birth*, but he is stuck in a
living nightmare. Those around him are watching … judging …
expecting him to break, but for Deans the terror is only just
beginning…

Book 3
THE BONE HILL

**A killer at large. A gift obscured by tragedy. One last chance for
justice...**
As Deans pieces together the fragments of his shattered life, the
North Devon tide washes up another decapitated corpse.
Determined to end the horror and avenge his own devastating
loss, Deans exposes an ancient cult with a thirst for blood and a
lust for human sacrifice. Staring down a terrifying evil, the like of
which he's never confronted, the biggest question still remains…
who will be next?

THE DI CHILCOTT MYSTERIES

A brand-new series set on the streets of Bristol.

Book 1
DEAD RINGER

They left him for dead. Now he's back. And he wants revenge...
When the discarded body of a young woman sparks a manhunt
on the streets of Bristol, striking similarities to another murder
suggest there's only one detective for the job. It doesn't take DI
Robbie Chilcott long to establish a shocking link between the
victims: both were daughters of SAS veterans. If Chilcott is to end
the bloodshed, he must break from the shackles of law and place
his trust in one of the most secretive and tight-knit military units.
But will they turn on one of their own?

THE BONE HILL

A DETECTIVE DEANS MYSTERY

by

JAMES D MORTAIN

PROLOGUE

Archie Rowland drove his trusted twenty-year-old Volvo estate back through the still blackness of the country lanes towards his home, seven miles from the nearest civilised settlement. He had lived with his wife at the ancient land holding for three decades. He loved the unspoilt solace of the moors, but his wife, Jen, had always favoured town life and discussions about moving back to a more vibrant way of living were never far from her lips. It was no doubt different for her; she was at home all day while he was generally at the North Devon Infirmary, or attending pathology meetings with his peers, or with the senior police staff in Exeter. That was a journey he hated and refused to drive. Instead, he would take the excruciatingly slow, but delightfully scenic route between Barnstaple and Exeter by 'snail train', as he called it.

This night, Archie drove with a mechanical vacancy as his troubled thoughts fogged his mind. His gloved fingers fidgeted on the steering wheel as he took the final left hand bend and slowed on approach to his farm entrance. His wife had already illuminated the outside lamps and he quickly checked the clock on the dashboard to ensure that he was still good to his word.

His Volvo clunked and spluttered to a stop and he fumbled

with his old leather briefcase and keys. The front door to the house opened for him, and stood in a sheer black gown and glistening jewellery was his beautiful wife of forty-one-years that very day, Jen.

'Thank you, Archie,' she said checking over her shoulder at the antique Grandfather clock ticking precisely in the hallway nearby.

'Yes, well,' Archie said. 'A promise is a promise.'

Jen leaned towards him and gave him an air kiss near both ears. 'Good day, love?' she asked.

Archie's bushy eyebrows twitched, but he smiled for Jen's benefit. 'Yes, yes,' he said, placing his briefcase behind the door next to the Welsh dresser.

'Is fifteen minutes long enough for you?' Jen asked. 'I took the liberty of ordering a taxi, not knowing whether you would make it in time, or not.'

Archie nodded and smiled.

'At least you can have a nice glass of something if somebody else is driving,' Jen said.

'Fifteen minutes. Right, okay.' Archie made his way through the hallway towards the stairs with his wife in his wake informing him a fresh shirt and pressed suit were waiting for him on the bed.

He reached the top of the stairs and paused outside of his youngest daughter's bedroom. His shoulders sank and he looked down at his feet before continuing on to his room, where he quickly freshened up and dressed in the clothes Jen had prepared for him.

The sound of crunching shingle and the flash of headlamps alerted him to the taxi arriving outside. He shook his head, they were never *on time*, probably due to the fact they were so far out of town.

'It's here,' Jen shouted up the stairs.

Tying the knot of his tie as he walked down the stairs, he saw Jen waiting in the hallway.

'When are we going to do away with all these Christmas decorations?' he commented as Jen smoothed down his lapels and ran her thumbs around the back of his collar. 'We only did it for the kids' benefit,' he said.

'Now shush that nonsense,' Jen said. 'We have this every year, and every year you get the same response; Christmas isn't just for the children, it's a celebration, a time for giving, a time for loving—'

'Oh, God, you're not going to sing *that song* again, are you?'

Jen laughed, opened the door and waved across to the taxi driver. 'Come on, Mr Grumpy,' she said. 'Let's go and have a nice meal with our children.'

It was almost midnight by the time they took the return lift home. Their two eldest daughters had met them at the hotel with their respective partners and gone their own way home. Archie's youngest daughter was spending the weekend with her boyfriend, but at least the offer had been there for her to join them. She always distanced herself from the family engagements despite the fact they had done everything they could to make her feel as wanted as their biological children. Archie didn't push, he'd learnt the hard way through her adolescence and knew she was best left well alone.

'You've been unusually quiet tonight, darling,' Jen said taking Archie's hand in hers as the taxi neared their home.

Archie looked down to her hand and twitched his brow.

'Something's bothering you, isn't it?' Jen said, squeezing his hand.

'Oh, it's nothing,' Archie said.

'It must be *something*?' Jen pressed. 'I haven't seen you like this for years.'

Archie coughed behind closed lips and shifted his bottom in the seat. He looked directly at the rear view mirror into the driver's eyes, which focussed on the road ahead, and the muted sound of late-night radio was playing in the front. Archie dropped his head. 'Today's job,' he said softly. 'Well, it was quite... distressing. That's all.' He released Jen's hand and centralised the knot of his tie.

'Would you like to discuss it?' Jen asked.

Archie glanced at the driver's reflection once again. 'Yes. We need to. We *have* to.' He faced his wife with watery eyes. 'But not here.'

Archie paid the driver and gave an extra ten-pound note as a Christmas tip. He walked with his wife to the door and assisted her with her coat.

'Would you like a nightcap, darling,' Jen asked.

'We need to talk about this, Jen,' Archie said.

'Can I get myself a drink first, I am sure it can wait.'

Archie turned Jen to face him. 'Please,' he said. 'I need to tell someone...'

'Okay, okay. Come on, you can tell me anything.'

Archie looked away.

'Arch, what is it?' The volume in Jen's voice increased.

Archie walked into the lounge and stood in the middle of the room. Jen, wide-eyed followed silently behind.

'Sit down,' he said.

Jen did as requested and perched on the lip of the luxurious leather sofa.

Archie blinked quickly several times and swallowed away his anxiety. 'Jen,' he said, 'Do you recall when the children were younger, I taught them suturing. Do you remember?'

'How could I possibly forget, I was forever finding rotting chicken breasts and banana skins lying about the place. Disgusting—'

'That's right,' Archie said softly, 'We practised on chicken breasts and bananas.' He dipped his head, hesitated and then lifted his sombre eyes to meet his wife's. 'I saw something today on a murdered victim that I haven't seen in a long time.'

Jen stared back.

'An unusual suturing technique, seldom, if ever, used in general surgical practice...' He waited to see if his wife was going to say something. She didn't.

'Jen, there's only one person who can replicate that technique – I know that to be a fact, because I invented it.'

Jen didn't speak.

'And the last time somebody else tried it, to my knowledge,' Archie said, 'they were stitching chicken breasts.'

Jen's eyes were unblinking. 'That was over fifteen years ago, Archie. Are you trying to tell me that no one else is capable of copying those stitches?'

Archie nodded.

'Are you certain?'

'It was something I experimented with at Med School,' Archie said. 'I was forever trying new ideas, pushing the limits of my abilities, and I created a method of stitching that was strong, clean, but time consuming and expensive.' He narrowed his eyes and moved over to the sofa sitting down next to his wife, taking her hand in his. 'I've thought about this, Jen. I should inform the police.'

Jen tugged her hand away from his. 'You most certainly will not,' she snapped.

'I must,' Archie said, his voice fractured.

'Can't you get rid of this body? Incinerate it, or something?'

'No,' Archie whispered. 'I'm afraid this is going to be one job that simply won't go away.'

'Why not?' Jen barked.

'Because the victim was the wife of a serving police officer.' He looked deeply into her eyes. 'And she was beheaded...'

Jen recoiled and sat back against the sofa.

'And the sutures I talk of... sealed a surgical wound to her womb and the decapitated body of her unborn son.'

Jen covered her mouth with a hand and dashed out of the room.

Archie didn't try to follow. There was nothing more he could say that would make the problem go away. He knew Jen would return when she was ready, and he didn't have to wait long for that to happen.

She searched his face for answers, but Archie had none. 'What do we do?' she uttered.

Archie rubbed the back of his neck with slow and deliberate passes. 'I need to complete a report,' he said. 'The police will expect one, especially given the nature of the deaths.' He saw Jen squirm and withdraw. 'There are only three people that know about that stitching,' he said reaching out and holding Jen by the rounded tips of her shoulders. 'And that includes you and me.' He gently guided his wife backwards towards the sofa, his hands remaining on her shoulders directing her movement. He gently pushed down and Jen took the seat once again.

'Promise me we won't talk about this again,' he breathed.

Tears welled in her eyes and she shook her head. 'Never,' she whispered.

'Very well,' Archie said. 'Then I will do the *right* thing.'

CHAPTER ONE

Ingrid Andrews loved this time of year. It wasn't for the lack of tourists, or "grockles" as they were colloquially referred to, nor was it for the fact she could park pretty much wherever she wanted. It was because the North Devon coastline in the depths of winter made her feel *alive* with energy. The rumble of the Atlantic Ocean, the flat expanse of the golden-brown sands, the biting nip of the onshore breeze – and it was a haven for dog lovers, like her and her faithful Springer Spaniel, Nelson.

This day was perfect; powder blue skies, a low-slung sun, vast marbled sands and the gentle lap of an incoming tide. Ingrid sloshed through the milky fringe of water, her ruby-red Hunter wellies leaving deep patterned trenches in her wake, only to be licked away with each gradual encroach of the tide. Small beige-coloured shellfish rattled against one another as they rolled back and forth on the leading edge, and tiny waders and sanderlings scampered away as Nelson careered through the shallows as if it was the first time he'd seen the sea. It wasn't. They came every chance Ingrid had, come rain or shine.

'Go on, boy,' Ingrid yelled, hurling another soggy tennis ball through the air with a colour-coordinated ball-launcher to match her wellington boots. Nelson needed no second invitation and sprinted off like a guided missile towards his prize.

Ingrid breathed in the salty freshness of the day. This beat her usual Monday morning slog as a checkout assistant at the local Morrisons superstore. She had pulled all of the busiest shifts over the Christmas period and as a reward for her efforts she had been given a few unexpected days off by her unusually festive boss.

Nelson returned – his liver and white coat matted with Demerara brown sand. He dropped the ball in front of her feet and nudged it closer with his nose.

'Come on, Nelson,' she said dotting the ball with the end of the launcher. 'We need to head back the other way, boy.'

Nelson planted his front feet and prepared to spring back into action. Ingrid giggled. He was like a nine-year-old pup.

'Again?'

She looked briefly at her watch.

'Is nothing going to tire you out today? Okay – one last throw, but we need to head back.' She gave Nelson a hard stare and then tossed the ball into the shallows. Nelson darted off and Ingrid turned to make tracks back to the slipway.

She watched the foamy water lap over her toes and her mind turned to her poor mother, recently diagnosed with Alzheimer's disease. She would have loved the serenity of this place, but she was in Birmingham, in a nursing home. She had tried time and again to convince her to move into one of the local homes, but Mum was as stubborn as they came and refused to leave.

'Nelson,' Ingrid shouted. 'Come on, boy. Time to go home.' She didn't need to turn about, the stiff wind was at her face.

She continued onwards, but strangely, Nelson didn't come back.

'Nelson. Nelson. Come on boy let's go home.' Ingrid stopped and looked back. 'Nelson. Nelson.'

She scanned the beach but Nelson was nowhere in sight. She

looked up towards the pebble ridge, but due to the low tide, it was too far away to see anything clearly. Checking her watch again, she doubled back and called out Nelson's name as she went. Then she saw him in the waters beyond the shallows, a hundred metres ahead.

'Nelson, come here,' she shouted sharply. 'Nelson come.' But whatever Nelson was up to, he had no intention of returning on command.

'Come on Nelson, fetch your ball.'

As she got closer, she could see Nelson was out of his depth, his nose barely above the waterline and although the waves were tame by Sandymere Bay's standards, they were still buffeting little Nelson around.

Ingrid stepped deeper into the water, now inches from the top of her boots. An energetic wave came rapidly towards her. She tried to retreat, but water splashed above her knees and slopped into her wellies.

'Bollocks,' she spat. 'Come on, Nelson, that's enough now. I don't care if you can't find your ball. Mummy is wet through.'

She padded back towards the beach, her feet soaked and frozen from the eight-degree waters. Then she saw Nelson's tennis ball washed up on the sand ahead of her.

She bent down with a mumbled expletive and picked it up. 'Here it is, Nelson. Here it is. Come on Nelson. Come and get your sodding ball.'

Nelson had other ideas. The waves were pushing him closer to the shore and Ingrid could sense his determination to retrieve something from within the water. She trudged to the dry sand; her feet absolutely soaked and removed her wellies, one at a time, pouring the seawater out onto the sand. Nelson was now back on his feet, his jaws clamped around a submerged object, his head tugging with single-minded eagerness.

Ingrid could see a much larger wave approaching that would undoubtedly engulf Nelson. She quickly returned her boots to her feet and ran back into the water, but she was too late and water crashed against Nelson and he was lost to sight. Ingrid held her breath and frantically searched the top of the water for her little dog.

'Nelson,' she shouted and started to run deeper into the sea, her legs and feet moving as fast as the thick waters would allow.

'Nelson. Nelson,' she screamed, now wading beyond knee depth. 'Oh my God, Nelson.' Her legs were heavy and weighed down completely by her water-filled wellington boots.

'Nelson.' Her voice was now frantic.

She looked around anxiously for help, but she was still alone.

'Oh, God,' she wept, raking the waters aside with her hands, and then she saw him bob back to the surface.

'Nelson!'

She thrust her legs through the surf, the cold water no longer registering with her brain. Her dog was just feet away.

Ingrid reached out – all she needed was a scruff of fur to hold. He was now tantalizingly close, but each time she lunged forwards, another wave took him away from her desperate grasp.

She took another step, the surf splashed into her chest and face. She timed her reach and caught Nelson by his hind leg. His weight took her by surprise and pulled her off her feet, face first into the chilly waters.

She thrashed out with her legs and felt the seabed beneath her feet. She still had her dog's leg in her grip and heaved him back, lifting her own head above the water line. Gasping for breath, she planted her feet and got a second hand around her dog. She turned for the shore and heaved him slowly inwards with each laboured step. The briny waters stung her eyes and she struggled to see if Nelson was alive or dead. Either way, his jaws were still connected to the heavy object his jaws were clamped around.

Finding an inner strength, Ingrid dragged Nelson back to knee depth. She reached for his head, lifting his face clear of the water, dislodging the attached object that at first disappeared and then bobbed clear of the waterline into view.

Ingrid took a sudden intake of breath and fell backwards. Water covered her face and gushed into her open mouth. She choked as water went down her throat and she let go of Nelson, her legs kicking wildly in a desperate attempt to get out of the water as quickly as possible. She clawed at the sand and dragged herself clear.

Her eyes fixed wide on a spot in the water. She coughed and at the same time vomited onto the sand beside her, and dragged her body clear of the unpleasant slick.

She composed herself and lifted her body onto her elbows to gain a clearer view of the water. She felt her heart pounding through the saturated and heavy layers of clothing.

The object inched ever closer with each surge of the waves.

Ingrid dragged her legs up to her chest, and rolled onto her hands and knees. Her neck was frozen stiff and wouldn't allow her to look in any direction other than directly ahead, as the object scuffed and slewed against the sandy seabed.

She slowly rose to her feet, her eyes glued to what she could now clearly see was a human arm floating on the surface.

She stepped hesitantly back into the water and shuffled towards it. The hand on the arm was curled, as if it had once held a honeydew melon. Her breathing accelerated, as she got closer. She bent forwards but then stopped. She inhaled a lung full of chilled air, puffed out her cheeks and grabbed the stiff hand.

The arm was weighty, and as it came towards her, suddenly rolled beneath the water and the connected torso bobbed to the surface.

Ingrid jumped backwards and fell into the water once again, her face stricken with fright. Motionless, she couldn't tear her eyes off the body, now bouncing gently on top of the passing waters. She picked up an object in her peripheral vision and turned her head like it was on a fine-tooth ratchet, though her eyes stayed transfixed to the corpse moving ever closer. The realisation of what was to her side broke the spell of the dead body and she looked away.

There in three inches of water, Nelson lay on his side, his little legs unmoving and stiff.

CHAPTER TWO

Detective Andrew Deans looked himself up and down in the full-length bedroom mirror. He brushed a hand over his shoulder and straightened his black tie. It was less than five weeks since the train crash and he was still tolerating the bulky orthopaedic boot on his leg. Thankfully, he was able to remove the boot and place it over the top of his freshly laundered suit.

He tilted his head, closed his eyes and drew a long slow breath from the sombre air.

'Alexa,' he said to his bedside companion. 'Play me some happy music.' The small round smart-box came to life with a single rotation of lilac light.

"I am sorry," the electronic voice said. "Another device is currently streaming music. Would you like to stream from this device instead?"

Deans looked deeply into the eyes of his own reflection. There was only one *Alexa* device in the house, other than the application on his phone, which was inside his trouser pocket. Unless…

'Yes, Alexa,' Deans said excitedly. 'Repeat the last played song.'

He waited for the music to start and searched his face as the hairs on the back of his neck responded to the opening notes of the song being played through the small speaker. He closed his eyes and dropped his chin to his chest as Jennifer Hudson's voice broke into the introduction of *Golden Slumbers*.

A faint smile ghosted his lips and he remained unmoving, until every note and word of Maria's favourite song had finished. He looked up at the ceiling, tears pooling in his eyes. 'I love you, Maria,' he mouthed.

Detective Sergeant Mick Savage arrived on time with a gentle tap at the door. Some wonders never ceased to amaze Deans.

'Hello, Deano. How are you bearing up, buddy?' Savage asked, shaking Deans' hand and making his way through to the kitchen where he helped himself to the kettle. 'You look very smart, mate. Very smart.'

'Shit the bed, Mick?'

'I know, I know. You probably expected me to be fashionably late, but today I have a duty… to you.' Savage frowned, as he looked closer at Deans' face. 'Are you sure you are all right, Deano?'

Deans wiped moisture from the corner of his eye. 'Yeah. I'm fine, thanks.'

'Great,' Savage said looking at his watch. 'Time for a bacon butty.'

Deans turned away. 'Not for me, thanks.'

Savage hesitated. 'No, you're probably right. I'd only get ketchup down my front or something. How about a brew? Fancy a quick coffee?'

Deans nodded and Savage took two mugs from the kitchen cupboards and rummaged around for the instant coffee.

Deans took himself off to the living room.

'Did you sleep?' Savage asked joining Deans, holding out a coffee mug.

Deans shrugged and took the drink.

'Still having the dreams?'

Deans sipped and nodded.

'Should you see someone about it?'

Deans raised a brow.

'I'm just saying, Deano—'

'Nobody can fix what I've got.'

Savage didn't attempt to answer and they both sat silently finishing their drinks until the transport arrived.

They pulled off the main road and drove between the large pillars of the open-gated entrance. Deans looked directly ahead over the shoulder of the driver. A large crowd was already gathered at the front of the chapel and a smaller clutch of media photographers and TV cameras were camped in a line, two deep, and kept at respectful arm's length by several of Deans' uniformed colleagues. Interest in Deans' *story* had piqued following a mention the week before on Breakfast TV by Piers Morgan, who sent Deans the nation's thoughts and prayers. If it had been just the train crash, the media would have moved on by now and Deans wouldn't have had to become a relative recluse. But Maria's plight along with Deans' lone survival from his wrecked carriage had sent the world's media into a feeding frenzy, and now, everybody wanted a piece of him.

His wife's parents, Graham and Penny, were sitting alongside him. Deans adjusted the knot of his tie for the fourth time that journey and closed his eyes as the head of the procession slowed to a stop beneath a vine encrusted chapel entrance. The rear doors opened simultaneously and an arm reached towards him with an encouraging hook of the elbow. Cool air invaded the warm confines of the stretch limo. Deans looked towards his mother-in-law, who was being assisted up from her seat by a man wearing a long dark trench coat and sporting an equally long face.

Deans steeled himself with a deep breath. *This is it.* He looked out at the apologetic faces peering back his way. He had decided not to wear dark glasses, even though the sun was blindingly low in the cool blue sky, and now he was beginning to regret that decision.

Deans held his eyes shut for a soothing moment and wished he didn't have to go through with this. He leaned forwards and took the outstretched arm, his heart pounding beneath his suit jacket. He stood as tall as his body would allow and stared straight ahead. As he stepped away from the limo he became aware of the subtle backward movement of bodies in his peripheral vision, like a parting tide, and as he edged forwards, the ocean of guests filed back in behind him. He could see mouths moving, accepted outstretched hands and stood solid to the body hugs, but he was barely aware of what was going on around him.

He locked eyes with Mick Savage, who came forwards and took Deans gently by the elbow. He said nothing, but right then, *nothing* was just what Deans needed and he followed Savage without question. The others filed silently behind into the large acoustic room. The scuff and shuffle of leather clad feet and the occasional sob or blow of a nose was all that could be heard.

The head operative of the funeral procession stood in front of Deans with a knowing, sympathetic smile. He offered Deans a solitary nod and waited for Penny and Graham Byrne to shuffle in by his side. He caught Graham staring at him – Deans was sure they still blamed him for what happened to Maria. Savage released Deans' arm and left him with a gentle pat on the shoulder.

'Okay?' the funeral director said.

Deans nodded and the funeral director turned his back.

Deans stepped slowly forwards and the sombre notes of a string quartet filled the empty room with *Barber's, Adagio for Strings*. Deans chomped down and blinked tears from his lashes.

They followed the run of deep red carpet, being led at the front by the bald-headed director who walked with stiff purposeful limbs as the music got louder.

The pews were positioned in an L-shape. Deans was shown to the front row pew at the top of the 'L' facing a choir on the other side of the room. He took his seat and Graham sat alongside. Deans fixed his gaze on the stainless steel cradle positioned centrally, several metres directly in front of him, as mourners respectfully took their places. Deans did not try to mask or stifle his grief, and as the music continued, he noticed heads turning towards the entrance.

He tried to turn, but his neck would not allow him, and as the haunting music drew to a close, Maria's wicker coffin was placed gently onto the supporting frame before him.

Reverend Simms addressed the room.

'Dear friends,' he said with outstretched arms. 'We come together at the turn of a new year, on this saddest of days, to pay our final respects to our beloved, Maria Elizabeth Caitlin Deans. Our community and many others have been deeply affected by the sudden and horrific taking of our dear daughter, wife, colleague and friend.'

Deans' blurred eyes grew heavy, but they refused to look away from the coffin. *If I could swap places, my love, I gladly would.*

Reverend Simms continued speaking, but Deans was taking nothing in, and then in the corner of his eye he saw the fluttering wings of a white butterfly. Deans drew his head back and parted his lips. Others in the chapel began to notice and within thirty seconds, the ripple of whispers had reached the furthest most extremities of the room.

Reverend Simms stopped speaking and watched with seeming wonderment as the creature landed on the head of the cask and brought its graceful wings to a rest.

Maria, Deans mouthed and met the gaze of Reverend Simms, who allowed the congregation a brief instant of comment before continuing with the service. Deans stared at the small creature, which remained at the head of the coffin until the conclusion of the ceremony.

Deans was prompted to his feet, along with his in-laws by the Reverend, and as the choir sang *Ave Maria,* they slowly followed the casket outside through the centre of the mourners. As they reached the outer doors, Deans noticed the bank of media and felt his top lip curl into a snarl.

Savage hurried alongside him. 'Ignore them, Deano,' he said softly in his ear. 'Our boys and girls will keep them at bay, don't worry about that.'

Deans then noticed a man with a handheld video camera standing alone and separate to the others. He didn't appear to have an identity lanyard and there was no urgency to his actions, unlike the mob of photographers and reporters.

Deans stopped walking and squinted to focus. The man appeared to register Deans' attention and slowly lowered the camera from his face, and, motionless, stared back at Deans.

'Come on, Deano,' Savage said, grabbing Deans' arm. 'Come on, mate. Leave them.'

Deans took several steps away with Savage, but kept his eyes on the man with the small video camera.

The chilled air cut through his skin and Deans lifted the collar of his trench coat, tightened the scarf around his neck and turned away. He felt a tug on his arm – it was Denise Moon and she looked at him with a reassuring smile.

'Hello, Denise,' Deans said. 'Sorry… I didn't know you were coming.'

Denise squeezed his hand. 'I'm here for you,' she said. She looked behind. 'I don't know if you would have noticed, but Sergeant Jackson is also here somewhere.'

Deans shook his head. He really hadn't taken in any members of the congregation, if anything, he wanted to avoid eye contact with them.

Up ahead, the coffin bearers came to a halt and Deans saw an opening in the ground and the pea-green surface of artificial turf on either side. Mourners slowly squeezed together in considerate silence, Deans next to Maria's mother and father. He had lost his own parents years ago, and now, Maria's parents were the only family he had. He turned to Penny, her face was shattered and bereft. He reached for her hand and after a moment's hesitation, she took it.

As the Reverend gave his final blessings, Deans, for the first time, looked around those gathered. DS Jackson was looking right back at him. Jackson was the obtusely difficult skipper of the Major Crime Investigation Team in Devon. They hadn't seen eye-to-eye ever since Deans had been seconded to Devon for the Amy Poole murder investigation, but it had recently become clear to Deans that there was far more to Jackson than the asshole he portrayed.

Jackson extended Deans a nod. Deans reciprocated and then looked back down to the grave as tears once again dropped from his cheeks with each measured lower of Maria's coffin.

Maria's mother and father were the first to approach the graveside. Penny kissed a rose, dropped it into the pit and fell hysterically into the arms of her husband.

It was Deans' turn to approach the edge of the grave. He felt everyone's eyes bearing down upon him. He wiped his nose with a handkerchief, crouched down, and took a fist full of dry dirt. He ground the granules in his fist and bowed his head. *I won't stop until I've found all of you*, he promised Maria silently. *I know you are still with me*. He drew his hand to his lips, kissed his curled fingers and scattered the soil onto the surface of the casket like small marbles. He closed his eyes for a moment and again spoke silently to Maria; *Love is forever. Vengeance is now.*

CHAPTER THREE

Deans noticed DS Jackson turn away, one hand covering his ear while he attempted to hear the caller on his mobile phone. They were now at the wake in a pub about a mile from the chapel. Deans could count on both hands the number of times he had been to a wake at this particular pub, but never for a second imagined that his wife would one day be the mourned.

He studied Jackson for a moment and then he saw something that made his heart pound; Jackson lifted his head and as he spoke to the caller, he slowly turned and looked Deans straight in the eye with unease. Jackson turned away and made a hasty retreat for an outside door.

Deans apologised to the people surrounding him, placed his half-empty pint glass down on the table and followed Jackson out through the door, into the cold, still air.

Jackson was on the other side of the smoking area with his back to Deans, who closed the door quietly so that Jackson would not know he was there.

'Okay, okay,' Jackson said impatiently. 'I'll give my excuses and leave immediately. Take a statement from the witness and you'd better inform the DCI that we've got another one.' Jackson ended the call, twisted around and saw Deans facing him. His shoulders tightened and he coughed in an attempt to hide the tail end of the phone conversation.

'Alright, Deans?' he said.

'Another what?' Deans asked.

Jackson's eyes wandered around the patio tiles. 'It's nothing,' he said. 'But I'm afraid I have to go.'

'I heard you,' Deans said.

Jackson rubbed the side of his nose and gave off an insincere smile.

'There's another murder… isn't there?'

Deans noticed the slightest of twitches in Jackson's eye. He was right, there was another.

Jackson chuckled quietly and shook his head as he moved to pass Deans, all teeth and bullshit.

'It's not related,' he said.

'What isn't?'

Jackson stopped beside Deans' shoulder. His steel-blue eyes cutting deep.

'You don't need this, son,' he said. 'It's not your problem.'

'I *need* justice. It *is* my problem.'

'And you will get that. In time.'

'Remember who you are talking to. We both know anything could happen between now and the court case.'

Jackson pinched the bridge of his hooked and slightly off-centred nose.

'Tell me,' Deans said impatiently.

Jackson snorted.

'Tell me,' Deans said again, this time louder.

Jackson jogged his head. 'Okay.' He looked around Deans' face with narrow eyes. 'Another body has been washed up today,' he said. The tendons in his neck tightened and he stared into space beyond Deans' shoulder. 'At Sandymere Bay.'

'I'm coming with you,' Deans said.

'No, you're not.'

Deans gripped Jackson's forearm. 'This isn't over for me, just because I buried my wife today. It's not over by a long stretch.'

Jackson sniffed and looked down at Deans' hand clamped around his forearm.

'I can help you,' Deans said, 'like you can't imagine.'

'I know,' Jackson whispered. 'But—'

'No buts,' Deans interrupted. 'I'm going inside to find Denise and we'll follow you back down to Devon.'

Jackson's lips parted and he gazed at Deans. 'It doesn't sound pleasant,' he said, '…the job.'

Deans released his hand from Jackson's arm. 'I need to do this.'

'Shouldn't you ask your supervisor?'

'No. I'm off work on compassionate grounds.'

Jackson's harsh stare softened. 'Okay,' he said.

'Okay?' Deans repeated.

'I'll wait for you at Torworthy nick. I'll get the lowdown from the guys on the ground, and by the time you arrive, we should know a bit more.'

Jackson held the door wide for Deans to hobble through. Denise Moon was already waiting for them in the narrow corridor. Deans beckoned her over to them.

'We need to go back to Devon, right now,' he said. 'There's another body.'

'What?' Denise said.

'I'll be on my way,' Jackson said. He held out his hand and Deans shook it.

'I'm really sorry,' Jackson said. 'About all of this.' He squeezed Deans' hand a little tighter. 'But don't come down to my patch if you're going to screw up my investigation.'

Deans let go of Jackson's hand and gave him an uncompromising glare. Jackson walked over to his table, scooped his coat from the back of a chair and left without saying another word to anyone.

Deans moved across to the gathered mourners and stood in the middle of them.

'Listen in everyone,' he said loudly.

Sixty voices dampened to a stifled murmur.

'I'm afraid I have to leave you all.'

The room fell completely still.

'I have to go away for a few days.'

Deans noticed DS Savage forcing his way through the maze of motionless, open mouthed mourners towards him.

'Please stay and enjoy the food, get drunk and remember my beautiful Maria.' He caught a look of utter contempt in Graham's eye.

'We really appreciate all of your support and thank you for coming this morning. I *will* catch up with each of you individually in the coming days. I am sorry, but I really have to leave.'

Savage reached him, just as he stopped talking. The muffled conversations had already begun around the room.

'What are you doing?' Savage whispered. 'You can't leave now. These people have come here today for you.'

Savage looked at Denise Moon and his lips tightened. 'Might have guessed you'd have something to do with this.'

'Hold on right there,' Denise said.

'It was me,' Jackson said, striding in behind Deans. 'I need Detective Deans to help me out with… something.'

'He's not fit to work,' Savage said. 'He's just lost his wife and child—'

'It was my choice,' Deans cut in. 'Sergeant Jackson didn't ask me to go. But I *have* to.'

'For God's sake, Deano,' Savage flared. 'Look around you.' He pointed at the faces staring awkwardly back at them. 'What can be more important than *this*? You need these people. You need them to help you recover. You don't need more stress.'

Deans dropped a heavy hand onto Savage's shoulder. 'I'll be alright, Mick. I am doing this for the right reasons – Maria knows that.'

'No,' Savage said. 'You're not.'

Deans planted his crutches onto the beer-stained carpet, stared at Savage and gave the room one final fleeting look.

THE BONE HILL
Available now!

FREE EBOOK

Receive a FREE eBook!

Join my exclusive *Crime Scene Team* for news, updates and special offers and receive a FREE copy of **THE NIGHT SHIFT**, the gripping short story prequel to the *Detective Deans Mystery Series*.

Get your free copy by typing this link into a web browser
www.jamesdmortain.com

ACKNOWLEDGMENTS

A year ago, I didn't know if I would have an opportunity to write a second acknowledgements page following the release of my debut novel, *STORM LOG-0505*. But thanks to a great many people who read my book and kept me motivated, I am delighted to be able to do just that. In no small part, this has much to do with my wife, Rachael, who has tolerated the family sacrifice and frequent late nights spent in front of a computer. Dreams deserve to be experienced, and I am blessed that Rachael and our beautiful daughter, Gracie, allow me to pursue mine.

There are a number of key individuals, who I must thank without whom, this book would not have happened. Firstly, a fellow author – Chris Ryan. We met by chance in 2012 at a bar in Bath, and following our short conversation, he became my inspiration to write. Until that meeting, I had no aspiration of becoming a writer.

To my background team: Varun Sharma, Phil Croll, Terry Galbraith and Barbara Olive – you inspire me and continue to provide invaluable help and insight – I am eternally grateful to have you at my side. To my editor: Debz Hobbs-Wyatt, thank you for making the editing process such a joy and I look forward to working with you again in the future. Jessica Bell, my book cover designer – you are a gem!

I am also lucky to have recruited some excellent beta readers – you are so important to the publishing process – thank you all for your time, input and encouragement. To Walter Henry's Bookshop, Bideford, local libraries and other North Devon venues that supported me from the very beginning, you made me feel like a *proper* author.

I cannot complete this list without mention of a wonderful group of people who have embraced me as a one of their own and championed my writing – the community of Westward Ho! and surrounding area, among whom, a special thanks must go to Cath and Clive Shuttleworth, Sandra Ramsay and Lynsey Wheatley, Rifaat Mirza and Jane Hampson, and finally, Rob Braddick and Michael Cannon who kindly allowed me access to the magnificent Seafield House. You have all shown me great generosity and kindness, and I am lucky to know you.

Not forgetting you, the readers – you and you alone keep my dreams alive!

ABOUT THE AUTHOR

Photograph Copyright of Mick Kavanagh Photography.

Former British CID Detective, turned crime fiction writer, James D Mortain brings compelling action and gritty authenticity to his writing through years of police experience. Using his own real-life experiences within a busy CID department, James creates gripping, fast-paced crime thrillers that will keep you on the edge-of-your-seat until the very last page.

facebook.com / DetectiveDeansSeries

twitter.com / @jamesdmortain

instagram.com / jamesmortain

Printed in Poland
by Amazon Fulfillment
Poland Sp. z o.o., Wrocław